Finding Our Way Through the Fog

Jonathan B. Taylor

Finding Our Way Through the Fog

Jonathan B. Taylor

Cadmus Publishing

www.cadmuspublishing.com

CadmusPublishing.com

TABLE OF CONTENTS

Finding Our Way Through the Fog
Jonathan B. Taylor

CHAPTER 1, 'KYLE'

A sliver of sunlight found its way through the bunker style windows of the basement and struck Kyle in the face, disturbing his blissful slumber. Waking from a dream, he greeted the day as any typical eighteen year old would; with a heavy head and a raging hard on. He turned his crumpled face away from the annoying sunbeam and made a feeble attempt at returning to sleep and revisiting the exquisite dream world where moments ago, his deepest desires where playing out in the murky recesses of his mind. As the last few remnants of the dream dissipated, he surrendered to consciousness, and reluctantly kicked his feet free from the sheets before finding their way to the floor. Sitting on the edge of his bed, he observed the large digital display of the alarm clock on his nightstand and saw that it was 7:00am. An unsuspecting Patrick Connor would be over shortly to begin their morning workout, completely unaware of the erotic activities that occurred between them in Kyle's overnight fantasy world.

He went to his dresser and removed one of the four orange bathing suits that served as uniforms for his position as a lifeguard. He and Patrick were two of the four lifeguards that were posted on the main beach in the small Cape Cod town of Sunset Cove. The others were Allyson Lynch, who everyone called 'Ally', which was pronounced like an 'alley' between two buildings. She was Kyle's sort of girlfriend who was really more of a best friend with benefits. Then there was Patrick's current girlfriend, Amber Pierce with whom he was in a similar type of casual relationship as Kyle was with Ally. There were also two junior lifeguards named Steven and Casey Alves, who were entering their junior year of high school. They served as alternates and were referred to by the crew as 'the juniors'.

Kyle slipped out of his boxer shorts and looked at his naked reflection in the full length mirror that hung on the wall beside the bureau. He was pleased with his muscle development over the past few months since he had started working out with Patrick. His erection had subsided and was no longer standing at full attention. He turned his back to the mirror for inspection and peered over his shoulder while flexing his delts and lats. He was fair skinned and only had the faintest of tan lines, which drew a boundary between his lower back and the round ample gluteus muscles of his creamy white buttocks. He rubbed his ass cheeks and spread them apart to reveal his tender pink anus as he thought to himself, "This is what Patrick would see if he were to take me from behind." A wave of pleasure rolled through his body and then the moment passed. As he pulled on his shorts, he shook his head and wondered aloud, "What the hell is wrong with me?"

Kyle had known Patrick for years and while the two had always been on friendly terms, they had never exactly been friends. It was only over the past few months that they had begun spending an increasing amount of time together to the point that now they had become virtually inseparable. Patrick was the one who initiated their newfound friendship when he appeared from the woods one early spring day in Kyle's backyard. The two started talking and before he knew it, hours had passed. When they finally parted ways that afternoon, they made plans to meet up the following day to pick up the conversation again and so the dance began.

This was the only way that their friendship would have ever formed, as Kyle would never have been so bold as to approach Patrick in such a manner. He was too intimidated by Patrick's good looks and superior intellect to ever consider the possibility of a friendship forming between them, never mind the flirtatious fraternization in which they were now engaged. Patrick was an Adonis who looked like something that Michael Angelo may have carved out of marble. He was easily the most handsome boy that Kyle had known and someone he had often admired from afar, even making him the object of his fantasies during masturbation sessions in the past. At six feet tall and one hundred eighty pounds, he had a muscular build with washboard abs and a face that was easy to fall in love with. His short, blond hair was neatly parted on the side, with a reddish tinge, which appeared more pronounced in his facial and body hair on the rare occasions that he allowed it to grow out. He had dazzling blue eyes that were deep blue like the sea and his chiseled features consisted of pronounced cheekbones with full lips, a small pointed nose, and a square jaw line with a slight cleft in his chin. He looked like a male model that may have materialized from the pages of a men's fashion magazine with a flawless face, which you would otherwise find on a mannequin in a store display at a shopping mall. For Kyle, who always had a distant crush on Patrick, getting close to him was like attending some kind of relationship fantasy camp that he never wanted to end.

Patrick wasn't the first boy that Kyle had fallen for but this certainly was the hardest he had ever fallen for someone. Of his numerous crushes on other boys, only one had actually resulted in a sexual encounter. It was during his sophomore year in high school when he began spending a lot of time with Kevin McCoy who was a member of his swim team. As the two grew closer, the harmless flirtations began and eventually came to a head one night when they were walking home from a party at the home of a fellow classmate whose parents were away for the weekend. It started with them casually brushing their arms against each other as they strode along. This eventually led to an embrace and a passionate kiss beneath a street light. They spent the rest of their evening in Kyle's bed together performing oral sex on each other voraciously throughout the night.

In the morning, Kevin was gone and after avoiding Kyle for a few days, when they finally crossed paths in the parking lot after school, Kevin acted as if the whole thing never happened. Following that interaction, Kevin kept coming up with convenient excuses why he couldn't hang out and Kyle finally gave up on the budding friendship with benefits and allowed it to fizzle. A couple of times since then, Kevin had called Kyle out of the blue and attempted to get together but Kyle wasn't interested in being used and discarded like dish rag so, he declined those invitations. Now, he found himself in a similar situation of building sexual tension with Patrick and he attributed his bad experience with Kevin as the source for his current apprehension and contributing factor to his reluctance to take it to the next level.

While Kyle was very comfortable with his own sexuality, he knew that others weren't so lucky, and many would grapple with their sexual identity through a whirlwind of mixed emotions. Guilt or shame fueled by an unhealthy outlook on sexuality could condemn a person to a loveless lifetime of failed relationships and empty one-night stands. Kyle was fortunate to have progressive, open-minded parents who viewed sexuality as a fluid state where individuals could experience attraction to either sex on any given day, which allowed him to embrace bisexuality in a safe, nontoxic environment where he could flourish accordingly. Patrick, on the other hand, had deeply religious, ultraconservative parents, which made him a prime candidate for becoming one of those self-loathing, damaged types who can never quite accept the many layers of their ability to love.

Despite being comfortable with his bisexuality, Kyle wasn't really comfortable with broadcasting it and mostly kept the information to himself. He saw the world as largely homophobic and hostile toward the gay community and preferred the protection of anonymity to the potential of public ridicule. Outside of some generic references acknowledging the 'gray area' of his sexuality that he made to his parents, the only person he had actually 'come out' to, aside from Kevin, was Ally who had confessed her own bisexuality to him. He would never go so far as to deny his sexuality but he certainly didn't go out of his way to advertise it either.

One of the things that used to bother him about Kevin was his willingness to join in on the homophobic rants of their peers in vain attempts to conceal his own sexuality. Kyle always saw this as an act of betrayal to oneself and came to the realization that anyone who was outspoken against homosexuality was probably struggling with those issues themselves and were essentially announcing their true feelings to the world. He also figured that any misguided closet case who tried this tactic was ultimately contributing to their own self-loathing. Unfortunately, this was another one of those traits that Kyle had discovered in Patrick, which became an additional check in the 'reasons not to pursue this' column. Despite the mounting downsides, Kyle knew that the attraction was too great and there was no stopping this freight train from careening off the mountain.

Kyle made his way to the bathroom and turned on the faucet to the sink. After drinking a few mouthfuls of cold water from cupped hands, he splashed some on his face and then over his head before attempting to smooth out the parts of his short, dark hair that were sticking up in different directions due to a restless night's sleep. He stood for a moment and relished the reflection of his youth in the mirror. A snapshot in time that was fleeting. Having turned eighteen in May, he arguably had some of the best years ahead of him and felt excitement for the future but, there was a sense of loss over the carefree years of adolescence that were now just memories receding in the distance. For the recent high school graduate, who was technically an adult now, this was a transitional period that would mark the final summer of his childhood before testing his wings on the currents of independence when he headed off to college in the fall. Up to this point, life had been relatively simple and free from turmoil. However, his world was about to get a bit more complicated.

Just then, he heard a knock on the door. Patrick had arrived.

Finding Our Way Through the Fog
Jonathan B. Taylor

Finding Our Way Through the Fog
Jonathan B. Taylor

8

CHAPTER 2, 'PATRICK'

Patrick Connor traveled along the sun-dappled path through the dense forest of oak and pine trees that led to Kyle Jacobs' house. He was in full predatory mode and felt his senses heightened as he moved like a cat through the trees. The sound of his own breathing, echoed in his ears while his feet crunched loudly on the bed of dead leaves and fallen pine needles that littered the trail. The scent of pine was strong in the salty morning air and in the distance, he heard the sound of seagulls squabbling while nearby a woodpecker drummed rapidly on the trunk of a tree with its sharp, pointed beak.

Sunset Cove was a large beach community that was situated on a peninsula, which protruded from the southern coast of Cape Cod. Several acres of protected woodland covered most of the southern shore and carved out a large swath of land between the east and west sides of the small town. The east side was the more exclusive neighborhood which consisted of large luxury homes with private drives and sprawling grounds while the west side was more congested with densely packed, modest homes on postage stamp size property lots. A main road ran in a horseshoe pattern around the village and was divided into three sections aptly named East Main, West Main, and North Main streets. North Main Street was the heart of the village and home to several small shops and restaurants, some of which were seasonal establishments. While Patrick lived in the last house at the very end of East Main Street in what could only be described as a mansion, the Jacobs lived at the very end of West Main Street in a large cape style house that sat atop an above ground, finished basement. Set back in the woods, it was one of the nicer properties on the west side due to its seclusion and distance from the nearest neighbor.

Patrick navigated his way easily through the spider web network of paths that would have provided confusion for anyone who wasn't familiar with the layout of the winding maze. It was basically a straight shot to Kyle's house but the paths didn't make it that easy. At the halfway point, he passed a clearing where he and Kyle had built a stone fire pit and dragged some plastic lawn furniture out into the woods to create a secluded spot where they would go to be alone and get away from everyone. The most secluded spot they had discovered while exploring the forest together was an area just to the south of here through a wall of thorn bushes. That path led to the southernmost tip of Sunset cove, which was virtually inaccessible from any other direction.

Turning the corner onto the final path that led to Kyle's house, Patrick could feel his pulse quicken and the excitement start to build with the eruption of butterflies in the walls of his abdomen. Over the past few years, pursuing other boys had fast become Patrick's favorite pastime and several months ago, Kyle had become the target of his attraction. He wasn't sure if he was shifting more to the gay end of the sexuality spectrum but he knew that while his desire for boys was intensifying, his interest in females was fading. He still enjoyed sex with girls but straight sex didn't have the same intensity and gratification that guy on guy action provided. He supposed that part of the problem was how girls would often pursue him so there was no challenge and everything was out in the open so there was zero risk involved. This left his heterosexual hookups feeling somewhat generic and homogenized.

Being a closeted bisexual, Patrick kept his gay entanglements private so there was a certain risk involved with those highly clandestine encounters. As a general rule, Patrick only pursued other closeted gay and bisexual boys who were equally invested in keeping their secret safe. This presented its own set of problems since closeted individuals were harder to identify, which was the first and arguably most important step in the mating ritual process. Because they weren't wearing signs advertising their availability, Patrick had to find creative ways to identify potential partners. He would often elicit the names of previous lovers from his current conquests in order to gain an edge on his next unsuspecting target who had been unknowingly 'outed' through his devious tactics. His last hookup was a rather cute boy named Kevin whose pointed chin and thin nose gave him a somewhat elfish appearance. Kevin confided in Patrick that he had three previous gay experiences and among those names, there was one that stood out. That was Kyle Jacobs.

Kyle was the most beautiful person that Patrick had ever known and one of the first boys to whom he had found himself attracted. In junior high school, he would often steal glimpses of him in the hallway and try his best not to stare but always be somehow unable to look away. Now, as a young man, Kyle had become even more stunning. He had an angelic face with dark hair, greenish brown eyes, and full red lips that stood out on his flawless white skin. He had a lean, muscular build at five foot ten and one hundred sixty five pounds with the most perfectly developed ass that Patrick had ever seen on another human being.

Finding Our Way Through the Fog
Jonathan B. Taylor

Although he often fantasized about him over the years and imagined being with him, Patrick had no reason to think that Kyle was even the slightest bit gay and therefore, never dreamed that he would one day find himself on the verge of making those fantasies become a reality. That all changed when Kevin revealed that Kyle had been one of his past lovers. For Patrick, learning that information was like matching the winning lottery numbers on a multimillion dollar jackpot.

He immediately set his sights on Kyle and made numerous trips to the Jacobs' house through the woods in hopes of running into him. He wanted to catch him alone and the opportunity finally arose when he spotted Kyle sitting on top of a picnic table in his backyard enjoying the sun on a warm day in late March. Patrick approached him and struck up a conversation, pretending to have just been out exploring in the forest when he took this one path to see where it would lead. He played it off as though their meeting was by chance when in fact, he had orchestrated the entire encounter and every move he made was meticulous and methodical.

Now, after weeks of build up toward fulfilling one of his greatest desires to date, Patrick stood frozen on the brink, seemingly unable to follow through on his highly anticipated, erotic endeavor. This was uncharted territory for the usually cool contender who never had any trouble closing the deal on a sexual conquest. Kyle was sending some pretty strong signals which made it abundantly clear that he wanted Patrick every bit as much as Patrick wanted him but every time the two got close to crossing that threshold, they would both pull back and retreat to their respective corners. They were like two mimes performing on a street corner who were feeling their way around an invisible barrier while being unable to penetrate the imaginary force field between them.

Finding Our Way Through the Fog
Jonathan B. Taylor

Patrick didn't know what could be causing Kyle's hesitation but he had a pretty good idea of what was driving his own apprehension. Kyle was unlike anyone he had ever known, and Patrick's feelings for him had moved well beyond the overwhelming physical attraction that he felt and developed into something much deeper. Normally, by this stage of the game, Patrick would have made his move, had his fun, grown bored, and moved on but, something was causing him to linger in the wooing phase and prolong the pleasure of never ending anticipation. He was enamored with Kyle and afraid of losing him to that familiar pattern that brought all of his past liaisons to an end.

Kyle would swim through his thoughts like a playful dolphin when they were apart, urging Patrick to dive in and join him. The anticipation that grew before seeing him would be rewarded with the joy and excitement that he experienced when they were together. Patrick felt that Kyle's extraordinary attractiveness was exceeded only by his captivating personality. He saw Kyle as an uplifting and positive presence in the world whose ability to always see the best in people inspired Patrick to be a better person and strive to become that idealized version of himself that Kyle envisioned but he was conflicted. While a part of him wanted to violate Kyle sexually in unimaginable ways, there was an innocence and genuineness in Kyle that Patrick didn't want to defile. He wanted to preserve and protect that purity like the shiny new toy that was too cherished to play with and therefore kept pristine and in its original wrapper as a prized collector's item. Amid all of the blurry lines and swirling mixed emotions there was one thing that was perfectly clear. For the first time in his young life, Patrick had crossed the line and fallen in love.

Finding Our Way Through the Fog
Jonathan B. Taylor

CHAPTER 3, 'THE DANCE'

Patrick exited the woods and approached the door at the rear corner of the Jacobs' house that entered into the above ground finished basement of the three story home. Following a rapid three knocks, he heard Kyle's familiar voice inviting him to 'Come in'. He stepped inside and scanned the room. No sign of Kyle. He must be in the bathroom. The first floor of Kyle's house was basically a studio apartment and had been his living area since moving down there from his old bedroom when he turned thirteen. It was an open floor plan with the exception of a bathroom and adjacent utility room, which housed the boiler, hot water heater, and electrical panels. In the opposite corner were a double bed and a couple of bureaus. On the other side of the room, directly across from where Patrick had entered, was a makeshift gym, which had an adjustable weight bench with a leg curl attachment and a contraption for doing cable pulley exercises. There was also a squat rack, a preacher bench, and a wall mounted pull up bar as well as various weights, bars, and dumbbells on a rack next to a heavy bag which hung from the ceiling. In the middle of the room, were a sofa, two chairs, and a wall mounted flat screen television. Although there was no kitchen, Kyle had a small mini fridge and a microwave oven, which sat in a cupboard below a stairway that led to the upper floors where he could access his parent's kitchen if the need arose.

Finding Our Way Through the Fog
Jonathan B. Taylor

Kyle appeared from the bathroom. His partially tamed hair was darker than usual from being wet down but still had the slightly tousled 'bed head' look that he often sported in defiance of his beauty. Both of their faces lit up with wide eyes and beaming smiles when they saw each other as they dreamily said, 'Good morning.' before blushing and awkwardly looking toward the ground over the exposure of their obvious feelings for one another. This is where Ally would have urged them to 'get a room' had she been there to witness the spectacle of their daily ritual.

Patrick made his way toward the sofa and placed his small, black, canvas backpack on one of the cushions. During the school year, it served as a book bag but now it carried all of his supplies for a day at the beach. Kyle had a similar dark green model hanging on one of the hooks that were fixed to the wall beside the smaller of his two bureaus. He moved with a quiet confidence that was just shy of a swagger. Unlike Kyle, who seemed indifferent of his own attractiveness, Patrick reveled in his looks and carried himself accordingly. Watching Patrick walk across the room with his blond hair and dazzling blue eyes, reminded Kyle of the uplifting feeling he got from seeing the sun track across a cloudless sky for the first time following days of rain. Patrick pulled off his tank top in the most alluring way imaginable and said, "I thought we'd do some chest today. Are you ready to be abused?"

"Yes," Kyle responded enthusiastically, while throwing his head back and pumping his fist as though he had just won first prize at the fair.

"We'll start with some barbell flat bench, followed by incline dumbbell presses and flies. Then we can head to the beach and do the butterfly stroke for our swim."

"Sounds good," Kyle replied approvingly.

"Well, come on. Let's go! It's your set and we haven't got all day." Patrick issued his directives in a commanding voice but it was all done good naturedly.

"Yes, drill sergeant," Kyle responded as if a private attending boot camp in the Marines. He lay down on the bench and got beneath the barbell, which was already loaded with forty-five pound plates on either side for a warm up set.

"Give me ten, Private," Patrick instructed.

"Yes, drill sergeant! Ten," Kyle confirmed obediently. What seemed like harmless fun actually had a deeper meaning. Through this little bit of roll playing, they were solidifying their positions in any future relationship dynamic. Patrick was asserting himself as a 'top' and Kyle was confirming himself as the 'bottom'.

Patrick stood behind Kyle at the head of the bench to provide him with a spot. He leaned back slightly and projected his waist and hips forward so that the bulge of his genitals was thrust out over Kyle's forehead. Kyle looked up and saw the outline of Patrick's well endowed penis with a distinctive mushroom head that showed easily through his loose fitting nylon mesh lifeguard shorts with the silky shear undergarment that came standard in most men's swimwear. As he adjusted and positioned himself for his set, Kyle lifted his head off of the bench and gently nudged the tip of Patrick's awaiting penis which earned him an approving smile from his handsome trainer.

Kyle then performed his ten reps and when he finished they switched places so that Patrick was lying on the bench and Kyle was standing behind him in the spotting position. Now, Kyle leaned his shoulders back and his hips forward, waiting for Patrick to give him a 'genital' nudge in return. However, Patrick took it a step further when he lifted his head off the bench and began rubbing it vigorously on Kyle's awaiting penis, causing Kyle's eyes to widen with surprise and gleam with delight. Patrick looked up at Kyle affectionately and asked, "Will you be my girl," to which, Kyle looked down at Patrick, stared into his eyes and smiled with deepening dimples, as he began to slowly nod his head in agreement. Suddenly, Kyle saw the flimsy material of his own lifeguard shorts begin to rise from his growing erection. Looking at Patrick's shorts, he could see his erection forming as well. They both thought to themselves that it was finally going to happen. They were laying their cards on the table and passing the point of no return. Just then, Patrick suddenly sat up so that his back was to Kyle, concealing his now rock hard erection from view. Kyle followed Patrick's abrupt lead and made his own departure from the moment by turning his back on another potential consummation of their elusive union and shielding his suddenly throbbing erection from Patrick's sight in the process.

"I need some water," he said, walking over to the mini fridge to retrieve a bottle.

"Me too," Patrick seconded. "Can you bring me some?"

"Sure," Kyle said, still standing with his back to Patrick and slowly sipping his water while waiting for his obstinate erection to subside. For something that took only seconds to form, it was taking an uncomfortably long time to diminish. Meanwhile, Patrick's erection had rapidly relaxed and he was already growing impatient.

"Come on," he urged. "What's taking you so long? We gotta get this workout in or we're gonna be late again." They were both scheduled for lifeguard duty that day. Finally, Patrick finished with, "That's enough joking around."

Finding Our Way Through the Fog
Jonathan B. Taylor

That did it. "Oh, so that's what this was," Kyle thought to himself incredulously. "We were just joking around? Is this guy for real? What am I doing here? It's like Kevin two point oh." He knew however, that it wasn't like Kevin at all. Patrick wasn't like anyone or anything he had ever experienced before and it didn't matter if he never heard from him again after having sex with him. He would follow this through to the end because the true regret would come from never taking the chance.

Whatever Patrick had done, it seemed to have worked. Kyle was cured of his stubborn erection and he felt confident that he could resume the workout, free from any worries of recurrence. This is how it had been for the past several months of slow escalation. Each time they got close to crossing that line, they would both hit the brakes and pull back on the reins before pressing the reset button and doing it all again. They were like two planets, drawn to each other by gravity while being pulled apart by the vacuum of space, locked together in an endless orbital waltz as they danced around one another without ever actually colliding.

Finding Our Way Through the Fog
Jonathan B. Taylor

CHAPTER 4, 'WEST BEACH'

With their erections subsided, the two wishful lovers were finally able to finish their workout and avoid further interruptions, by skipping the suggestive roll playing of domineering drill sergeant and submissive subordinate and turning their attention to the business of exercise. When their sets were complete, they quickly grabbed their gear and departed Kyle's house where they walked down the long, winding driveway through the trees that led to West Main Street on their way to the sprawling sands of Sunset Cove's West Beach. The Jacobs' house was set far enough back in the forest to be obscured from the view of the street. It made for a pleasant, picturesque stroll on a bright, sunny day but it was the kind of spooky trail that you took with quick strides and your heart in your throat when made at night, as you half expected an ax murderer to leap out at you with every urgent step.

They reached the main road and turned right toward the beach and the bustling community of the West Side. A left turn would have taken them a short distance to a large parking area at the end of West Main Street that was a popular scenic overlook by day and a wild teenage hangout by night. As they walked along at a steady pace, Kyle posed a question to Patrick.

"If you could have any superpower, what would it be? And please don't say flying. Everyone says flying, which only shows a lack of imagination."

Finding Our Way Through the Fog
Jonathan B. Taylor

Patrick was never really a fan of Kyle's hypothetical scenarios, which always felt slightly psychoanalytical and seemed more like Rorschach tests than small talk. He was someone who enjoyed a comfortable silence whereas Kyle found quiet moments unnerving but Patrick indulged him and played along with his game.

"Okay," Patrick answered. "It's not flying but its pretty close."

"Really," Kyle replied with a sense of intrigue. "So, what is it?"

"My superpower would be teleportation," Patrick revealed.

"Why teleportation," Kyle questioned curiously.

"I don't know," Patrick pondered. "I guess it's because that's the one I think about the most so, it's the first one that comes to mind."

"Why do you think about teleportation," Kyle pressed as he attempted to understand the enigma that was Patrick Connor.

"You know, whenever I'm in a situation that I want to get out of I think, 'I wish I could teleport myself out of here,'" Patrick explained.

Kyle was silent for a moment as he considered Patrick's answer. It was somewhat similar to flying but he was satisfied that Patrick had at least put some thought into it and was only being honest. There was no right or wrong answer but, he couldn't help wondering how many times Patrick had wanted to teleport himself out of a situation involving him and whether he was thinking about it right then.

"So, what about you," Patrick asked in return. "What would your superpower be?"

"That's easy," Kyle answered. "If I could have any superpower, it would be the ability to read minds."

"You mean, like telepathy," Patrick asked.

"I guess you could call it that. Telepathy or clairvoyance. I just want to know what people are thinking. People seem to never let you know what they're actually thinking." Kyle wondered if Patrick was picking up on the fact that he was referring to him. "That's one of the reasons that I enjoy reading novels so much. In novels, the author gives us the power of clairvoyance by allowing us to peer into their character's minds and share their thoughts and feelings so we can see what's really going on behind all of those blank stares that we often face every day. Sometimes I wonder what it would be like to live in a world where everyone knew what the other was thinking and feeling. Deception would be off the table and all of our precious secrets exposed." Again, Kyle was hinting at the situation between them.

"Of course," Patrick pointed out almost defensively, "we would all need much thicker skin in a world where all of those comments that we keep to ourselves and are best left unsaid were suddenly spewed forth and unloaded on our companions, putting a tremendous amount of stress on all of our relationships."

Patrick had a point. Maybe clairvoyance wasn't such a good idea after all. Kyle realized that it had some downsides and began rethinking his choice, as they turned onto Access Road, which was the last stretch of their trek. A slight bit of laughter escaped Patrick's lips.

"What," Kyle asked in response to his snicker.

"I was just picturing you with a giant purple turban on your head and a deck of tarot cards."

Finding Our Way Through the Fog
Jonathan B. Taylor

"Sounds like 'worst superhero costume ever'," Kyle laughed as the two of them sized each other up. Both were wearing their bright orange shorts and white ball caps with the word 'Lifeguard' stenciled across the front and they each had on a backpack, sun glasses, and black mesh running sneakers. The only noticeable difference was their shirts. Patrick had on a white tank top whereas Kyle wore a black pocket T-shirt.

"We look like a couple of those guys who call each other up to see what the other is wearing so they can dress alike," Patrick said wryly.

"That's funny," Kyle replied. "I was thinking we look like a couple of not so undercover Secret Service Agents who are trying unsuccessfully to blend in with a crowd of tourists."

"Yeah, you're right. That's probably what people are thinking," Patrick droned sarcastically.

They reached the beach at a few minutes before 8:00am, which was the start of their shift. They still had to swim a lap to complete their workout but at least they were technically at the job site, even if they weren't actually at their posts. West Beach consisted of an immense strip of sugary white sand that was around a half mile long. It was a popular public beach that attracted many visitors from inland locations who would come for the day and spend ten dollars to park in one of the large lots, which were owned and operated by the town. Halfway down the beach, there was a picnic area set back from the shore, which was referred to as the 'pavilion' although there was no structure other than a large concrete pad with ten wooden picnic tables spread out in a uniform pattern. Behind that, a small, concrete bunker style building provided restrooms and an outdoor showerhead where beach goers could rinse the salt and sand off themselves under bone chillingly cold water. There was also a small wooden lifeguard shack that housed various types of equipment such as floatation devices, emergency aid kits, and radios for communication. There were two Lifeguard chairs, one situated a quarter of the way down the beach and the other, three quarters, which received a fresh coat of white paint every year resulting in a thick latex shell.

Just offshore, about five hundred yards out and five hundred yards apart, were two large, red marine buoys that contained special sensors for detecting any tagged sharks that entered the area. Over the past decade, with an increasing seal population, Cape Cod had become a hotspot for Great White Sharks, which enjoyed snacking on the plentiful marine mammals. Every year, a marine conservation group would place special tags on any previously unidentified sharks that it was able to locate. This allowed them to track and record data on the apex predators. The buoys were a vital tool in protecting swimmers from the threat of shark attacks. If a tagged shark were to enter the safe zone, it would trigger an alarm that sounded along with a flashing red light to alert beach goers of the danger. The lifeguards would then use their bullhorns to order everyone out of the water and the beach would be temporarily closed to swimming until the Harbor Master and other local officials could make a threat assessment. It was a good system with only one major flaw. It only worked on tagged sharks and every week during shark season, the conservationists would locate and tag new sharks, which indicated that there were still plenty of the untagged beasts patrolling these waters, that could easily slip past the safety net. This thought always loomed in Kyle's mind when he and Patrick would swim out to the southern buoy and back. An alarm wouldn't do them much good at that distance. Even if it were to go off, they would never make it back to shore before being easily overtaken by a hungry shark and becoming it's lunch.

It was still early and the beach was relatively empty but this was generally the time when people would start arriving and they knew that it would be filling up soon. They removed their backpacks and left them in the sand at the base of the first lifeguard chair along with their hats, sunglasses, shirts, and sneakers. Just as they were about to take off for the water, they saw Ally and Amber approaching from the direction of the pavilion. The two girls were a vision of loveliness walking across the sand in their bikinis with their hair blowing slightly in the gentle morning breeze. Ally looked particularly stunning in a bright canary yellow bikini which contrasted nicely with her beautiful bronze skin and showed off her curvy, toned body and voluptuous chest. She was a classic beauty with long, dark, curly hair and light blue eyes that were the color of the sky. Amber was equally breathtaking with shoulder length red hair that was like a warm orange sunset and which she would often use her entire arm to flip over to one side. She had bright green eyes that were the color of emeralds and a perfect upside-down heart shaped ass that Kyle would steal glimpses of whenever he had the chance. She was wearing a lime green bikini and unlike Patrick and Ally, who tanned up easily, she was fair skinned like Kyle and had to apply copious amounts of sun block to prevent from burning. Both girls had the same type of natural earth tone shading and contouring around their eyes as Kyle and Patrick, which gave all four of them the appearance of wearing lightly applied eye makeup where none was required.

"So, you guys finally showed up," Ally chided.

"Yeah. We thought we were gonna have to cover for you," Amber joined in.

Finding Our Way Through the Fog
Jonathan B. Taylor

"You may still have to," Kyle said with mildly pleading eyes. "Can you get our stuff for us from the shack?"

"What's wrong with your legs," Ally balked.

"Nothing, but we did a chest workout this morning and we still have to swim a lap. It's only to the first buoy and back." He tilted his head and gave her an inquisitive puppy dog face.

"Oh, so you want us to do your jobs for you while the two of you go frolic in the water," she scoffed.

"Does that mean you'll do it," Kyle smiled.

"Sure. We'll do it," Ally agreed, "for a kiss."

"Okay," Kyle shrugged and began to lean toward her when she held up her hand to stop him.

"Not us," she said. "You have to kiss each other."

"What," Kyle's face reddened as he laughed nervously. He looked at Patrick and saw that he too was blushing although his tanned skin made it less obvious.

"Come on," Amber pleaded. "It would be so hot!" The girls looked at each other and nodded in agreement.

"Relax," Ally said, sensing their discomfort and deciding to let them off the hook. "I'm only joking. Of course we'll help you out. Don't we always?"

They then turned and began walking toward the lifeguard shack to retrieve the radios and other equipment that the boys would need for their shift. As they walked away, Kyle and Patrick watched them for a moment, mesmerized by the sway of their backsides, before finally heading down to the shore for their swim. The sea was still relatively cold in early July and took a bit of their breath away with each plunging step into deeper water. When it reached their waists, they dove in and began to swim. As Patrick suggested, they did the butterfly stroke to target their chest muscles. Kyle was the stronger swimmer and could have easily taken Patrick in a race but this was just a workout so the two of them stayed in stride. Kyle tried to focus on his breathing and form but he kept thinking about the interaction with Ally, which had occurred moments ago. She seemed to be aware of the sexual tension between him and Patrick as she was continually making suggestive comments like the one about them kissing, which really wasn't helping matters. Kyle saw Patrick as being extremely skittish over the prospect of gay sex and figured that any threat of exposure would make it that much harder to coax him from the closet. He had a false image of Patrick as being inexperienced with other boys, having no knowledge of the turned out trail of teenagers he had left in his wake throughout high school.

As they arrived at the buoy, they heard the familiar sound of a motorboat approaching and saw Nick Barros' eighteen foot Boston Whaler coming toward them from the direction of South Point. Nick was the local Harbor Master and although he was technically their boss, he treated them more as coworkers than subordinates. He was like the adolescent babysitter who pretty much let the kids do whatever they wanted while occasionally cracking down and telling them to get the fork out of the toaster. He pulled up alongside them and threw the twin outboard motors into reverse for a split second to stop his forward momentum. The boat was an open skiff with two swivel seats at the midway point where the steering column was located. The rest of the boat was bare except for some first aid and safety equipment such as life jackets and a lightweight aluminum frame stretcher, which had cylindrical Styrofoam floats attached to its sides.

Nick was fidgeting with something on the other side of the boat, and Kyle was wishing that he would hurry up as he and Patrick treaded water to hold their positions by the buoy.

Being this far out, Kyle felt extremely vulnerable and didn't want to linger. He knew that floating objects like buoys were magnets for marine life, drawing one fish after another, right up the food chain. Now, they were suspended in twenty-foot-deep water with their arms and legs dangling like delectable lures for any passing ambush predators that felt like making a meal out of them. Kyle could feel his heart pounding in his chest while the dreaded theme music from 'Jaws' played ominously in the back of his mind.

Just as Kyle was about to say 'fuck it' and start swimming back to shore, Nick appeared at the side of the boat, leaning over the edge and looking down at them. He was tall and lanky at six foot four and one hundred eighty pounds with leathery skin and curly, windblown, salt and pepper hair that made him look older than his thirty-five years.

"How'd you know we were out here," Patrick asked.

"Your girlfriends gave you up," he said, holding out his radio as if it were a prop to his explanation.

"Dirty snitches," Patrick shook his head disapprovingly.

"Why? It's not like I was going to believe that bullshit about you both being in the bathroom anyways," Nick laughed.

Suddenly, fear swept over Patrick's face as he was the first to see the telltale, dreaded dorsal fin, with tail fin in tow, slowly making their way into view from behind the boat. He started shrieking, "Shark! Shark!" in a high pitched falsetto as he scrambled toward the boat in a thrashing panic. Kyle instinctively launched himself toward the boat as well before turning his head to glance at the two fins carving their way through the water. Reaching the boat first, he pulled himself over the side, landing on his back with a thud inside the craft. He then reached over the side and took hold of Patrick's hand, attempting to pull him to safety but, he lost his grip and Patrick fell backwards, disappearing under the water. Kyle panicked and started to jump over the side when Patrick resurfaced and took hold of his hand again. This time they interlocked their thumbs in an arm-wrestling grip and were able to hold on to each other while Kyle pulled him out of the water and into the boat. They both looked at Nick, who offered no help during the ordeal, and saw that he was laughing uncontrollably as he walked to the stern of the boat and began pulling on a thin, nylon string to retrieve the floating fins that were attached to either end of a long, plastic tube.

"You guys fell for the oldest trick in the book," Nick gloated. "I just confiscated this off of some kids near the East Side Marina and, when I heard that you were out here swimming, well, it was too good to pass up. What do you think," he asked, holding it up for inspection. "They did a pretty good job on this thing. It looks realistic. Right?"

"Real funny, asshole," Patrick fumed.

"No shit," Kyle added. "What are you, some kind of fuckin' psychopath, ripping off old horror movies?"

"You're just pissed 'cause I got you," Nick continued to laugh.

"Well, it's not exactly the kind of shit that you'd expect the HARBOR MASTER to pull," Kyle responded, downplaying their gullibility.

"I know," Nick said proudly. "That really sold it. Huh?"

"Yeah, real fuckin' responsible," Patrick concurred with Kyle's point.

"Oh, really? You two want to lecture me about responsibility while you're out here swimming on the taxpayers' dime when you're supposed to be at your posts."

Finding Our Way Through the Fog
Jonathan B. Taylor

"Look at what you're doing? You're cruising around fuckin' with people on the taxpayers' dime," Kyle shot back.

"You're a dick," Patrick shouted as he and Kyle reluctantly jumped back in the water, with their nerves still on edge, to begin the swim back to dry land.

Before pulling away, Nick yelled to them, "Just remember the old saying, 'You don't have to outrun a bear in the woods, you only have to outrun the guy you're walking with'."

These words of wisdom offered some comfort to Kyle but didn't sit well with Patrick who shouted a final, "Fuck you!" before breaking back into the butterfly stroke toward the shore.

The girls watched from the beach and critiqued Patrick and Kyle as they walked toward them from the water after finishing their swim. Both were lean and muscular with no visible body fat and sported six pack abs with well developed shoulders, chests, arms and legs that were flanked by prominent lat muscles which gave their backs the classic vee shape that is prized by body builders. Patrick was slightly more muscular with an athletic build whereas Kyle was sinewy and boasted more of a swimmer's build. As they waded through the knee deep water, Kyle saw that Ally and Amber had them in their sights and were clearly making comments to each other. Kyle suddenly felt self-conscious, realizing that his wet shorts were clinging to him and revealing the effect that the cold water was having on his package, which had withdrawn as far into his body as it could possibly get. He looked at Patrick's privates to see if he was having the same issue and saw that he was not. His impressive member was still swinging menacingly from the motion of his stride. Kyle pulled the waistband of his shorts away from his body in an attempt to peel the material from its revealing grip and take the triggering source for his feelings of inadequacy out of the equation. Patrick, however, made no such effort. He was also aware of the revealing grip that his wet shorts had on his body but he took tremendous pride in the size of his well-endowed penis and welcomed any opportunity to show it off. They approached the girls who were standing at the base of the southernmost lifeguard chair and Kyle asked, "Did you see what that lunatic just did to us? I think he's gotta have a couple of screws loose."

"Of course we saw," Ally answered. "Nick gave us front row tickets."

"So, you knew he was going to do it," Patrick sounded annoyed.

"Yeah. He gave us the heads up not to sound the alarm. You gotta give it to him. It was pretty funny," Ally shrugged.

"You thought that shit was funny," Kyle said in disbelief. "Then, you're just as twisted as he is."

"Oh, hell yes, it was funny. And, you would have laughed too if you saw it happen to someone else."

Kyle and Patrick looked at each other and laughter escaped the both of them as they nodded in agreement with Ally's point. After gathering their equipment, which included a first aid kit, a radio, a bullhorn and a florescent orange, torpedo shaped floatation device to assist in rescues, Patrick and Amber headed down the beach to take up position on the other lifeguard chair while Ally joined Kyle on the bench style seat of his chair.

"So, what were you girls talking about when we were coming back from our swim," Kyle asked, not really sure if he wanted to know the answer.

"We were discussing how hot you two are and trying to decide who's hotter," Ally answered.

"So, who won," Kyle pressed.

"It was a tossup. You're cuter but, Patrick has the nicer body. Except for the butt. You definitely have the nicer butt. Although," she paused, "there's one other area where he's got you but, I won't say what that is."

"You don't have to," Kyle said with disillusionment. "I already know what it is. You're talking about his big dick. Out of everything, I'd say that's the one that hurts the most."

"Oh, I'm sure it does," Ally concurred. "Just try to relax your muscles and use lots of lube."

Kyle laughed and nodded his head approvingly over the pun, which he had so carelessly teed up for her. He enjoyed spending time with Ally. Her personality made it feel like hanging out with one of the guys and he couldn't help wondering how much of a role that may have factored into his attraction to her. Suddenly, Kyle had a sobering thought as the reality of Ally's words began to sink in and he wondered how he would be able to handle Patrick's potentially painful penis if they were to follow their current course of action and finally complete the elusive deed. Kyle winced as he imagined his asshole being torn open by Patrick's massive member and Ally, immediately took notice.

"You're thinking about it right now aren't you," she said as if having just caught him in the act of masturbating.

"What? No," Kyle insisted as his red face betrayed him.

"You really shouldn't play poker," she advised. "You have absolutely no poker face and everybody can see what you're thinking by your facial expressions and body language."

"Well, that sucks," Kyle, thought to himself. Here he had been wishing he could read minds and Ally just told him that he was doing the complete opposite. Instead of knowing what others were thinking, he was walking around broadcasting his own thoughts to everybody else.

"Look, it's obvious you two are into each other so, why don't you just get it over with and do it already," Ally suggested.

"I'm not saying that I don't think about it," Kyle admitted, "but, Patrick would never go for it," he lied. He didn't like having to deceive her however, the situation with Patrick had put him in a difficult position. He usually told her everything, including the details of his experience with Kevin but, in that case, he never mentioned him by name and was able to protect his anonymity. Ally already knew Patrick so he couldn't reveal any intimate information without betraying a confidence and exposing his secret.

"Trust me, he wants you," she insisted. "I see how he looks at you."

"Even if that were true, wanting is different than doing. Just because somebody wants to do something, doesn't mean they would ever actually do it." Kyle continued his efforts to throw her off the trail. "Besides, you're just trying to change the subject from the fact that you think Patrick's dick is better than mine because he's hung like a porn star." Kyle said in an attempt to change the subject.

"I never said his was better," Ally corrected him. "I just said that there was an area where he had you beat."

"What difference does it make," Kyle shot back. "Either way, it says that you're into farm animals."

"No. I'm not interested in horse cock," she insisted.

"But, I thought that all girls like big dicks," Kyle replied.

"Yeah, whores maybe," Ally, said. "But, don't look at me. I got a tight pussy. The girls who like big dicks are the ones with big pussies."

"Yeah, not a big fan of the 'roomy vagina'," Kyle confessed,

"I don't know why you're making such a big deal out of this anyway. You have a nice size dick and it's really handsome too. Besides, just because Patrick's got a freakishly big dick, doesn't mean he knows how to use it."

"Why do you say that? Did Amber say something," Kyle was eager to get some intel on Patrick's sexual prowess.

"Let's just say that he only goes the distance about half the time," Ally dished, "and, I know that's never been a problem for you. With you, I've gotten off every time we've done it."

"Really? So, he doesn't finish her off?" Kyle was only half feigning surprise as he took in the information. As a competitor, he liked hearing that he was better in bed than Patrick, but as a potential partner, he was a little disappointed by the prospect.

"Not always," she said shaking her head. "Unfortunately, a lot of guys don't. I hear girls complain all the time how most guys are only interested in getting themselves off."

"But, wouldn't that imply that they preferred masturbation," Kyle picked at her words.

"You know what I mean. Guys generally make selfish lovers," she concluded.

"What's ironic is that, by not bringing a girl to orgasm, they end up cheating themselves out of the best part," Kyle reasoned. "When a chick orgasms, her vagina sends waves of muscular contractions up your dick which are designed to stimulate male ejaculation and draw the semen up into the uterus to achieve fertilization. That is the coolest feeling in the world and there's nothing that comes close to it."

"How scientific," Ally said dryly.

Kyle continued, "I bet if I could design one of those pocket pussies like they sell in the back of smut magazines, which feels like the real thing and simulates the contractions of a chick's orgasm, I could make a fortune."

"You should do it," she encouraged. "Then you could go on that show where people go to get financial backing for their ideas and inventions."

They both laughed. "I'm not sure how that would go over," Kyle said doubtfully, "although, it might work in a late night satire skit."

"Look," Ally said, returning to the subject, "the bottom line is, you're better looking so, you win. At the end of the day, isn't that the one that everybody would take over all the others?"

"Well, that's debatable," Kyle shrugged off her compliment, as he didn't really see himself to be more attractive than Patrick. "If I'm better looking, then why do all the girls swarm around him?" Kyle questioned as they both looked down the beach and saw three girls standing at the base of Patrick's lifeguard chair, looking up and talking to him while Amber sat beside him taking little notice. She was neither jealous nor possessive which, was the only way to be with Patrick.

"Oh, I don't know, maybe because he's rich," Ally pointed out as though the answer should have been obvious.

Kyle figured that she had a point. Attractiveness was often amplified by a sizable bank account and the kiss of wealth had probably turned more than a toad or two into princes. However, whether Patrick's looks were naturally better or being enhanced by his money didn't matter. The bottom line was that he had won. The only way for Kyle to win now, would be for him to bag Patrick.

Finding Our Way Through the Fog
Jonathan B. Taylor

CHAPTER 5, 'A SEDUCTIVE SHOWER'

After spending much of the morning hanging out with Kyle and Patrick in their lifeguard chairs, Ally and Amber made plans to meet up with them that night and then headed off to play volleyball on one of the impromptu courts, which had popped up along the beach. These sources of recreation would often become the bane of beach goers who suddenly found themselves under threat from errant balls that rolled and bounced through their staked out areas. Once their shift ended, the two boys returned to Kyle's house and found themselves back in his basement where their day began with a close call on his weight bench that only resulted in further frustration for the disjunctive duo. They were each sitting on either side of the sofa with their feet up on the coffee table, while Patrick restlessly surfed through the channels using the remote. As Patrick watched the television, Kyle was watching him and studying the symmetry of his handsome facial features as he often did. He wanted to go to him and be with him but, the few feet of couch cushions between them felt like an ocean that he was unable to cross. Instead, he decided to lob a ball into Patrick's court and see if he wanted to play.

"Well, I'm gonna take a shower," Kyle announced, still staring at Patrick, whose ears pricked up when he heard the words. As their eyes met, Kyle tried to use his betraying body language to his advantage for a change by broadcasting the message of wanting Patrick to join him using only his facial expression, just as Ally had suggested he was doing involuntarily all along. He went to the bathroom and left the door wide open to extend the invitation, as he got undressed. The shower was a four foot square, glass enclosure which was located in the back corner of the bathroom. He stepped inside and turned on the water, keeping it lukewarm to avoid fogging up the glass. He glanced at the open door, hoping to see Patrick entering the bathroom but instead saw that he had taken up position on Kyle's bed, which was the only location that provided a clear view of the shower from the main living area. Patrick was leaning back, propped up on one elbow and massaging his crotch with his free hand. Kyle didn't let his stare linger however, he held it long enough for both to establish that they had seen one another. It was time to put on a show and extend the invitation a little further. With his back to Patrick, he began to caress his ass cheeks and spread them apart like he had practiced in the mirror that morning. Next, he took the soap and began to lather himself, sliding his fingers in and out of his anus with his head tossed back as if in the throws of ecstasy.

From his relocated vantage point on Kyle's bed, Patrick pulled down his shorts and began to stroke his throbbing erection as he watched Kyle run his hands all over his own ass, which appeared as true perfection through the glass walls of the shower stall. This was the first time that he had seen it in the flesh and it was even more spectacular than he'd imagined. Kyle's creamy white ass cheeks were so perfectly round and muscular, they reminded him of two honeydew melons that were ripe for picking. Now, Kyle stood just yards away, finger fucking himself in the shower, practically begging Patrick to come and take him from behind, and all he could do was sit there on the bed like a deer frozen in the headlights, and pleasure himself like some sort of pervert at a peep show.

Suddenly he heard a door open and Kyle's mother calling down from the top of the stairs. Patrick quickly pulled up his shorts and sprang from the bed. He dashed to the couch and hurdled himself over the back, landing in a seated position. He then grabbed a small throw pillow and placed it on his lap to cover his noticeable erection just as Kyle's mother began descending the stairs.

Claire Jacobs was a stunning woman of forty years who could easily pass for thirty. She bore a remarkable resemblance to Kyle and it was clear that he took after her in the gene pool. "Oh, hi Patrick," she said, smiling. "Where's Kyle," she asked, scanning the room.

"He's in the shower," Patrick motioned with his head toward the bathroom. He was wishing for a bigger pillow and hoping that there wouldn't be any reason for him to stand.

"Can you tell him to come see me when he's done?"

"Sure," Patrick agreed, hoping that she would leave now.

"How are you doing," she asked, making polite small talk.

"Good," he responded. "Got no complaints."

"How are your parents? Is your mom still working as a Nurse?"

"No. She's pretty much retired." He didn't want to tell her that his mother had taken to self-medicating and was popping too many pills to pass the drug screening.

"And what does your father do? Isn't he like a CEO or something?"

"He's a corporate vampire," Patrick said nonchalantly. "He takes over corporations and merges them with other companies for a profit."

"Oh," she paused for a moment as though processing the information. "Well, tell them I said hello." She proceeded back up the stairs and Patrick was relieved to hear the door close on the awkward moment that could have been much worse.

Meanwhile, Kyle, who had been trying to entice Patrick to join him in the shower, was disappointed to discover that he had disappeared from view at some point during his seductive performance. He wondered if this was just another case of Patrick pumping the brakes as he got too close to hitting Kyle's bumper or, had the shower show been a complete turn off for the indecisive suitor? After stepping out of the shower and toweling off, Kyle put on a clean pair of boxer briefs and some lightweight, navy blue, cotton gym shorts. He preferred wearing boxer shorts but being around Patrick was like being thirteen years old all over again. He found himself prone to constant, potentially embarrassing erections which boxer briefs made it easier to conceal. Kyle came out of the bathroom and saw Patrick sitting back in his seat on the sofa with the remote in his hand as though he'd never left.

"Your mom was just down here," Patrick offered as an explanation for his early departure from the theater.

"Oh, she was," Kyle, said as if relieved over suddenly gaining insight to a puzzling situation. "What did she want," he questioned, now slightly annoyed by her untimely intrusion. His parents almost never came down to the basement and she had picked the worst moment to break with tradition.

"I don't know. She just said that she needed to talk with you when you were done in the shower."

Kyle ran upstairs and then returned a few minutes later. "She just wanted to tell me that her and Phil are going to New York for the week to attend the opening of a new art gallery that's supposed to feature some of her work." While Kyle's father was a noted journalist and author, his mother was a successful artist and sculptor whose works, which she created in a studio above the family's two car garage, sold for a considerable amount of money in different galleries around the world.

"Oh, dude, you have to throw a bash," Patrick suggested with a devious smile.

"Oh, hell no," Kyle retorted. "I don't want a bunch of drunken assholes trashing my house so I can live out some tired old tradition that's become nothing but a cliché."

Patrick shrugged, "It was just a thought. I'm gonna take off," he said, getting up from the couch and stretching his arms, "but I'll be back around seven o'clock."

"Sounds good," Kyle said, imagining a goodbye kiss between them at this point, if they only had the type of relationship for, which he had been longing.

Finding Our Way Through the Fog
Jonathan B. Taylor

CHAPTER 6, 'PHIL AND CLAIRE'

That evening Kyle sat down to dinner with his parents at one of the six captain's chair style swivel stools that surrounded an island counter in their upstairs kitchen. There was a formal dining room with a large table but they seldom used it except for dinner parties and other special occasions. It was rare for Kyle to be dining with them these days, as he would usually grab something to eat with Patrick either at one of the North Main Street restaurants or they would get takeout and bring it back to his basement. On this night, his mother made a nice linguini with white clam sauce and steamed asparagus spears, which he dusted lightly with freshly grated parmesan cheese. His parents drank white wine and offered him a glass, which he declined. Neither he nor Patrick used any type of drugs or alcohol. Kyle had tried smoking pot once with Ally but didn't enjoy it and Patrick said that he wasn't interested in anything that was going to 'dumb him down'.

While his mother Claire looked young for her age, his father Philip, who went by Phil, looked every bit of his forty years. His dark hair had gray patches on the sides, which were more pronounced in his shortly cropped goatee although they both stayed in excellent physical condition by jogging and going to the gym together a few times a week. They were always there for Kyle but were never big on imposing rules or restrictions and pretty much let him find his own way in the world. They felt more like a couple of old friends than parents and he had been calling them by their first names ever since he turned thirteen and moved into the basement.

"I saw Patrick today," Claire mentioned. "That boy is so handsome and he just gets better looking every time I see him."

"Oh, yeah, he is really good looking," Phil nodded in agreement. "If I was twenty years younger, I would be all over that."

"Okay, can we stop," Kyle pleaded, waving his arms in front of him like overlapping windshield wipers. "Look, I like that you two are so open and cool but, I don't need to listen to you lusting after my friends. It's a bit much!"

"How did this kid get to be so uptight," Phil asked Claire. "He didn't get that shit from us?"

"I think they pick this stuff up on the street," She reasoned. "Who knows, maybe this is just his way of rebelling. You know, by being a repressed prude. Anyway, nobody is lusting after anyone. We were just saying that he's attractive."

"Really? 'Cause it sounded to me like Phil wants to do him," Kyle replied.

Phil was nodding his head in agreement again. "I would totally bone him!"

"Good to know," Kyle shook his head and laughed.

Claire started clearing the plates while Phil rinsed and placed them in the dishwasher. "You know, September is going to be here before you know it," she pointed out to Kyle, "and you still have a lot to do as far as getting ready for school. Have you decided what you want to do about housing?"

"I don't know," Kyle said with frustration in his voice. "I just don't want to live in the dorms with a bunch of rambunctious adolescents who act like their parents left them home alone for the weekend. The ideal thing would be to get an apartment."

"Well, apartments in the city are really expensive," Phil noted.

"I know but, I was thinking I could get a roommate to split the cost."

"Did you have someone in mind," Claire asked.

"I'm working on it." Kyle had wanted to pitch the idea of sharing an apartment to Patrick but he kept getting cold feet just as he did with everything else, which felt like a step toward the edge of that cliff where the unknown future of their complex relationship teetered. Over the course of their time together, Kyle had discovered that having Patrick for a friend could be kind of like having a genie in a bottle where all he had to do was suggest something and, 'poof', Patrick would make it happen. The first example of this occurred when Kyle suggested that the lifeguard positions at West Beach were the ideal summer jobs because they allowed you to hang out at the beach all day. Patrick took this information and used his family's influence to land him and his friends the coveted posts. Patrick obviously didn't need to work but, he reasoned that this type of public service thing looked good on a resume when in fact, it was merely an excuse to get closer and spend more time with Kyle. Now that Kyle recognized the fact that Patrick could turn his suggestions into reality, he found himself reluctant to use this newly discovered power as it felt like manipulation when he did.

"What about Patrick? He's going to be attending school in Boston, isn't he? I know you'll be in different schools but you'll both be in Boston," Claire interrupted his thoughts.

"I'm way ahead of you," he said, as the wheels continued to turn.

Finding Our Way Through the Fog
Jonathan B. Taylor

Kyle made his way back to the basement with his mother's words weighing on his mind. She was right, September was coming at him like a comet and he needed to act. He had often heard the concept of time moving faster as you got older and now he was experiencing it firsthand. He was only eighteen and no longer felt like there were more than enough hours in the day to accomplish the things he needed to get done. It was as if the tired old hourglass was yawning and allowing the sand to gush forth through its gaping gorge as the hands on his watch spun like tops, spawning little tornadoes to peel off the calendar pages like leaves blowing in the wind. He needed to float the idea of being roommates to Patrick and he needed to do it that night.

Finding Our Way Through the Fog
Jonathan B. Taylor

Finding Our Way Through the Fog
Jonathan B. Taylor

50

CHAPTER 7, 'THE PAVILION'

At around seven o'clock, Kyle heard the familiar sound of Patrick's Dodge Challenger in the driveway. He wasn't a fan of environmentally unfriendly vehicles but he had to admit that the powerful machine with its black and red custom paint job was incredibly sexy and he liked the way it pinned him to his seat when Patrick gunned the motor. They cruised around town and took in the sights, stopping for ice cream at a stand on the North Main Street strip, which they ate seductively while staring at each other's eyes. Patrick swirled his tongue around in slow circles on the top of his scoop while Kyle ran his tongue up the side of his cone to catch a trickle of melted ice cream as though he were running it up the shaft of Patrick's prick to catch an escaping drizzle of come. Once again, Kyle could hear Ally's voice in the back of his mind, urging them to 'get a room' and this gave him an idea. Somehow, her tiresome, played out, catch phrase could prove useful by providing the perfect segue into broaching the subject of being roommates with Patrick. "This is ridiculous," he finally thought to himself. "I don't need a gimmick to accomplish something so simple. I'll just mention it and see what he thinks." However, once again, the words got stuck in his throat and he felt all of his confidence drain from his body and scurry away with his balls. Maybe he was over thinking it or, maybe a segue to break the ice wasn't such a bad idea? The indecisiveness wasn't helping matters either and the whole situation was becoming as maddening as the rest of their complicated relationship.

Eventually they made their way to West beach as the clock continued to run on the evening and Kyle wasn't any closer to finding his lost nerve. Patrick parked in the employee lot at the end of Access Road, which was actually closed to parking at that hour, but one of the perks of being a lifeguard was that local law enforcement tended to let certain indiscretions slide. Kyle was curious where Patrick had been earlier in the day when he disappeared at dinner but he was being vague about his whereabouts so, Kyle didn't press. He didn't want to be one of those boyfriends or best friends or whatever the hell they were to each other. He didn't even know what to call it anymore. It felt like they were in a full on relationship at this point with all the boxes checked except for that elusive physical intimacy one. Meanwhile, Ally and Amber had fallen to the wayside as the two boys turned their full attention toward each other.

It was just after sunset and there was still a dark orange glow in the western sky, which reflected nicely on the shimmering blackness of the relatively calm water creating the type of picturesque scene that gave Sunset Cove its name. Patrick and Kyle trudged across the soft sand that gave way beneath their feet and provided a leg workout through the lack of leverage as they made their way toward the pavilion, which was the epicenter of West Beach nightlife. Already, a group of about sixty young people had amassed under the powerful stadium style lights that flooded the area of the picnic tables and concrete pad. The lights had been installed as a deterrent to teens find were meant to drive them from the area after dark. However, they ended up having the opposite effect and, instead served as tractor beams, drawing them in like moths in the night.

The boys caught up with Ally and Amber who were sitting in the sand at the base of the southernmost lifeguard chair passing a joint back and forth to one another. Neither of them drank but, unlike Kyle and Patrick who never used any type of drugs, the girls would sometimes smoke marijuana if it was given to them for free and this was one of those rare occasions. The girls seemed overly excited to see them as an obvious side effect of their current condition. Amber held out the joint to Patrick, asking him if he wanted some.

"Are you alright," he asked rhetorically as he furiously waved away the cloud of smoke that she had blown toward his face.

Ally looked up at Kyle and started to say something but, suddenly appeared completely stumped before declaring, "I forgot what I was gonna say." This caused her and Amber to burst into uncontrollable laughter, as they fell into each other, with Ally laughing so hard at one point that no sound was coming out because she was momentarily unable to breathe.

"What the fuck," Kyle said, shaking his head in disbelief. "How much of that stuff did you smoke?" This prompted another round of hysterical laughter from the girls while Kyle and Patrick rolled their eyes at each other over the absurdity of it all. Watching the girls lose their minds like this, Kyle could see how the infection of drug use was spread. To the outside observer, the girls were inadvertently enticing others to join in their apparent good time. However, if anyone were to look beyond the laughter, they would see that there was really nothing funny about the onset of drug-induced dementia.

"Well, you can kiss those brain cells goodbye," Patrick said indifferently to which Kyle nodded in agreement.

Finding Our Way Through the Fog
Jonathan B. Taylor

As the girl's erratic laughter eased, Patrick and Kyle sat down beside them in the sand. Kyle gave Ally a friendly peck on the lips while Patrick and Amber broke into one of their over-the-top marathon make out sessions, prompting Ally to drop a 'get a room'. That was the opening Kyle had been hoping for but, he suddenly found himself caught off guard as he struggled to find the words, which he had been rehearsing in his head all night. When he was able to regain his footing, he realized this wasn't exactly the opportunity that he was looking for. With Patrick and Amber continuing to go at it, he may as well be talking to the lifeguard chair if he were to mention the roommate idea at that moment. By the time they stopped, the segue had expired but, Kyle was confident that he could count on Ally for another 'get a room' before the night was over. Party animals could play drinking games based on her overuse of that line.

"Are you two pot heads coming back down to earth yet," Kyle asked playfully.

"Hey, I seem to remember you smoking a joint with me one time so, you're not all clean and innocent," Ally pointed out.

"No way," Patrick said with genuine shock. "You, Mr. won't even take an aspirin."

Kyle nodded shamefully. "Yeah, she was able to corrupt me that one time but, I hated every minute of it and never did it again."

"What was so bad about it," Amber asked with a curious laugh.

"I don't know," Kyle considered the question for a moment. "I just felt this wave of anxiety and paranoia come over me and spent the whole time wishing I could feel normal again."

Finding Our Way Through the Fog
Jonathan B. Taylor

"Well, it's not for everyone," she shrugged.

"You two are going to be the only completely straight people in college," Ally predicted.

"I know," Kyle, sighed. "Don't remind me. I'm really not looking forward to the thought of living in the dorms around all of that drinking and partying."

"Me neither," Patrick seconded and, the two of them looked at each other as if waiting to see who would blink first. Kyle figured this was the perfect time to suggest the roommate idea when Amber suddenly hijacked the conversation and started pulling the train away from the station.

"Why do you think that is," she questioned. "Why do so many kids go to college and start drinking like fish?"

"That's a good question," Ally concurred. "Why is there so much drinking on college campuses?"

"Probably because a lot of these kids are getting out from under their parent's control for the first time and are just letting loose," Patrick surmised.

"Well, that's definitely part of it," Kyle agreed, "but I read somewhere that the number one reason college kids say they drink is because it loosens them up for what they refer to as 'recreational sex', which they are otherwise uncomfortable having."

"So, does that mean college students are basically plying each other with alcohol in order to have sex," Ally responded.

"I don't know if they're plying each other but, it certainly sounds like they're plying themselves," Kyle smiled at them and nodded but if he had looked closer at Patrick and Ally, he may have seen the little light bulbs appear above their heads as their eyes narrowed and the wheels began turning. At the moment, he was more focused on trying to steer the conversation back to the downside of dorm life and, as Kyle contemplated his next move, Ally suddenly saved him the trouble.

"Look, you're both going to school in Boston and neither of you wants to live in the dorms so, why don't you just get an apartment together in the city?"

Kyle and Patrick's eyes widened along with their smiles as they looked at one another with joy and relief that someone else had suggested the idea which they had each been agonizing over how to propose and seemingly unable to present themselves. Patrick quickly composed himself and spoke first. "You know, that's actually not a bad idea," he said, shrugging his shoulders.

"Why didn't we think of that," Kyle said as he tried to match Patrick's matter-of-fact tone but, without a poker face, he was unable to contain his elation. The pressure he had felt to get Patrick on board with being roommates was suddenly lifted and his hope for them living together was going to become a reality.

"I'll set the wheels in motion," Patrick declared but, the truth was that the wheels had already been in motion because, earlier that evening he had finalized a deal which secured them an apartment in Boston for the coming Fall and he had spent the past few hours fretting over how to broach the subject with Kyle. The hesitation that they both felt in moving forward on something as simple as suggesting that they get an apartment together was an extension of the issues they were having with trying to break through whatever barrier was preventing them from engaging in physical intimacy. This small victory gave them each a sense of optimism that they could knock down that other wall and finally consummate their feelings for one another. If they could break through one barrier, why not the other?

Ally, who had emerged as the hero of the night, spoke up. "So, this means that after all this time, you two are gonna finally take my advice and,"

"Get a room," they all said in unison.

The four young travelers, who were embarking on the journey into adulthood, sat in the sand and gazed out at the horizon as they looked ahead to their futures. The waxing moon was nearly full as it hung in the night sky and cast a wavy beam across the water while in the backdrop, the Milky Way enchanted the evening with its countless stars that resembled sparkling diamonds strewn across a blanket of black velvet. To the north, a shooting star slashed through the frame, prompting them to point their fingers as if identifying a culprit.

"Look, it's a meteor or, is it a meteorite," Amber asked. "I can never figure that out."

"Yeah," Ally continued, "what is the difference?"

They all turned to Kyle and awaited the answer. "Well," he began, "they're the same thing but, the terms distinguish the different stages of the object. For instance, when it's traveling through space, it's a meteoroid but when it enters the earth's atmosphere, it becomes a meteor and, once it reaches the ground it becomes a meteorite.

"You're so smart," Amber smiled. "You're like the super-hot nerd."

"That's why he's 'Kyle my, the science guy'," Ally said, putting her arm around Kyle and resting her head on his shoulder affectionately.

"Thanks pot head. That means a lot coming from someone who probably couldn't recite the alphabet without singing it right now," Kyle said to Ally before turning back to

Amber. "And, for the record, we prefer the term 'geek' as the word 'nerd' conjures up images of certain social inadequacies."

"But, I said 'super-hot'," Amber pointed out.

"Yeah, but, a compliment doesn't count when you water it down with an insult. It's like saying someone's a 'really hot lame ass'," Patrick admonished her.

"Look at you, coming to your boy's defense," Amber noted. "Is this part of the 'bro code'? Bro's before ho's?"

"That is one of the articles," Kyle acknowledged.

"Well, for the record," Ally spoke up, "we prefer the term 'bitches' because 'ho's' conjures up, well, I think you know what it conjures up."

"Yeah," Amber added, "and not just 'bitches' but, 'bad ass bitches'."

"Okay, then," Patrick said approvingly, "'Bro's before bad ass bitches' it is. All in favor?"

"Aye," Kyle raised his hand.

"The motion passes. You girls just changed the 'bro code'. How does it feel to be a trailblazer," Patrick asked.

"It feels fucking amazing," Ally emoted. "I feel like we can do anything now!"

"The world is your oyster," Kyle quoted the old cliché.

Eventually they broke up the private party and made their way to the pavilion where they could mingle with the mass of people, which had swelled to over seventy and continued to grow. The coed portion of the evening had ended and so, the girls would gravitate toward the other groups of girls and the boys would tend toward the pockets of male clusters that formed throughout the arena. The air seemed to crackle with electricity as the whole place was filled with positive energy that emanated from the crowd of gatherers. Patrick and Kyle were in high spirits with the plan to live together firmly in place and, both were pleasantly imagining the upcoming scenario in the back of their minds. They found an empty picnic table to sit on while using the bench for a footstool. They were sitting close enough for their legs to be touching and, they each began to press steadily against the other which was code for, 'I want to have sex with you'. They kept this up for several minutes as they silently broadcasted their intentions to one another, neither wanting to break the enticing connection until suddenly, Patrick heard one of his favorite songs playing and the moment was over as he was gone in a flash.

One guarantee to West Beach nightlife was that someone would always supply the music by way of a radio or some other form of portable sound system. This would usually be set up in an open area of the concrete pad, creating an impromptu dance floor where the young night owls would give into their primal urges to move with the music that provided the personal soundtrack for the three-dimensional movies in, which they each existed. This was where Patrick was in his element and whenever he took to the dance floor, Kyle couldn't take his eyes off him. Kyle was mesmerized by Patrick's ability to spontaneously choreograph his movements with the music. He seemed to be one with the music as if the music itself had taken on a physical form and materialized on the dance floor, providing the perfect blend of audiovisual stimulation for those who witnessed the show. Patrick appeared to be well trained at his craft as one who tirelessly practiced his moves but Kyle knew that Patrick was a purely instinctual dancer who improvised his actions on the fly. The song, which had stolen Patrick away from Kyle's provocative moment with him, was a vintage tune by a legendary Boston band in, which the singer boasts of having a big ten-inch blues record along with an insatiable girlfriend who is constantly urging him to 'whip' it 'out'. Patrick's enthusiasm for this particular tune, left Kyle and probably a few others thinking, "Okay, we get it. You've got a really big dick."

As Kyle sat on his perch atop the picnic table and watched Patrick shine, his friend Dylan, who was a fellow math and science geek, came over to say hello. Dylan had always been slightly overweight with thick glasses and bad acne but, in the last year, he had slimmed down and his complexion cleared up so that he was looking attractive and confident.

"Oh, hey, Kyle. How are you doin'," Dylan greeted him.

"Dylan, my boy. I'm doin' alright. Just enjoying the summer and getting ready for college," Kyle said. "It's great to see you. You look really good."

"Thanks," Dylan smiled. "I notice you've been spending a lot of time with Patrick." Dylan gave one of his 'yikes' expressions. "I never thought I'd see that."

"What do you mean," Kyle said, confused by the revulsion. "Why does that surprise you?"

"I don't know." Dylan shook his head. "I guess 'cause he seems like one of those rich, stuck up, jock, douche bags who I can't picture you associating with."

Dylan's words indicated a sense of betrayal on Kyle's part over his friendship with Patrick however, it wasn't a betrayal of the mathletes and science club but rather a betrayal of himself and his own principles. "I understand what you're saying but, he's really not like that. If you gave him a chance, you'd see that he's actually pretty cool and down to earth. Especially, when you consider how he grew up." It was true that Patrick had become more down to earth these days but it was only through Kyle's influence that he had started to view the world through a different lens than the one of the spoiled rich kid. "And besides," Kyle added, "he doesn't even hang out with those other assholes anymore." Kyle was defending Patrick along with his own integrity by downplaying the notion that he was some kind of a self sell out.

"I guess I'll take your word for it," Dylan shrugged.

Suddenly, almost as if on cue, around ten representatives from the 'rich, stuck up, jock douche bag club' to which Dylan had been referring decided to make an unwelcome appearance at the pavilion and instantly shift the mood to the negative polarity. The infiltrators were seen by most as mindless meatheads who crashed their way through life much like out-of-control bulls running through metaphorical China shops. It was unusual for them to show up here and Kyle assumed it meant that the cops had probably thrown them out of their preferred stomping grounds at the scenic overlook so, now they were descending on this gathering to everyone's dismay. Kyle and Dylan looked on as Patrick left the dance floor to greet the newcomers. He seemed to be the only one who welcomed their arrival as he eagerly doled out the handshakes and half hugs.

"Hey, look who we found," one muscle bound meathead announced upon seeing Patrick emerge from the crowd, "hiding out among the lames."

Dylan rolled his eyes and promptly walked away from the scene with obvious discontent while leaving Kyle with the feeling that all of his credibility was now being called into question. To say that Kyle was disappointed in Patrick would be an understatement. His conversation with Dylan was working away at his brain as he watched Patrick interact with the obnoxious intruders and he found himself starting to view him in the same light, which Dylan had described. For the first time since they had gotten together, he was seeing Patrick as one of 'them' and, his ever-intensifying attraction to him was beginning to falter.

Just then, one of the offensive linemen said, "I can't believe you ditched us for these homos. Does that make you a homo too?"

"Fuck you," Patrick shot back with a shove. "I'm not a fuckin' faggot!" The moment the words left his lips, he regretted them, even before he caught sight of Kyle looking back at him with hurt and disgust in his eyes. Patrick had only seen joy and adoration reflected back at him when he gazed upon Kyle and, to see the look of disdain on his face at that moment, left Patrick with a sick feeling deep within the pit of his stomach.

Kyle had seen enough. The spell, which had been slowly cast over him for the past few months, was abruptly broken by all of the bile that had just spewed forth from the depths of Patrick's soul. Kyle turned his back on Patrick along with their entire pseudo relationship, which had been teasing them both with repeated broken promises of ecstasy for what felt like an eternity now, and he started heading home. In a panic, Patrick went after him.

Kyle made his way back across the beach toward Access Road with the replay of what had just transpired at the pavilion looping continually through his thoughts while his mind reeled from the whiplash of having such an intense attraction turn to instant repulsion in one quick crack. It seemed that he and Patrick had been living in somewhat of a dream world for the past few months in, which they were the only occupants but they had just been given a dose of reality when their two separate worlds of origin came crashing together like high speed particles crossing paths in a supercollider. With these stark differences suddenly visible,

Finding Our Way Through the Fog
Jonathan B. Taylor

Kyle was convinced that it never would have worked between them and walking away was the right move but his heart and legs became heavier as the lights and sounds from the pavilion grew fainter in the distance and with each labored step, Patrick began to slowly creep back into his system. Kyle was losing momentum from his initial launch and the trajectory was turning back on him like a boomerang finding its way home. Until now, the two potential lovers had only been growing closer and this was the first time they faced the threat of something actually pulling them apart. However, that cataclysmic event that abruptly tore them away from one another would ultimately serve as the catalyst that would finally bring them together. Faced with the prospect of losing him, Kyle quickly came to the realization that he didn't want to live in a world without Patrick and when he heard the sound of his voice calling to him in the night, the magnet was instantly turned back on and the attraction was stronger than ever.

For Patrick, the thought of losing Kyle was equally distressing which was evident in the sound of his pleadings as he scrambled across the sand to catch up with him. "Kyle, wait up! Please," he called out desperately.

Kyle's pace slowed to a crawl, allowing Patrick to easily overtake him and when Patrick finally did reach him, Kyle felt as though his entire body would melt from the touch of Patrick's hand on his shoulder as he was brought to a stop and turned around by his determined pursuer. Patrick held Kyle in place by his shoulders as if preventing him from escaping while he pleaded with him for another chance. "I'm sorry! I don't know why I said that. I thought I had put that person to rest and buried him by the side of the road but, just as you bring out the best in me, those guys bring out the worst and that's what you saw tonight when that zombie crawled out of the ground and reared it's ugly head." Patrick paused for a moment to search Kyle's eyes for anything other than what he had seen in them earlier. The anger was gone but the hurt remained. "When I saw you looking at me tonight as if all of the affection had gone from your face and left only scorn, I felt so empty inside and I don't ever want to do anything to have you look at me like that again."

Kyle could see Patrick's eyes welling up with tears while he slowly wrapped his hands around the back of Patrick's head and felt his soft hair between his fingers as he pressed his lips against Patrick's in a slow, tender kiss. Patrick gently lowered his guard and placed his hands on either side of Kyle's slim waist as both of their bodies trembled slightly in the moment. Neither made an attempt to penetrate the other with their tongues but, rather reveled in the softness and sensuality of the other's lips touching their own. In the distance, the whoosh of a bottle rocket being launched, was followed by the crack of an explosion while a burst of sparks lit up the sky, seemingly right on cue.

Following the kiss, they wrapped their arms around each other tightly and locked their necks together for added leverage as they held on for dear life. After a moment, they unhooked their necks and rested their foreheads against one another while continuing the embrace of a lifetime. As their gazes met, each saw the other's watery emotions glistening at the brim and they both smiled, knowing that unlike the tears of anguish that had previously welled up in Patrick's eyes, these were the kind of joyous tears that came from a triumphant climax or a happy ending to a good book or epic movie. They had reached a milestone by finally breaching the invisible wall, which had stood between them for so long, and, all it took was a momentary threat of losing one another to snap them back together and hurdle them past that troublesome sticking point.

Their precious moment was suddenly interrupted by the sound of voices and the realization that they were standing out in the open, barely obscured by a few shadows, which caused their bond to be abruptly severed as they instinctively separated before turning and walking away from the oncoming interlopers. They made their way back to Patrick's car and headed for Kyle's house, driving the short distance in relative silence while periodically turning to one another and smiling with excitement before blushing and turning away. The emotional rollercoaster, which carried them here, had taken them through a series of corkscrew loops and was now inching them up the tallest hill on their way to the grand finale. When they pulled up to Kyle's house, Patrick shut off the motor and sat for a moment, holding onto the steering wheel with white knuckles. Kyle recognized the hesitation and felt his heart sink in anticipation of the expected disappointment. Patrick was about to flake on him again.

"Aren't you coming in," Kyle asked, already knowing the answer.

"I probably shouldn't," Patrick replied reluctantly.

"Why not," Kyle pleaded as if a child on the verge of a tantrum. "I know you want to!"

"I didn't say I didn't want to," Patrick admitted. "But, we can't! It's too risky!"

Kyle was confused by this response. "What are you talking about? What risk?"

"I don't wanna risk losing you," Patrick had genuine dread in his voice.

"You won't," Kyle assured him.

Finding Our Way Through the Fog
Jonathan B. Taylor

"You don't know that," Patrick said to the steering wheel, unable to look Kyle in the eyes. "Sex always changes things and you never know how until it's too late and the damage is already done."

Kyle was still misreading the situation and believed Patrick's trepidation to be based on inexperience, which meant it would have been a mistake to push him. "Hey," he said, putting a hand on Patrick's shoulder. "It's okay. Whenever you're ready, I'm here." And with that, a dejected Kyle got out of the car and headed into the house.

Patrick wanted to follow Kyle but something was still preventing him from taking that final step. However, he still had to do something about his throbbing erection or there was no way he would be able to leave so, he pulled it out of his shorts and began masturbating in the car. As he stroked himself, he envisioned coming up behind Kyle in the shower and sliding his engorged erection into Kyle's eagerly awaiting ass. He ejaculated quickly in what had become a familiar routine, following many frustrating occasions with Kyle. After relieving himself, Patrick reached for the packet of travel tissues that he had started keeping in his glove compartment for these situations but he found an empty wrapper instead. "Damn! I gotta stock up on those fuckin' things," he thought to himself. "At this point, I should probably just keep a roll of paper towels on hand." As a last resort, he removed one of his socks to use as a catch rag. "Clean up on aisle five," he joked as he wiped up the messy masturbation aftermath. He then folded up the sock and stuck it under his seat. If the cops ever swabbed the interior of his car for DNA samples, he supposed it would probably light up like the Vegas Strip from all of the unsatisfied endings to evenings with Kyle he had endured.

Finding Our Way Through the Fog
Jonathan B. Taylor

While Patrick was busy rubbing one out in the car, Kyle lay in bed and waited to hear the sound of him leaving but no sound came. He suspected that Patrick was still sitting in the driveway trying to talk himself into or out of finishing what they had started. "Come on Patrick!" Kyle was willing him to make the trip inside. "Get your ass in here so we can do this!" Finally, after what seemed like an extended period of time, he heard the engine turn over and the sound of Patrick's motor fading into the night as he backed down the driveway. Kyle then went to the bathroom and retrieved a box of tissues and a bottle of lotion from the cabinet beneath the sink, before settling down on the sofa with the memory of the kiss still fresh in his mind. "Jacobs, party of one," he said unenthusiastically and then proceeded to masturbate.

Finding Our Way Through the Fog
Jonathan B. Taylor

CHAPTER 8, 'STEVEN'

The next morning, Kyle received a troubling text message from Patrick, just around the time he was expecting him to arrive for their morning workout. 'Can't make it today. Visiting aunt in hospital. Talk to you later. – P'.

"Oh, what the fuck Patrick," Kyle thought to himself. "Visiting your aunt in the hospital! Really? That is one of the lamest excuses in the book. It's right up there with my dog ate my homework. What the hell is wrong with you?"

With no appetite and his stomach in knots over the situation with Patrick, Kyle skipped breakfast and headed straight for work. He wondered what was going through Patrick's head at that moment. Was he missing Kyle as much as Kyle missed him or was he intentionally avoiding a meeting because of the kiss? If he was this freaked out over a kiss then sex was probably out of the question as it could easily lead to him suffering some kind of nervous breakdown. When Kyle reached West Beach, he saw Amber was there in her lifeguard uniform which was a bright orange sport style one piece woman's bathing suit with the standard 'lifeguard' stenciled across the front and back in white letters.

"You're covering for Patrick?" It was more of a statement than a question but it warranted a response.

"Yeah," she said, gravely. "Did you hear what happened? His Aunt Karen, who he's always been super close with, was in a really bad car accident. She's in a coma and they don't know if she'll make it."

Finding Our Way Through the Fog
Jonathan B. Taylor

"Oh, wow! That sucks!" Kyle suddenly found himself deeply concerned for Patrick. The thought of him in distress was worrisome but he also felt a sense of relief that Patrick was telling the truth about visiting his aunt in the hospital and he felt guilty for doubting him and also for his selfish response to the situation.

After smearing sun block on each other's backs, Amber left Kyle to take up position on the north lifeguard chair while Kyle posted up on the southern one. At around nine o'clock, Ally stopped by to say hello but also said that she wasn't staying.

"You're leaving me," Kyle asked with a combination of surprise and disappointment. "Where are you going?"

"I'm going to hang out with Amber," she said matter-of-factly.

"What? You're ditching me for her? That's messed up," Kyle complained.

"Hey, you and Patrick have been ditching us for your little 'bromance' so, don't get you're nuts in a twist if we do the same to you."

"So, this is some kind of payback," Kyle asked. "In response to our 'bromance' you two are having your own little 'homance'?

"Hey," Ally cautioned him with a disapproving leer.

"Sorry, I meant to say 'bitchmance'," Kyle quickly corrected himself and Ally only responded with a half a leer this time, prompting him to add, "bad ass 'bitchmance'." That got him a smile before he went on, "Of course, 'bitchmance' doesn't really rhyme with 'romance' so it doesn't actually work. In this case, you need something that rhymes with 'romance' like 'flowmance'. You know. Then you could say that the two of you are involved in a 'heavy flowmance'.

"Ah, because of our menstrual cycles. That's clever but, no. Keep trying."

"How about 'blowmance'," Kyle suggested.

"That doesn't even make any sense," Ally said confused.

"It would if you two were doing a sixty-nine," Kyle reasoned.

"Okay, time to go," Ally said, realizing that Kyle was merely keeping her there with his usual banter so; she cut it short and gave him a quick kiss before heading down the beach to join Amber. He was sorry to see her go but he couldn't blame her. He and Patrick had been prioritizing each other and it was only natural that the girls would gravitate toward one another to fill the void. As he sat by himself and looked down the beach at the girls on the other lifeguard chair, he felt like he was both looking back on the past and seeing ahead to the future in the same frame. Ally and Amber had moved on and he was all in on Patrick now. Still, he could have used some company that morning as a distraction from the situation with Patrick, which had grown increasingly complicated and was becoming borderline maddening.

Relief from his incessant dwelling came when Steven Alves, one of the two junior lifeguards who worked West Beach, climbed up on the chair to join him. Steven and his brother Casey were twins and although they weren't identical, they bore a striking resemblance to one another. He and his brother worked some of the odd shifts and provided extra support on some of the busier weekends and holidays. They were both good kids in Kyle's eyes, but Steven was his favorite of the two. He was only sixteen years old and, at six feet tall; he had already grown into his man size body although he was still thin and rubbery at one hundred fifty pounds. He had dark, curly hair that hung over his large, brown eyes and reminded Kyle of the style a skateboarder may wear. He was a good-looking kid with an infectious smile and a nose that was slightly large but handsomely shaped.

"Hey, junior," Kyle greeted him as someone who was way too eager to see another person.

"Hi, Kyle," Steven replied with equal enthusiasm. Like many of the people who encountered Kyle, Steven couldn't help but develop a bit of a crush on him. Kyle noticed this and found it endearing, although he would never take advantage of the situation outside of engaging in some harmless flirtation. "I can't believe I get a little one on one time with you," Steven said excitedly. "Usually, you're with Patrick or Ally so we never get a chance to talk." Steven often came to Kyle for advice on work, school, and life in general.

"Hey, I'm the lucky one here for getting a chance to hang out with you," Kyle insisted. "Besides, I'm always here for you anytime you want to talk. You know that. So, tell me, what's on your mind," he asked with a friendly smile.

Steven was looking for advice and he got right down to business on soliciting it. "Well, I like someone and," he scrunched up one side of his face, "I think that they like me but, it seems like we're both too scared to make a move. Have you ever been in a situation like that," Steven asked.

"Oh, yes," Kyle said with ironic certainty as he thought about his ongoing saga with Patrick. "So, who is she," he asked, turning to Steven's predicament.

"I didn't say 'she'," Steven pointed out.

"Oh," Kyle said as if he were just getting up to speed on the realization that Steven had just come out to him. "Okay," he said, nodding affirmatively.

"I'm sorry. Is this weird for you?" Steven sounded worried.

"What? No! Of course not," Kyle said as if he was deeply offended. "If anything it makes it so much cooler!"

"Really," Steven said with relief and excitement. "You're not just saying that?"

"No, I really mean it," Kyle assured him. "I couldn't be more impressed with you right now!" Feeling somewhat inspired by Steven, Kyle decided to reciprocate. "It takes a lot of balls to do what you just did in a world that can be a pretty unwelcoming place for us but, don't worry, you're not alone. There's more of us out here than you think," and he gave him sly a wink.

"Wait, you too," Steven wasn't so much surprised to hear that Kyle could also be into guys as he was surprised to hear him say it. "I know I see you with Ally so, does that mean you like both? I mean girls and boys?"

"Yeah," Kyle smiled and nodded. "I like both."

"Which do you like more," Steven asked. "Do you have a preference?"

"It depends," Kyle shrugged. "It mostly has to do with the person I'm currently interested in. If that person is a guy, then my overall sexuality will lean to the gay side and vice versa. Contrary to popular belief, sexuality is not a fixed state but, rather a fluid one that fluctuates with a multitude of factors."

"That's how I feel," Steven said as though it suddenly all made sense for the first time. "Ever since I've wanted to hook up with this kid Billy, it seems like all I think about is gay stuff."

"Ah, so his name's Billy. Tell me more about this Billy the kid."

Finding Our Way Through the Fog
Jonathan B. Taylor

"Well, we met at a swim meet," Steven explained.

"Ironically enough," Kyle interjected.

Steven laughed before continuing, "He came in first and I was second in the fifty-meter butterfly. Anyway, after the race, we were giving each other a congratulatory hug and it was as if we both instantly felt something. We got to talking and ended up making plans to start training together and we've been getting closer ever since but, like I said before, we can't seem to make that initial move to take it to the next level. Any advice on how to do that?"

Kyle was shaking his head in disbelief at the similarities to his own experiences with both Patrick and Kevin. It felt like he and Steven were existing in parallel universes where everyone was following different versions of the same storyline. Now, Steven was asking him for advice in a real-life version of 'what would you say to your sixteen year old self if you had the chance'. The only problem was that he didn't have any answers and there was no one he could turn to with the same questions. "I wish I knew what to tell you," was all he could muster. "The truth is, I've been in similar situations and, while one didn't go well, the other remains unresolved. But, whatever happened in my case or someone else's has little bearing on your situation. Everyone's journey is unique and some things you just need to figure out for yourself." Kyle felt like he had let Steven down with his cryptic answer but he figured that sometimes the best advice you could give, was no advice at all although he was pretty sure that Steven would have preferred actual advice over some useless philosophical bullshit.

"So, let me ask you this," Steven continued his quest for enlightenment, "when you say that sexuality is a fluid state, are you saying it's that way for everyone?"

"Pretty much," Kyle confirmed. "While, there may be some people out there who lean so far to the straight or gay ends of the sexuality spectrum that they have no discernible attraction to the other side, the vast majority of us are all just varying degrees of bisexual. And, this isn't some new concept. This is what progressives have been saying for years. Back when my parents were young, they used to say that sexuality was not all black and white and there was a whole 'gay' area."

"You mean 'gray' area," Steven corrected him.

"It works both ways," Kyle grinned.

"Oh, I see what you did there." Steven nodded approvingly. "But, this is all just theory, right? I mean, there's no way of knowing what people are actually thinking and I don't see too many of them admitting to this."

"Actually, there is a way of knowing what people are thinking in this case and scientists have used that ability to back it up with facts."

"Wait, you're saying that scientists have found a way to read people's minds," Steven said doubtfully.

"In a way, yes." Kyle then provided an explanation for his statement. "Back in two thousand eighteen, there was a news story that broke, which said that scientists had determined that human beings are generally bisexual in nature. I'm sure you can find it online if you want to read the story for yourself. Basically, what they said at the time was; after conducting a study in which electronic sensors were used to detect sexual arousal in test subjects who were shown erotic images of both their own and the opposite sex, it was found that virtually every one of the participants displayed some degree of bisexual attraction. Obviously, this doesn't mean that all of these people are out there living double lives and acting on these underlying impulses but, it certainly shows us that there's a lot more going on in the backs of people's minds than they're willing to admit."

"Well, I would die if anyone ever saw what goes on in the back of my mind," Steven admitted. "Sometimes, when I jerk off, my imagination is so fucked up that I start to think that there may be something wrong with me."

Kyle laughed. "There's nothing wrong with you. I'm pretty sure that most of us would say the same thing if we were being honest. I think we're all pretty freaky when it comes to our sexual fantasies. I don't see too many people just imagining missionary position every time they jerk off. I bet if we could all see what was really going on in people's minds when it comes to their sexual fantasies, everyone of us would be afraid to leave the house. But, that's the great thing about sexual fantasy. It can be as wild as you want, and that's perfectly healthy. It's when you start trying to act it out in reality that it becomes a problem." Kyle heard his own words echoing ominously in the back of his mind and wasn't sure why but, he could see himself easily going down a road of sexual experimentation with Patrick where anything goes and that could put him in one of those positions like he was currently warning Steven to avoid.

Suddenly, they heard the sound of a boat approaching from the north and saw that it was Nick doing his daily drive by. Kyle quickly grabbed his radio from the seat and keyed the mic. "Breaker-one-balls, breaker-one-balls," Kyle began in a trucker's drawl. "This is the Harbor Master here and, I'm just out cruisin' around lookin' to break some balls, c'mon back."

Nick slowed down to a drift, before reaching under his console to retrieve a giant orange foam finger that he had altered so that the middle finger appeared to be extended instead of the index finger and he held it up for them to see as he slowly floated by.

"Oh, that's real professional, dick! Oops, I mean Nick!" Ally's voice came over Amber's radio.

"Yeah," Kyle joined in. "What are you, like a prop comic?"

"You know, there are kids on this beach, dick. You're gonna have a lot of pissed off parents on your hands if you keep up your shit," Amber said, leaning into the radio while Ally held it.

Nick grabbed a handful of his package with his free hand which was the international symbol for 'Suck it!', while holding the foam finger high on display with his other. When he was done making his point with the high visibility communication device, he returned it to the console and then opened up the motors to full throttle as he raced off toward South Point without ever having said a word.

"There's nothing like a game of charades with your overgrown adolescent boss," Kyle said approvingly while Steven nodded in agreement.

Eventually, it was time for Steven to go for his planned morning swim but, before leaving, he hugged Kyle in solidarity of their new found bond. As he climbed down the rungs on the front of the chair, he paused for a moment and looking up at Kyle he said, "There's one thing I don't understand. If everyone has a little bit of bisexual in them, then what's up with all these homophobes? Wouldn't that mean they're all just hating on themselves?"

"That's exactly what it means," Kyle confirmed. "Unfortunately, we live in a homophobic society which normalizes disdain for homosexuality so, many people feel guilt or shame over their underlying attractions to members of their own sex and that leads to self loathing, which they then project onto the gay community. Then there are other closet cases who try to conceal their same sex attractions with outspoken displays of homophobic rhetoric but, the louder their objections, the more obvious they make their true feelings."

"Thanks Kyle. I really enjoyed our talk. I hope we can do it again soon," Steven smiled.

"Definitely," Kyle agreed and, as he watched Steven walk toward the water, he felt exhilarated by their shared experience of coming out to one another. In the midst of savoring the moment, he heard his phone vibrating and retrieved it from his backpack. It was a text message from Patrick, written entirely in capitals and it simply stated, 'TONIGHT! I'M READY!!! – P'.

Finding Our Way Through the Fog
Jonathan B. Taylor

80

CHAPTER 9, 'A SECLUDED SPOT'

Following his interesting day at the beach with Steven, Kyle returned home to prepare for his eagerly awaited rendezvous with Patrick. The stage was set for this to be the night when they would finally unleash their desires on one another and enter a world of unbridled lust where love and passion collide. However, Kyle was cautious of letting his hopes get too high in light of the growing number of strikeouts, which had already piled up between them. Still, he went through the motions as someone who expected success.

First, he cleaned himself out with an enema which he performed by injecting warm, soapy water into his rectum with a makeshift device, fashioned from a water bottle that was equipped with a dish liquid style pop up top. After flushing out his system, he proceeded to shave the stubble from his pubic area to make it nice and smooth. He had always kept his pubic hair trimmed but, started shaving it completely after learning that it was part of Patrick's shaving routine. Patrick had told him that body hair had gone out in the seventies and it was common courtesy to keep the area clean for anyone who may be giving you a blowjob and to ensure that they wouldn't have to stop in order to remove a hair from their mouth. All of his reasons made sense but, the main reason Kyle shaved it off was because he thought that if Patrick didn't like pubic hair on himself then, chances are he wouldn't like it on someone else.

Finding Our Way Through the Fog
Jonathan B. Taylor

When he finished taking a shower, Kyle got dressed and was sitting on the sofa wearing a thin, gray, cotton T-shirt with matching gym shorts that were constructed of the same flimsy material but were timeworn to the point of being almost transparent. He wasn't wearing any underwear so, the shape of his penis was well pronounced through the light fabric making the head easily visible. He decided to skip the restrictive boxer briefs this evening along with any other attempts to conceal his inevitable arousal. If and when he got an erection, it would be in plain view for Patrick to see.

As he sat in front of the television, mindlessly clicking through the channels, he was unable to focus on anything other than the anticipated event, which was set to take place shortly. He had imagined this moment for so long that it no longer seemed real and now his mind was flying around in circles as he sampled every sentiment on the emotional buffet. He was filled with excitement one moment and nervousness the next before transitioning to fear and doubt, then back to excitement in a vicious cycle of rinse, and repeat. His palms were sweaty, and it felt like a bevy of butterflies were fighting over flowers within the walls of his stomach. He had never experienced a buildup of this magnitude to anything else before and he wondered what effect it would have on the overall outcome when and if it ever occurred. Would so much anticipation culminate in inevitable disappointment? Would the event ever live up to the hype or was he selling the whole thing short in his head while in reality, it was on course to exceed all expectations and be everything he hoped for and more?

As Kyle continued to chase his tail around in circles within the walls of his mind, the endless search for unobtainable answers became irrelevant when he heard the familiar sound of Patrick's rapid succession of sharp knocks, which he supposed were similar to what the cops may do, seconds before kicking in a criminal's door to execute a search warrant. Patrick didn't wait for an invitation and instantly appeared through the doorway. He was wearing black mesh shorts, a dark green T-shirt and had his backpack strapped to his shoulders. Kyle looked at him and thought how his mother had been right. Patrick really did get more handsome every time you saw him.

They did their customary greeting with overly excited expressions upon seeing each other followed by red faces and awkwardly avoided eye contact. After the moment of silence, Kyle broke the ice and spoke first. "I didn't hear your car pull up. Did you walk here?"

"Yeah," Patrick answered.

"Through the woods," Kyle said, sounding slightly surprised.

"Yeah, through the woods," Patrick shrugged. "Why should that surprise you? Don't I always come through the woods?"

The reason for Kyle's surprise was that a dense fog had rolled in over Sunset Cove as it occasionally did during the summer months. "I was just thinking about how foggy it is out there. It's like zero visibility. How is it you didn't end up lost?"

"Shit, there's no way I could get lost in those woods. I could probably find my way through there blindfolded," Patrick boasted. "But, enough about that. We've got an itinerary so let's get to it. Are you ready to go?"

"Sure. But, where are we going," Kyle asked.

"You'll see," Patrick said, mysteriously. "I've got something special planned," as he motioned his head toward the door.

Finding Our Way Through the Fog
Jonathan B. Taylor

Kyle eagerly jumped to his feet and, when he stood, he saw Patrick's eyes focus on his noticeable package and smile approvingly at the revealing view through the flimsy material of his timeworn gym shorts. Under normal circumstances, this would have most likely triggered an erection but Kyle was too nervous at the moment, which worked out for him, as he wasn't quite ready to display one so boldly just yet.

"So, really, where are we going," he asked again as he followed Patrick out the door.

"All in good time," Patrick continued his evasiveness.

Once they were outside, it quickly became evident that Patrick was leading them back into the woods from where he had just come. Kyle never would have attempted to enter the forest in a dense fog bank by himself but, being with Patrick, he had no worries and felt completely at ease. He didn't know where Patrick was taking him and he didn't really care. He just wanted to be with him, and he had fallen so deeply under Patrick's spell by that point he would have followed him into shark-infested waters to see where this night was going. As he trailed behind Patrick, Kyle detected a slight hint of some expensive cologne in his wake, that he had probably helped himself to off his father's dresser. The aroma was captivating and blended nicely with the scent of pine and brine that wafted in the air and seemed to be amplified by the fog along with the other scents and sounds that filled the forest as if their minds were compensating for the visual impairment imposed by the murky mist.

Wandering through the woods with Patrick under a blanket of fog, Kyle thought of Ally and Steven and Amber and, how in some ways, they were all out here roaming through the forest, trying to find their way through the complex maze of sexuality where the gray area of fog could be so disorienting.

Finding Our Way Through the Fog
Jonathan B. Taylor

"What are you thinking," Patrick asked, breaking into his thoughts.

"I was just thinking about life and how we're all just finding our way through a dense fog bank at night, where perilous rocks threaten to sink their teeth into our hulls and swallow us up in the deep as ghostly shapes play tricks on our minds and eerie foghorns moan in the distance. Why," Kyle asked curiously. "What were you thinking?"

"I was just thinking, 'so, this is what it feels like to be inside a cloud'," Patrick said and they both laughed.

Suddenly, Kyle realized that he had been so caught up in the moment that he hadn't even thought to ask Patrick about his aunt. "Listen, I was sorry to hear about your aunt. How's she doing?"

"She's messed up pretty bad. We don't know if she's gonna make it," Patrick's voice cracked. "Right now she's in a coma and they have her on life support."

"Oh, man. That sucks," was all Kyle could muster. He knew that Patrick was hurting and he wished he could somehow take the pain away. He had heard how people would sometimes turn to sex as a coping mechanism for dealing with tragedy and he wondered if this was playing a role in Patrick's plans for them that evening.

For Patrick however, it was more about the realization that life was too short and he didn't want to waste another moment that he could be sharing with Kyle in the way he truly wanted to be with him. He had also concluded that he was in love with him and no amount of sex would ever weaken those feelings. He only hoped that Kyle felt the same.

When they reached the clearing with the fire pit and plastic lawn furniture, Kyle realized where Patrick was taking them. They were headed out to their super secluded spot at the very tip of South Point but, in order to get there, they needed to get past the menacing patch of thorn bushes, which guarded the entrance to the path and, in order to do that, they needed to get down on the ground and belly crawl about twenty feet through a two-foot high tunnel that snaked through the hazardous underbrush. They were both careful to stay low as they slithered along, having previously made the mistake of raising their backs too high and receiving a harsh lashing from the vicious vines for their careless behavior. When they were finished crawling under the coils of barbed wire, the rest of their basic training involved an easy jaunt through the pine trees, where there was very limited underbrush to impede their progress. The trail ended at a small sandy patch of beach, which was nestled between jagged rocks and tall marsh grass on either side of the secluded spot. It was the perfect place for what they had planned. The area was virtually inaccessible from every direction leaving little chance of anyone interrupting them. The jagged rocks extended for a few hundred feet out into the water so boats avoided it and no one ever came on foot along the shoreline because the mud was like quicksand and the tree line was overgrown with poison ivy.

Patrick pulled a folded green army blanket from his backpack and spread it out on the small patch of soft, white sand. After removing their sneakers and socks, they both sat with their arms folded around their slightly bent knees, which they had pulled up in front of them. Kyle felt that it was on Patrick to make the first move and he was not looking forward to the walk of shame out of the woods if they were to come up short again. Patrick reached into his backpack again to retrieve two bottles and handed one to Kyle.

Finding Our Way Through the Fog
Jonathan B. Taylor

"What's this," Kyle asked, inspecting the label. "Strawberry wine coolers? But, we don't drink," he protested, as if pointing out the obvious.

"Tonight we do," Patrick replied with authority as he cracked open his bottle.

Kyle's memory flashed to their previous discussion about the use of alcohol on college campuses to loosen things up for recreational sex and suddenly it all made sense. Patrick was taking a page out of the college kid's playbook and using a little alcoholic leverage to get them past that bitch of a sticking point that had plagued them for all these weeks. Kyle, who was willing to try anything at this juncture, cracked open his bottle and tapped it against Patrick's while echoing, "Tonight we do!" He then took a healthy swig of the bittersweet elixir and winced slightly from the taste of the alcohol. As he continued to drink, Kyle noticed that his motor skills were being affected, causing a slight delay in the response time between his body and brain. It felt like he was moving in slow motion through a world that continued to run at normal speed. He couldn't help feeling somewhat vulnerable in his weakened condition and thought of how a predator would make an easy meal of him if he were to encounter one at that moment. Patrick had brought a six-pack, which they downed relatively quickly, and by the time they had each finished their third bottle, they were feeling the full effects of the alcohol on their virgin systems.

"I feel like my head is buzzing," Kyle said with a slight slur. "Hey, that must be why they call it 'getting buzzed' or is it 'catching a buzz'? I forget." As Kyle heard himself speaking, he was reminded of Ally and Amber, stoned on the beach and he said, worriedly, "Oh, god! This stuff has turned me into an idiot!"

Finding Our Way Through the Fog
Jonathan B. Taylor

They both started laughing and when they turned to face each other, their faces became serious as their eyes met and, they were suddenly reminded of why they were there. As their gazes dropped to each other's slightly parted lips, their faces slowly followed and they both leaned in for another soft, sensual kiss like the one they had shared on the beach the night before. Kyle hoped the moment would last forever but, Patrick interrupted it when he broke away and started taking off his shirt. He had been planning this evening out in his head all day and was determined to stick to the script without being sidetracked by tantalizing improvisation. Once he had his shirt off, he stood up and said, "Come on, let's go swimming," as he slid his shorts and boxer briefs down his legs, momentarily losing his balance while kicking the garments free from their final hold on his feet.

When he stumbled, Kyle watched Patrick's impressive penis become animated as it danced and jiggled before his eyes. This was the first full image he had of it other than some brief glimpses and he was savoring every second of the spectacular view. It was pastel pink in color and had a well-defined head, which was slightly triangular with a softly shaped torpedo tip. After spending so much time and effort trying to picture it through his clothing, the thrill of actually seeing Patrick's magnificent member in the flesh was exhilarating and comparable to the rush that would come from downhill skiing or parachuting from a plane for the first time. Kyle watched as it slowly swelled and stiffened, beginning it's steady climb toward rigidity. Just as Kyle was about to make his way over on his knees, Patrick turned and started walking down to the water. Kyle dropped his head in exasperation and said, "Well, I guess we're going swimming." He removed his clothing and started walking toward the water with Patrick leading the way. Patrick was about ten paces ahead in knee deep water and, Kyle watched his starkly white buttocks, in contrast to his golden bronze back and legs, as the well developed muscles bounced and flexed from his leisurely leaps over the small waves like a white tail deer bounding through the forest on a spring day. The analogy seemed fitting to Kyle who felt as though he had been chasing a deer through the forest and now he was running in a stream, trying to catch a slippery fish with his bare hands.

"There's got to be an easier way," he thought to himself as he unsteadily tried to avoid the treacherous rocks, which were encrusted with razor sharp barnacles that threatened to slice his feet with every step. Each time he placed a foot, he half expected a lobster or blue crab to clamp down on his toes and more than once, he felt something moving which caused him to jump in a panic. There were other dangers in these waters to consider as well. Due to it's seclusion, this spot was a favorite haunt for seals which could be dangerously territorial wild animals who always brought the added risk of shark encounter with them wherever they went. Just throw in some alcohol with a little low visibility and you had the perfect recipe for disaster.

As he continued to run the gauntlet in pursuit of passion, Kyle stepped cautiously around the minefield of hazards, which stood between him and the object of his desire. When he momentarily lost his footing after stumbling over a slippery stone that was covered with a slimy coating of algae, he finally voiced his concerns. "Dude! What are we doing? We're gonna break our necks out here! Are you trying to get us killed or what?"

Patrick stopped for a moment and considered the question before realizing that he didn't have an answer. What exactly were they doing out there? He had planned to use swimming as an excuse to get their clothes off but hadn't really thought it through beyond that. Once they were naked, there really wasn't any reason to actually risk their necks swimming in these conditions so, maybe it was time to stop this madness and finally get down to the business at hand.

So, this was it. After so many build ups to so many let downs, the rollercoaster had reached the top of the tallest hill and was ready to plunge them into the ultimate thrill. It had all come down to this. For weeks, the two had been shielding the sight of their hard-ons from one another and now, Patrick stood on the verge of exposure with a fully engorged erection while a few feet away, Kyle stood behind him on the same ledge, equally aroused. Despite having already kissed and, having signed a letter of intent, Patrick still felt like he was jumping from a plane with no guarantees that his chute would open as he slowly turned to face Kyle with their arousal on full display. With the truth laid bare, they trudged toward each other steadfastly as if suddenly obtaining their sea legs and finally finding their footing while leaving all of their reluctance and uncertainty by the wayside. Their erections were seen as open invitations to ecstasy and neither could take their eyes off the other's prize as they tightened the last remaining gap between them. Kyle watched Patrick's impressive member swing ominously from side to side with each step and was filled with a dizzying degree of both excitement and dread over the potential for pleasure and pain that it presented.

As they drew closer, Kyle couldn't help but make the obvious comparison between their erections and feel woefully inadequate over the fact that Patrick's dwarfed his own although it was admittedly less enormous than he expected. Whereas his own erect penis would grow by an easy sixty percent over its flaccid state and closer to ninety in comparison to it's frightened, frigid phase, Patrick's erection only appeared to be twenty to thirty percent larger than it's baseline. This was somewhat of a relief to Kyle who had been calculating the foreseen expansion according to his own numbers, which would have put Patrick somewhere in the thirteen to fourteen inch range, and probably landed Kyle somewhere in the nearest hospital. Now he saw Patrick's monster size erection as menacing but, manageable.

When they eventually reached one another and came together, all of their impertinent thoughts were cast aside and they became completely absorbed in the moment. With their eyes locked in a lovesick gaze, they each placed their hands on the other's hips and cocked their heads slightly as they locked lips and began exploring each other's mouths with their soft, velvet tongues. Unlike their previous kisses that were of a sensual nature, this was a kiss of pure passion and a prelude to unbridled ecstasy. As their tongues rolled and writhed up above, their erections poked and prodded down below, sending waves of pleasure through their bodies with every point of contact. Patrick slid his hands around to Kyle's ass and gently caressed his puckering hole with his fingertips, running them in soft circles around the rim while he slipped his engorged erection between Kyle's legs along his undercarriage and used his fingers to press the head of his swollen member against Kyle's sensitive asshole causing him to whimper with anticipation for what was to come. This prompted Patrick to place his hands on Kyle's shoulders and spin him around forcefully so that Kyle's back was now turned to him. He then wrapped his arms around Kyle tightly, pinning his willing recipient's own arms to his sides while holding him closely and working his erection between Kyle's supple glutes to tease his hole some more with the soft head of his hardened tool. He then slid it up between Kyle's cheeks as though placing a hot dog in a bun and began dry humping the crack of his smooth, white ass. Patrick then proceeded to slide his erection down and back through Kyle's legs again only this time from the rear so that the base of his shaft was rubbing against Kyle's sweet asshole while the head of his dick was rubbing on the underside of Kyle's balls, hitting them like a punching bag with each stroke. Kyle craned his neck around to find Patrick's mouth and began to suck on his outstretched tongue as if he were giving it a blowjob. As Patrick continued to slide his dick back and forth along Kyle's undercarriage, he began to tenderly kiss his shoulder, slowly working his way up Kyle's neck to his earlobe which he sucked and nibbled on before whispering through clenched teeth, "I'm gonna fuck you in the ass!" This prompted Kyle to tilt his head back and nod vigorously in approval.

Patrick then placed his cupped hands on Kyle's plump ass cheeks and prodded him toward the shore. As he waded behind him through the shallows, Patrick watched the striations appear in Kyle's muscular ass while saucer size dimples appeared on the sides from the tantalizing motion of his walk. They both moved with a purpose, knowing that their greatest desire was about to take place. Kyle was about to be fucked in the ass and Patrick was going to give it to him. When they reached the beach and, were back at the blanket, Patrick stood behind Kyle and placed his hands on his shivering shoulders while jutting his knees into the back of Kyle's, causing him to buckle as Patrick pushed down, forcing Kyle into a kneeling position. He shoved Kyle face first into the blanket where he laid with his ass in the air, as an offering to Patrick for him to do with as he pleased.

Finding Our Way Through the Fog
Jonathan B. Taylor

Patrick kneeled down and positioned himself behind the catcher like an umpire awaiting the wind up. He then forced Kyle's legs apart with his knees to give himself a little more room for his task. Placing his hands on Kyle's hips, he began teasing Kyle by pressing the head of his hard dick against Kyle's tender, pink asshole without actually penetrating him, which drove Kyle wild and caused him to beg Patrick to enter him. "Oh, dude! Fuck me! Please," he pleaded.

"Are you sure you're ready," Patrick prolonged the agony.

"Yes! I'm definitely ready," Kyle, continued his urgings as he looked back at Patrick over his shoulder. "I even douched myself out for you so I'd be nice and clean."

"Oh, sweet," Patrick said approvingly as he bent down to place his mouth on Kyle's asshole, which he began sucking on and tickling with his tongue, eliciting another round of whimpers and moans, from his receptive subordinate. He then worked his tongue down to Kyle's balls which clung tightly to his body and began sucking and licking them as well.

Finally, when he felt that he had put Kyle through enough torturous foreplay, Patrick proceeded to fuck him. He began by reaching into his backpack and pulling out the tube of lubricant that he had brought and placing a generous amount of the clear jelly on his swollen erection. He then repositioned himself behind Kyle and lined up his shot, forcing himself inside of Kyle with three months worth of aggression released in one explosive thrust. The resulting pain that erupted in Kyle launched him like a rocket off of Patrick's monstrous member and caused him to recoil onto the blanket where he lay wincing in agony.

"Oh, shit! Are you alright," Patrick asked with concern as he attempted to stifle his laughter.

Finding Our Way Through the Fog
Jonathan B. Taylor

"It felt like you shoved a hot poker up my ass and it's still in there burning," Kyle grimaced through clenched teeth.

"I don't understand. What are you like a virgin," Patrick asked.

"Back there I am," Kyle admitted.

"Hey, we don't have to do that if you don't want to. There's other stuff we can do," Patrick said with feigned enthusiasm but, clear disappointment in his voice.

"No, I want to! Believe me I want to! It's all I've wanted for awhile now," Kyle assured him. "I just don't know if I can," He said with a little disappointment of his own.

"Well," Patrick shrugged, "if you want to try again, I think I know what to do."

"Definitely," Kyle replied as he eagerly scrambled back into position on his hands and knees in front of Patrick. "I'll do whatever it takes," He said looking back at him again and staring into his eyes.

Patrick smiled approvingly and repositioned himself at the helm. He then smeared some of the lube onto his fingers and slowly slid his middle finger into Kyle's anus prompting a resounding "Yes!" in response to the enjoyable intrusion. Patrick probed and twirled before sliding a second digit into Kyle's ass with his index finger. As he slowly and methodically finger fucked Kyle, he gave him a moment to adjust before inserting his ring finger next. When all three fingers were fully penetrated, he began to expand them slightly as he continued to slide them in and out of Kyle's widening hole while twisting them around in a circular motion as if boring out a shaft. Once it was sufficiently dilated, Patrick was able to replace them with his enormous erection, which he slid in with relative ease. There was a brief growl of pain from Kyle when Patrick passed through the inner o-ring of his anus and entered the realm of his rectum but Kyle grit his teeth and withstood the momentary agony, which he happily endured in order to provide Patrick with the pleasure that he desired.

"You like this, don't you," Patrick said as he thrust himself inside of Kyle. "You like having my hard dick in your tight ass! Don't you," Patrick said, demanding an answer.

"Yes," Kyle said, between gasps. "I just wish it didn't hurt so much!"

"I don't know what you're talking about," Patrick said indifferently. "It feels pretty good to me!" He laughed with the words. "Don't worry though. We just need to stretch those muscles out. You'll see. In a couple of weeks, I'll have your ass so blown out; you won't even notice me back here," Patrick continued to laugh as he amused himself. Then he abruptly withdrew himself from Kyle before grabbing his ankles and spinning his legs, forcing Kyle's limp body to flip over violently so that he was suddenly lying on his back, looking up at Patrick who was kneeling before him. It was thrilling for Kyle to be manhandled by Patrick in this way and he gave an approving smile to encourage more of the mistreatment. Once Patrick had him repositioned, he folded Kyle's legs back, exposing his previously tender pink asshole, which was now a gaping red maw. He reinserted himself into Kyle's ass and resumed his relentless thrusting, bottoming out his giant dick against the back wall of Kyle's rectum where it made the sharp turn into his colon. Kyle's ankles were rested on Patrick's shoulders and the undersides of his legs were braced against the soft skin of Patrick's torso. Patrick stroked his hands up and down Kyle's thighs while he punished him for wanting to be fucked in such a manner. Kyle looked up and saw the smug smirk of satisfaction on Patrick's face from watching his dick slide in and out of Kyle's ass and the image drove Kyle wild as he relished the thought of being used by Patrick for pleasure while enduring pain for him in the process. Serving Patrick in this way was intensely gratifying for Kyle and made his own dick throb and pulsate while waves of ecstasy radiated through his body and overrode the stabbing sting of Patrick's intrusive erection. Kyle rolled his head around in both agony and ecstasy as Patrick's massive member massaged his prostate, causing his body to convulse and finally begin to orgasm, sending several streams of ejaculate shooting onto his stomach. Patrick watched in amazement as Kyle climaxed entirely from anal stimulation.

"Oh, shit," Patrick said in a state of shock. "Did I just make you come? I didn't know you could do that!"

"Me neither," Kyle said with equal excitement.

"I never made a dude come like that before," Patrick said proudly as though he had just set a new world record in a most obscure event. "Usually you gotta give 'em a reach around or suck 'em off afterward."

The words stung like Patrick's prick when Kyle heard them because they came with the realization that his little fantasy of this being a first time for both of them was suddenly shattered as Patrick made it clear that he had done this before. Now that Kyle had climaxed and was feeling the slight crush of disappointment, he was no longer enjoying a mixture of pleasure and pain from Patrick's onslaught and was now merely enduring the latter. Patrick could see that the level of discomfort on Kyle's face had intensified as he continued to thrust himself into his gaping wound and he felt a slight twinge of guilt for inflicting the pain on his willing recipient but not enough to want to stop. Finally, when Kyle had reached the limit of his endurance, Patrick climaxed and Kyle felt the warm rush of his semen squirting against the walls of his rectum, signaling an end to his suffering. Patrick pulled out and lowered his face to Kyle's abdomen where he licked up the remnants of his anally induced orgasm as if he were doing Jell-O shots off his belly. He then reached into his backpack and pulled out a travel pack of handy wipes, which he used to clean off his genitals before tending to Kyle's ass and stomach. By now, the fog had lifted and night had fallen so, the two spent lovers lay together on a blanket of wool and spooned beneath a blanket of stars.

Finding Our Way Through the Fog
Jonathan B. Taylor

CHAPTER 10, 'ALLY AND AMBER'

While Kyle and Patrick were having a boy's night out on the private shores of their own deserted island, Ally and Amber were across town, enjoying a girl's night of their own in Ally's upstairs bedroom of her family's cape style home. The Lynch family home was one of a handful of oceanfront properties that were situated on a tract of land just north of West Beach. Ally lived there with her father and an older sister but both were out for the evening and neither was expected to be back anytime soon. Ally had her windows open to take advantage of the Cape Cod night air, which was known as 'nature's air-conditioning' for the cool ocean breezes that it provided. It billowed through the curtains and made them dance seductively in the dim lighting. Both girls were wearing white tank tops but Amber had on red bikini underwear with lacy frills and Ally wore scotch plaid print, men's boxer shorts. They each sat in one of the two upholstered armchairs that faced the window and looked out over the water.

"I wish we had some weed," Amber said longingly.

"How about this," Ally responded as she went to the small mini fridge beside her bed and retrieved two bottles of strawberry wine coolers.

"What's this," Amber asked as Ally handed her one of the sixteen-ounce bottles. "Since when do we drink?"

"Since Patrick asked me if I could get someone to buy for him tonight and I figured that since I was in the neighborhood," Ally curled the side of her mouth up and shrugged her shoulders.

"Wait a minute," Amber said, poking one flattened hand into the palm of her other as if signaling for a timeout. "Patrick needed someone to buy for him? How is that even possible? When did Patrick start drinking? Or was it even for him?" As Amber reached for the bottle, her memory flashed to the previous night's discussion on the subject of college kids using alcohol in order to have recreational sex. When she took the bottle from Ally's hand, their fingers touched slightly and lingered on the handoff.

"Oh, I'm pretty sure it was for him," Ally said confidently.

"Why would Patrick suddenly want to drink," Amber asked, still trying to process the information.

"He didn't say. Maybe he was having a hard time handling what happened to his aunt or maybe," she paused for a moment, "he just needed a little leverage, if you know what I mean?" She nodded her head to indicate her opinion that the second scenario was the more likely of the two.

"Oh, so you think him and Kyle might be finally getting a room together? That is if they haven't already," Amber said, smiling.

"I hope so," Ally said, toasting Amber with her bottle before taking a swig. "Because that would be the hottest guy on guy action ever!"

"You got that right," Amber agreed as she poured a healthy dose of drink into her open mouth. "What do you think the chances are that they'd let us watch?"

"They might." Ally said as she guzzled down the rest of her bottle and got up to retrieve a couple more from the mini fridge. "If we used the right approach."

"What did you have in mind," Amber said as she took the second bottle from Ally and enjoyed the prolonged touch of her fingertips once again.

"I don't know," Ally thought about it for a moment. "Maybe if we were to get them into a foursome, they wouldn't be able to resist each other and start going at it right in front of us." Ally said with a devious smile.

"Yeah," Amber agreed, "and especially if they saw us going at it first" she added before giving Ally a sideways glance in search of a reaction.

That was all the invitation that Ally needed. "You just read my mind," she said, getting up from her seat and walking over to Amber where she placed her hands on the armrests and leaned over her menacingly. Amber tilted her head back and moistened her lips as their mouths met and they slowly penetrated each other with their tongues. Ally straddled Amber's legs and sat on her lap as they both slid their hands under one another's shirts and caressed each other's braless breasts while continuing to glide their tongues around in each other's mouths. They had been building up to this for weeks but, unlike the boys who suffered a series of setbacks along the way, their progression from countdown to launch was smooth and seamless.

They paused their passionate kiss while Ally pulled off Amber's shirt to reveal her supple breasts and then Amber did the same to her. They each savored the thrill of seeing the other exposed as Amber caressed Ally's firm, white, D-cups, which appeared like two falling, tear drops amid the tan lines from her bikini top. Ally took one of Amber's slightly smaller C-cups in her hand and began kissing it while slowly swirling her tongue around the soft, pink nipple before sucking on it gently as if she were a nursing infant mammal. As they found their way back to each other's mouths and resumed kissing, their bare breasts pressed against one another like soft bumpers while their erect nipples teased and titillated as they jostled and jousted in the skirmish. Amber slipped her hand between Ally's legs and began to rub her crotch lightly before moving to the inside of her thigh and sliding her fingers up through the leg of Ally's boxer shorts, sending a shiver down her spine. As Amber found her way to Ally's creamy lips that were wet with anticipation, she penetrated Ally with her middle finger and coaxed a soft moan from the eager beaver who bit her lower lip in ecstasy over the welcome intrusion. Amber then removed her finger and brought it to her mouth where she licked Ally's glistening juices from her fingertips and began sucking on the middle one like a lollipop, as a clear indication of where she wanted to go from there.

Ally accepted the invitation with a smile as she stood up and slid her shorts down her legs to reveal her tender pink vulva, which was framed, in the hairless, white triangle of her tan line. She subsequently extended her own invitation by placing her left foot on the seat of Amber's chair and pointing her bended knee out, which was like spreading half her legs open. Ally then placed a hand on the back of Amber's head and guided her face into her eagerly awaiting crotch. Amber complied and began French kissing Ally's vagina with a vengeance, thrusting her tongue deep inside and sucking on Ally's fully erect clitoris. Ally then pulled away and stepped back a few feet, enticing Amber to pursue her which she did by sliding off the chair onto her knees and shuffling toward Ally with her mouth open and tongue extended. Ally widened her stance and folded Amber's head back as she straddled her face like a bicycle seat while Amber braced herself by wrapping her hands around Ally's upper legs and resumed her voracious licking and sucking. Ally was now whimpering and moaning loudly as Amber brought her to the brink and finally pushed her over the edge to climax. As the waves of pleasure rolled through Ally's body, the spasm of her lips released a flood of secretions into Amber's mouth, which she lapped up greedily like a thirsty kitten over a saucer of milk.

Still reeling from the orgasm, Ally stepped back and took hold of Amber's hands, pulling her to her feet and then sliding her lacy bottoms down her legs to reveal the soft pink petals of her delicate flower. Ally observed the orange stubble around Amber's pubic area and said, "Looks like someone needs a shave."

"Yeah," Amber agreed. "I guess I've gotten a little lazy with Patrick all into Kyle and everything."

"Don't worry," Ally smiled. "We'll fix you up." She took Amber's hand and led her into the adjacent bathroom where she pulled out her electric razor and began shaving Amber's pubic area. The tingling vibrations excited Amber and made her breathing become slightly erratic. When she was finished, Ally removed the hand held mini vacuum from it's wall mounted charging station and ran it across the floor where Amber had stood. She then held it to Amber's crotch for a second, allowing it to grab her flesh with its suction. "There," she said as she returned the vacuum to the wall. "All clean. Now, let's eat."

The girls walked to Ally's bed where she gave Amber a playful shove causing her to fall backward onto the mattress. Amber then pulled her knees toward her chest and spread her legs apart, extending an invitation for reciprocal cunnilingus to Ally, which she immediately obliged. She climbed onto the bed and positioned herself in front of Amber on her knees. She then took Amber's legs and slung one over each shoulder, placing her in the stirrups and giving Ally the leverage to lift Amber's ass off the bed so that only her head and upper back remained in contact with the mattress as if she were swinging on the trapeze with Ally serving as the apparatus. Ally began to kiss Amber's sweet lips softly, running her tongue gently around the labia and flicking it rapidly on Amber's swollen clitoris. After a moment of teasing, she slid her velvet appendage deep inside of Amber and tasted her free flowing juices while she thrust and swirled, causing Amber to yelp loudly as she began to orgasm repeatedly in Ally's open mouth.

When the girls were finished pleasuring each other, they laid together in the afterglow, savoring the moment they had shared. Although there was no cuddling or spooning, there also weren't any feelings of awkwardness or regrets between them. They were simply two good friends who had just added the benefit of recreational sex to their repertoire. Unlike Patrick and Kyle who had fallen in love with one another, the girls hadn't changed the nature of their relationship but merely modified the dynamic of it.

Finding Our Way Through the Fog
Jonathan B. Taylor

CHAPTER 11, 'AN UNEXPECTED VISITOR'

Back on the beach, at their secluded retreat, the sun was rising and, Kyle awoke to find himself alone on the army blanket with Patrick nowhere in sight. He looked around and wondered if Patrick had flaked on him again and whether that was the last he would see of him when he suddenly noticed that his missing lover was standing right behind him looking down and smiling. Patrick laid down on the blanket and pulled up next to Kyle for a kiss. Both were still naked and Patrick propped himself up on one elbow to take in the scene before him.

"Seeing you naked is definitely one of my new favorite things," he told Kyle.

"Same," Kyle smiled. "So, what are the others?"

"Pretty much everything that goes with that one," Patrick replied. He then slid his hand around the back of Kyle's neck and gave him a long, sensual kiss before declaring, "There's number two."

Kyle was relieved to learn that Patrick's feelings had not changed in the light of day and, he was happy to find himself walking through the same dream from last night that had now become his reality. As Kyle propped himself up on his own elbows, he felt the weight of a slight hangover hit him on the head. "Oh, man! My head feels like a ton of bricks! I thought that wine coolers were supposed to be weak," he said, struggling to keep his head erect.

"They are," Patrick reassured him. "Unfortunately, we're just weaker. We have zero tolerance," he explained.

"I hope we're not gonna have to drink every time we want to do it," Kyle said.

"No. I think we're good," Patrick smiled. "How are you doing otherwise? Are you sore?" He sounded sincere but, Kyle was sure that there was a hint of gloating in his tone.

"What do you think," he said with a note of resentment. "Of course I'm sore! You completely pulverized me! You literally tore me a new asshole and, I should probably be getting stitches right now. You try going fifteen rounds with an anaconda up your ass and, let me know how you feel." Kyle smiled to show he was only playing.

"Oh, hell no," Patrick retorted. "I don't get fucked. I do the fucking! You got a problem with that?" He leaned over Kyle menacingly. "You certainly didn't have a problem with it last night," he laughed, brandishing his smug smirk once again.

"You're asking if I have a problem with being your bitch? No way! I'm totally okay with it," Kyle insisted as Patrick watched his dick begin to stiffen at the same time that his own was becoming engorged. Just as their submissive and domineering role playing had aroused them in the past, the effect was amplified now that they had put it into practice. Now it was Patrick who felt like he had discovered a genie in a bottle with Kyle as his submissive lover and the endless array of sexual fantasies that could be played out in reality were flying through his mind like snowflakes in the headlights on a highway in the night. He was like a little kid on Christmas morning with piles of presents that were waiting to be opened.

As their erections formed, Kyle fanned the flames. "In fact, whenever I've imagined us together, I've always pictured you fucking me in the ass. It's all I ever think about," he confessed.

"Really," Patrick said with obvious approval. "That's great because whenever I picture us together, I imagine myself fucking you!"

"That's why we make such a good couple," Kyle smiled. "The very thought of having you inside of me makes my dick get hard!"

"And, the very thought of being inside of you makes me get hard," Patrick responded.

They were both fully erect now and it seemed like the obvious move was to pick up where they had left off the night before and follow through with their freshly declared desires. Patrick reached into his backpack to retrieve the tube of lubricant and began to position himself between Kyle's upright, bended knees. Patrick's swollen erection was laying directly on top of Kyle's so that the undersides of their shafts were touching and he began to slide it back and forth, sending light waves of pleasure through both of their bodies. He then picked up the tube and was preparing to apply some to his fingers when Kyle held his hands to stop him.

"Please, dude! Not again! I'm still hurting from last night and I don't think I can go another round just yet. I need a little time to recover," Kyle pleaded.

"How much time?" Patrick was making no secret of the fact that he didn't like the idea of waiting.

"I don't know," Kyle answered. "At least until the burning stops. Right now it feels like I sat on a nest of angry hornets."

"So, you're denying me," Patrick said in his domineering voice, hoping that it would trigger Kyle to succumb.

Finding Our Way Through the Fog
Jonathan B. Taylor

"No, never," Kyle quickly reassured Patrick of his willingness to please. "I'll do whatever you want and it's ultimately your call! If you decide to take it, I won't resist." His words were making them both grow rock hard as their erections began to throb and pulsate. "I just really want to suck you off," Kyle said, trying to steer Patrick's focus to his mouth and away from his aching ass. "I've been dying to taste you!"

"Alright," Patrick agreed, letting Kyle off the hook. "I'll throw you a bone," he said, moving from his kneeling position between Kyle's legs toward his chest by walking on his knees roughly over Kyle's stomach, causing him to grunt with pain from the crushing force. Patrick then sat on Kyle's chest with all of his weight and his monstrous erection looming before Kyle's open mouth. "From now on you will provide me with blowjobs on demand," Patrick commanded. "Whenever you see me look down at my dick, that will be the signal for you to immediately get down on your knees and begin sucking! Is that understood?"

Kyle nodded eagerly as his mouth began to salivate in anticipation.

"And, don't keep me waiting! If I don't like your response time or if any part of your performance displeases me, you will receive punishment," Patrick said sternly.

Kyle continued to nod his head vigorously in agreement to Patrick's terms as he attempted to reach his gaping mouth toward his undulating erection, which Patrick kept just out of reach. Finally, after deciding that he had tortured Kyle long enough, Patrick slid himself into Kyle's mouth and began to rock back and forth with his balls rubbing on Kyle's neck. Kyle was forced to open his mouth extremely wide to the point of discomfort in order to accommodate the massive girth of Patrick's member, which he continued to thrust deeper into Kyle, causing it to bottom out on the back of his throat while making him gag and choke as he gasped for breath on the backstrokes. Fortunately, the water boarding didn't last too long due to the arousing foreplay which had brought Patrick to the brink and caused him to climax relatively quickly. In a matter of minutes, Kyle felt Patrick's erection stiffen and grow even larger in his mouth as hard ridges formed on the shaft, the moment before hot come erupted on his tongue and in the back of his throat as Patrick continued to fuck his mouth while he ejaculated. Kyle swallowed and gulped the fluid greedily as he milked every last drop from Patrick's spasmodic spigot.

When he had finished unloading, Patrick withdrew and repositioned himself back between Kyle's legs. "There's something else you should know about me," he said as he began to go down on Kyle. "I love to suck dick!"

Kyle watched Patrick's eyes grow wide with excitement as he engulfed Kyle's erection in his mouth. Although it wasn't a surprise to learn that Patrick liked to suck dick after seeing him lick the load off of his stomach the night before, Kyle was a little surprised to hear him make the declaration, which provided an extra thrill to the moment. He propped himself up on his elbows and watched Patrick's handsome face sliding up and down on the shaft of his dick. His cheek bones appeared even more pronounced beyond the borders of his sunken cheek muscles, which were drawn in by the suction he provided in executing his task. Patrick performed like a sword swallower in the circus, taking Kyle all the way down his throat so that he was able to lick Kyle's balls when he bottomed out and when he came back to the top, he swirled his tongue around on the head, just as he had done to his ice cream cone two nights prior. Kyle could see how much

Patrick truly loved sucking dick as he had claimed, even elevating it to an art form, by applying the perfect amount of suction and making moves with his mouth and tongue that were comparable to those he demonstrated on the dance floor. He wished it could have gone on forever but immediate climax was inevitable as the waves of pleasure flowed freely from Kyle's dick to his brain, making the connection between body and mind that reverberated through his entire being, causing his toes to curl like clenched fists as he convulsed and climaxed. At the moment of orgasm, Patrick took him all the way down his throat again, triggering his gag reflex to spasm and shudder on the head of Kyle's organ while hot come squirted all over the tops of his tonsils. When Kyle was finished ejaculating, Patrick continued to squeeze his pumping fist around the shaft of Kyle's softening dick while sucking on it hard like the straw in an extra thick milk shake as he coaxed every last dewdrop from the tip of the sweet spout. Once Kyle was sufficiently depleted, Patrick laid down beside him and propped himself on his elbow again to gaze at Kyle's beauty.

Kyle turned his head to Patrick and noticed the tube of lubricant still lying on the edge of the blanket behind his head.

"I can't believe you walked into a store and bought butt lube," Kyle said, shaking his head and smiling.

"I didn't buy it," Patrick replied.

"So, how'd you get it?"

"I stole it," he explained.

"What do you mean? Are you saying that you shoplifted? What if you got caught," Kyle asked.

"Then I would have offered the clerk a few hundred bucks to forget the whole thing."

"Okay, so what if they asked for a thousand," Kyle continued with the hypothetical scenario.

'Then I would have pulled out my phone and told them, I just recorded you trying to blackmail me so, it looks like we're even."

"Well, I can see you thought this through but, wouldn't it have been cheaper to put on a pair of sunglasses and make the two dollar purchase," Kyle reasoned.

"How is that cheaper if I got it for free," Patrick said slyly.

"Well, it may have been cost free but, it certainly wasn't risk free," Kyle pointed out and, as he looked out toward the water, alarm rang through him when he saw a head quickly disappear behind a rock. "Oh, shit," he said in a panic. "There's someone out there behind that rock!" He pointed in the direction of where he had glimpsed the fleeting figure. They both scrambled to locate their discarded shorts, which were lying in the sand beside the blanket. The two of them had been so caught up in each other, that they hadn't even considered the possibility of being discovered. As they rushed to get dressed, they continued watching in the direction of the rock where Kyle had spotted the spying intruder. Suddenly, they saw the elusive head rising from behind the rock once again.

"There he is," Kyle pointed just as the seal's head popped back up over the rock.

Patrick laughed when he saw the curious animal looking back at them from its vantage point. "That sucks," he said gravely. "He's gonna go and tell everyone!"

They both enjoyed a relaxing laugh over the false alarm and proceeded to gather their belongings to make the hike back out of the woods when Patrick's phone began vibrating in his backpack. He retrieved it and checked his messages. "It's a text from Amber," he announced. "It says that she's taking her family's boat out today and wants to know if we feel like doing some waterskiing with her and Ally. What do you say?"

"Fuck yeah! Let's go," Kyle replied enthusiastically.

"Alright then," Patrick agreed. "She says to meet them on the East Side Marina dock at nine a.m.."

Waking toward the path, they paused and exchanged one last kiss before returning to a world where their true feelings for each other would be hidden from view.

Finding Our Way Through the Fog
Jonathan B. Taylor

CHAPTER 12, 'A DAY ON THE WATER'

After changing into proper swimming attire and having a bowl of instant oatmeal for breakfast, Kyle made his way back through the woods to meet up with Patrick and the girls at the East Side Marina. The boatyard was located in a small inlet on the southernmost end of East Main Street, directly across from Patrick's house. There were dozens of boats moored in the tiny harbor of various size and value from small pleasure crafts to luxurious cabin cruisers. Kyle walked down the long, concrete pier toward the floating dock, which sat at the end of the wharf where Patrick and the girls were already waiting. He observed a worker with a scrub brush and hose, locked in a never ending battle with the local seagull population to remove their droppings from the decks and docks of Sunset Cove's elite.

When he reached the end of the pier, Kyle climbed down the short wooden ladder onto the large floating platform and hopped into the modest pleasure boat that Amber's family kept moored at the marina. The fiberglass Wavecraft was fifteen feet long with an open deck and a pointed bow that housed a small storage area in the nose, which could be accessed through a panel beneath the dashboard console. This was where the lifejackets and various other equipment were stored. There was a Plexiglass windshield that sat before two swivel style captain's chairs at the fore and a park bench style seat with padded boat cushions, which was situated along the stern. In large black letters, the name, 'Yellowfin' was stenciled on the sides and stern. The girls were both dressed in ultra skimpy bikinis while Kyle and Patrick wore their usual board short style swim suits. Ally's bikini was hot pink and Amber's was neon green.

"What do you think of my new bathing suit," Ally asked Kyle as she twirled around for him slowly.

"I like it," he said approvingly. "You look bubblelicious!"

They both laughed while they unfastened the mooring lines and prepared to head out for their trip. Once they were off, the two boys took their seats on the bench while the girls opted to stand, with Amber at the helm and Ally beside her riding shotgun. They slowly taxied out of the marina, observing the strict speed limit within it's confines as they headed for open water and a day of waterskiing or as Kyle liked to say, 'trolling for sharks'. What Kyle and Patrick didn't know, was that waterskiing was only part of the plan and the girls had other ideas in store for them that afternoon.

"So, where are we headed," Kyle asked as they puttered past the bevy of boats that tugged on their mooring lines while being pulled by the current.

"West Beach," Ally announced. "That was part of the deal to get Nick to agree to giving us the day off and letting the juniors work the shift by themselves. We told him that we'd be close by if anything happened."

"Oh, so, now we're babysitting," Kyle, said dryly. "If that's the case, then I think we should get paid for our services."

"Yeah," Ally smiled. "I tried that argument but he wasn't going for it. He just said that it was the price of freedom."

"Oh, well," Kyle shrugged and said, "At least Patrick will have an audience to show off for," to which Patrick nodded in agreement.

When they exited the Marina, Amber thrust the throttle to full power, pinning Kyle and Patrick to their seats while Ally clung to the chrome handle that was mounted on the console to prevent herself from somersaulting to the back of the boat and landing on the bench with the boys. As the boat skidded over the small waves of the relatively calm waters, Kyle and Patrick enjoyed the view of the girls' shapely backsides bouncing and jiggling in their surfing stances. Making their way past South Point, Kyle and Patrick smiled at one another and did their customary blushing as they silently acknowledged the significance of the secluded site.

Amber made good time and they arrived at West Beach rather quickly but only to discover that the waters were overrun with flocks of wind surfers and squadrons of jet skis leaving little room for waterskiing. They would have preferred to find a less crowded location but duty dictated that they stick with their present stomping grounds so, they went against their better judgment and picked a lane to begin their run. Kyle scanned the beach to look for Steven and saw him waving excitedly from his lifeguard chair so, Kyle waved back to him with equal enthusiasm.

Following a round of rock, paper, scissors which Patrick won, it was determined that he would start things off. Kyle handed him the life vest and said, "You're up, shark bait. Let's give 'em a good show!"

"You know it," he replied as he suited up and jumped in the water. Kyle handed him the one ski, which was all that Patrick ever used and once his feet were secured in the rubber boot attachments, Kyle passed him the handle of the tow rope.

Finding Our Way Through the Fog
Jonathan B. Taylor

Lying on his back in the water, with the top half of his ski pointing up from the surface, Patrick gave the thumbs up, signaling Amber to slowly tauten the rope before gunning the motor just enough to pull him out of the water into an upright position as if by magic.

"The lord has risen," Kyle said while raising his arms in a celebratory fashion. "Now watch him walk on water."

Patrick began to loosen up by fishtailing in a slalom pattern and then he proceeded to swing wide of the stern and jump the curl of the tail wake while performing a series of corkscrew flips, which he alternated between the port and starboard sides of the boat. He also threw in some three sixties where he spun around in the air like a pirouetting ballet dancer while passing the towrope handle around his back in the process. For his main attraction, he did a few of his more tricky maneuvers, which involved some acrobatic back flips with some shaky landings but, he managed to stay upright and avoid any wipeouts. When Patrick was finished wowing the crowd with his aerial feats, the remainder of the show was pretty boring for the onlookers as the rest of the crew just did straight skiing on two skis with no special stunts in their bags of tricks.

After a few hours and several turns apiece, the crew was spent and decided to call it a day so, Amber drove them all out to South Point where they dropped anchor just beyond the rocks and enjoyed some roast beef sandwiches, which Ally had brought along in a small cooler. When they were finished eating, Patrick challenged Kyle to a race, which Kyle easily won after they dove in the water and swam about two hundred meters to the nearest rock and back. Swimming was the one area where Kyle had Patrick beat and he reveled in his small victory as he hung his arms over the starboard side of the boat with his lower body dangling in the water and panted rapidly in an attempt to catch his breath. When Patrick reached the boat, he took up a similar position directly across from Kyle on the port side. The two exhausted swimmers stared at each other from opposite sides of the craft while the girls reclined in their captain's chairs and soaked up the sun.

Kyle saw a mischievous grin appear on Patrick's face as he lowered his gaze downward in the direction of his fast forming erection. Kyle quickly recalled the image of Patrick instructing him to begin gratifying him immediately whenever he was issued that signal and he wasted no time in complying with the command. He took a deep breath and submerged himself before swimming under the boat to where Patrick's legs and waist were dangling just below the surface. Kyle slid Patrick's bathing suit down to his thighs and watched through the underwater blur as his erection popped up in Kyle's face when it became free from the clothing, which allowed him to take it in his mouth and begin sucking on it like a nursing baby dolphin. He was forced to ingest several mouthfuls of seawater in the process but, the risk was thrilling and he enjoyed the execution of his task, despite the difficulties. After about two minutes, Kyle was no longer able to hold his breath and was forced to resurface. He swam back to his side of the boat and popped his head out of the water to fill his lungs with fresh air before proceeding to repeat the process. He repeated this routine of diving, sucking and resurfacing several times for as long as his breath would sustain him. Finally, on the fourth effort, when he tried to resurface, Patrick wrapped his legs around Kyle's neck and clamped them against his back, holding him in a scissor grip and denying him the ability to replenish his lungs with air. Kyle struggled to get free but Patrick's legs were too strong. Kyle began to panic and in an act of desperation, he bit down on Patrick's erection with just enough force to leave temporary teeth marks without actually breaking the skin. This got Patrick's attention and he immediately released Kyle from his grip, causing Kyle to erupt from the water right beside him, gasping for air. Kyle had gone into survivor mode and was no longer concerned with the optics of suddenly surfacing on the other side of the boat right next to Patrick. He was attempting to wrap his head around what had just transpired and trying to determine if Patrick had just tried to kill him. He sought to put some distance between them by swimming around to the back of the boat and working his way to the starboard side where he was able to relax a little although he remained slightly on edge.

While Patrick had no intention of causing Kyle harm, there was a lack of concern on his part for Kyle's safety, which was demonstrated in his willingness to test the limits of his new power that he held over Kyle in their dangerous game of domination and submission. Kyle thought of his conversation with Steven and the warning he had issued about taking things too far. Now he found himself in one of those situations where he needed to take his own advice as he wondered what kind of relationship he had entered into, which had him vacillating between anger, arousal, and fear. This was only day two and, things were already getting out of control.

Whatever trepidations Kyle had were short lived and by the time he and Patrick were back in the boat and sitting on the bench, all was forgiven. Any negative feelings that Kyle had toward Patrick were washed away by his overwhelming love and devotion for him. The spell was recast and Kyle was once again willing to jump back in the water immediately and resume his suffocating duties if Patrick were to suddenly reissue the command with his eyes.

Finding Our Way Through the Fog
Jonathan B. Taylor

While Kyle and Patrick were preoccupied with one another on the back seat, they failed to notice that the girls had turned away to remove their tops before swiveling back around for the big reveal, which landed with a thud when they sat for a moment and shook their heads as they waited for the oblivious boys to discover them. This seemingly impossible scenario was the culmination of a steady progression over the past few weeks in, which Ally and Amber had increasingly become invisible in the presence of Patrick and Kyle. Just as the girls were about to peel off their bottoms and throw them at the boys faces to get their attention, Kyle did a double take as he suddenly caught a glimpse of the latest developments that were unfolding at the front of the boat.

"What the," Kyle said as he rapidly began tapping his knuckles on Patrick's leg to alert him of the sight and bring him up to speed.

"Oh, shit," Patrick, said with excited confusion as he followed Kyle's stare to the source of his urgings.

"Well, this is new," Kyle, said as they both wondered where the girls were going next.

That question was answered when Ally and Amber both stood up to remove their bottoms. Patrick then turned to Kyle and said, "Now, it's getting interesting," to, which Kyle smiled and nodded in agreement.

As the girls approached, Kyle found his eyes drawn to Amber's naked body while Patrick was locked onto Ally with this being the first time that either had seen the other without clothing. The seductresses moved in unison with Ally kneeling before Kyle and Amber in front of Patrick where they proceeded to slide the boys' shorts down their legs as Kyle and Patrick both wriggled in assistance. Ally watched Kyle's folded down erection spring to attention as it cleared the waistband of his lowering shorts and she immediately began sucking on it. Once it was coated with a glistening film of her saliva, she placed it between her breasts and squeezed them together as she slid them up and down on Kyle's rigid organ. Meanwhile, Amber had removed Patrick's shorts and was stroking him softly as she rolled his balls around in her mouth with her tongue like a couple of ice cubes on a hot summer day.

With both boys naked now and sitting beside one another on the bench, Kyle was no longer concerned with the comparison between their erections as he had fully accepted his lesser roll in all areas of their relationship, including dick size. He suddenly saw Patrick's enormous dick as his new favorite toy and embraced every opportunity to bask in its splendor. He also acknowledged the absurdity of salivating over something, which had caused him so much trauma the night before and wondered why everyone seemed to be so captivated by the mere image of monster size dicks when in reality, they were some of the most impractical things on the planet. Kyle watched as Amber struggled to fit Patrick's donkey dick in her mouth while Ally enjoyed a much easier time engulfing his less invasive organ and he started to see the advantages of having a standard size erection over a 'porn star's pride and joy'.

As the girls performed their synchronized routine, Kyle determined that it couldn't be a coincidence that they both decided to strip down and start performing oral sex on them at the same time when they had never done anything like it before, which could only mean that it was preplanned. For the second act of their intriguing endeavor, Ally and Amber continued with the choreography when they simultaneously stood up, turned around, and mounted Kyle and Patrick's laps, consuming their erections with their warm, wet vaginas. They then began riding the boys in unison as reverse cowgirls in an erotic rodeo with a slow and easy gait. The boys smiled at each other as they took in the exquisite scene before them. It was a beautiful day on the water and they were sitting back with two equally beautiful women, who were mounted on their laps like mermaid figureheads on the bowsprit, writhing up and down on their dicks in a smooth rhythm with the small waves that gently rocked the boat as they rolled beneath it.

It was a perfect moment for Kyle and Patrick who would have been content to ride out the rest of the afternoon in their current positions but the girls had other ideas in mind. They both dismounted the boys and stood together before them where they began kissing and caressing one another, causing Kyle and Patrick's eyes to widen as their eyebrows arched. The girls then circled around one another and passed the batons so that Amber took up position on her knees in front of Kyle while Ally knelt before Patrick. There was a momentary awkwardness upon the change of partners as they were entering uncharted waters but, the uneasiness was lifted the instant that the girls' mouths met the boys' erections. Kyle watched as Amber licked his dick like a popsicle while Ally did the same to Patrick and he realized that the girls were lapping each other's juices off of their glazed erections. Kyle was wondering what had gotten into the girls and now he knew. Apparently, they had gotten into each other.

"Oh, shit," Kyle, said to Amber. "Did you just lick the spoon?"

"That's right," she smiled. "Pussy frosted pricks. They're two great tastes that taste great together!"

"Yeah. They've been around forever and ever," Ally, continued the homage to an old eighties tune which had ripped off an even older candy bar ad.

Finding Our Way Through the Fog
Jonathan B. Taylor

As the girls continued to suck and lick each other's remaining traces off of the boys' joysticks, Kyle and Patrick were once again focused on each other and being overwhelmed by their desire to be together. They were inspired by Ally and Amber's open display of affection and saw it as a green light to lean in for a kiss of their own. The girls took note as the boys' open lips touched and their tongues twirled prompting Ally to hold out her hand while Amber slapped it with a 'mission accomplished' low five followed with some adolescent whooping and cheering which caused Kyle and Patrick to pause the kiss while stifling a bit of laughter between their pressed lips and reddened faces. Ally then stood up in front of Patrick and mounted him briefly in order to provide his dick with a fresh shellacking from her wet pussy. She winced slightly from the pain of the initial intrusion before sliding off his lap and informing Kyle that it was his turn to 'lick the spoon'. With Amber continuing to perform oral sex on him, Kyle leaned over and went to work on Patrick, taking his erection in his mouth and sucking Ally's tantalizing juices off it while enjoying the arousing combination of flavors just as the girls had described.

Meanwhile, Ally joined Amber on her knees in front of Kyle and proceeded to lick and suck on his shaft and balls while Amber focused her attention on the head. The two girls started caressing each other's breasts and making out on the head of Kyle's pulsating erection with their tongues rolling around on the tip. It was only a matter of moments before Kyle began climaxing in their mouths with Ally swallowing the bulk of the load and Amber licking up the drizzle. Within a few seconds of his own orgasm, Kyle felt Patrick's hot come erupt in his mouth, which he ingested eagerly in two large gulps.

Finding Our Way Through the Fog
Jonathan B. Taylor

With the two boys feeling satisfied, they sat back on the bench and watched the girls finish each other off in a sixty nine on the deck of the boat. Amber was on her back and Ally was over her as they worked on one another with their tongues and fingers like concert musicians performing a symphony of stimulation. Kyle and Patrick could see that they had a lot to learn in the art of cunnilingus. Although, they felt superior at sucking dick, they conceded that girls were far more masterful at eating pussy. Not only did they achieve climax much faster with each other but their orgasms seemed more intense as their entire bodies convulsed and they appeared to be experiencing grand mal seizures.

When the party was over, the four exhausted adventurers retreated to their original positions and observed their new world from the safety of those corners. Ally and Amber were back in their swivel seats while Kyle and Patrick were resituated on opposing ends of the backbench. Now that everything was out in the open in the post foursome picture, Kyle took advantage of the opportunity to speak freely.

"Well," he declared, "in the past twenty four hours, I've been back doored and now I just had my first orgy. Scratch two off the bucket list!"

"Whoa," Ally interjected. "Are you saying that you had that thing up your ass," pointing at Patrick. "I'm impressed! But, how is it you're not in the hospital right now?"

Kyle shrugged. "Honestly, I don't know how I pulled it off but I probably won't be walking right for the next week."

Patrick nodded in agreement with the same smug smirk of satisfaction that he had sported when he was fucking Kyle. He enjoyed having others boast about his penis size even when it was in a disparaging way.

"Well, Amber, it looks like our boat's come under attack from butt pirates," Ally said slyly.

"That's cute," Kyle replied with a wry smile before retorting, "Oh, look Patrick, the carpet cleaners have arrived."

"Yeah, about that," Ally said doubtfully, "I don't see any carpets here. Do you," referencing the fiberglass deck and their shaved crotches.

"So, what then, you're just here to mop the floors," Kyle inquired.

"Or, swab the decks," Patrick elaborated.

"That's more like it," Ally said approvingly before switching subjects. "You know, I couldn't help noticing that we did all of that work on you guys and neither of you got off but, the moment that you engaged with each other, you both blew your loads in a matter of seconds. Am I wrong or, is that how it is for you two?"

"No, that's how it is," Kyle conceded. "I guess we just really do it for each other," he added as he slid across the bench over to Patrick and wrapped his arms around his torso while laying his head on Patrick's chest. Patrick reciprocated by wrapping his own arm around Kyle's shoulder and holding him close while kissing the top of his head.

"It's true," Patrick confirmed. "Whenever we come together, it's instant orgasm. No pun intended."

"You two are so cute together," Ally smiled as her and Amber took in the sight of the two boys embracing on the back seat of the boat.

"Yeah," Amber concurred. "You really are the hottest guy on guy couple ever! You should do porn together. You two could make a fortune in the gay porn industry."

"Really," Kyle laughed. "That's what you think we should do with our lives? Become gay porn stars? That's like me suggesting that you should become a life coach."

"Or, a Guidance Counselor," Patrick threw in as a devious leer flashed on his face and then vanished.

"I think you may be overselling it," Kyle said, questioning Amber's reasoning. "I'm not sure if there's a fortune to be made there. I don't think that guy on guy porn has the wide ranging popularity of girl on girl action so, you're dealing with a much more limited market."

"Why is that," Patrick posed his question to the group. "Why is there so much more stigma around gay men than there is around gay women?"

"Honestly," Ally said, "I think it has a lot to do with the different reactions from the opposite sexes. If you notice, most guys will admit to being turned on by the image of two girls together but the same can't be said for a lot of girls who will openly cringe at the sight of two guys going at it. Guys will then pick up on those adverse reactions, which leave them feeling like their own bisexuality is somehow unacceptable so they join in on the self loathing and help perpetuate the homophobia against themselves."

"So, what is it that all of these girls have against gay guys anyway," Kyle asked Ally. "I mean, you and Amber don't seem to have a problem with it."

"I think it has a lot to do with jealousy and their own insecurity," Ally reasoned. "A lot of girls are threatened by the closeness that guys have with their male friends so the idea that guys could be physically attracted to one another is seen as an even bigger threat. This causes them to attack the very notion of male homosexuality as they would any rival."

"That sounds twisted," Kyle said. "So, how do we fix it? What's the solution?"

"I think guys should stop worrying about what other people think and just come out as bisexual if that's what they're into," Ally surmised. "They should stop depriving themselves and letting these insecure ladies manipulate them. Guys need to realize that they can have a cock in each hand as well as one in the bush. Just think," she added, "if everybody was to suddenly stand up and admit that the emperor has no clothes then homophobia would cease to exist."

"It sounds like we're a long way from equality among the sexes within the community," Kyle concluded.

"Well, now you know how women feel in virtually every other aspect of life," Ally smiled.

Eventually, their day on the water came to a close and, they made their way back to the marina from where their journey began. As the boat skipped along the surface like a well thrown stone, Kyle thought of the water racing beneath his feet and how his life was rolling right along with it at the same breakneck speed. Fall was coming fast and these carefree days of youth and summer would be left behind as nothing more than a trail of foam in their slowly fading wake. While one world was laid to rest behind him, another was opening up before him and he suddenly felt slightly exposed in his new surroundings. The number of people who were in on the secret of his sexuality had practically doubled in the past day as he slowly crept his way out of the closet. There was a bit of unease as each revelation posed the threat of possible exposure. The problem with sharing secrets is that you never know how safe they are in another's hands. Kyle figured that this concept was probably weighing on Patrick's thoughts when he had sworn the girls to secrecy regarding the afternoon's activities and the resulting revelations. They all agreed that it was unforgivable for one member of the community to out another and they each swore their silence on the subject however, Kyle wasn't convinced. Although, he had always trusted Ally with his secret, he couldn't shake the feeling that she had betrayed his confidence to Amber based on the days events and how they unfolded. Now he began to wonder who else she may have told.

Finding Our Way Through the Fog
Jonathan B. Taylor

CHAPTER 13, 'AN UNEXPECTED EXPOSURE'

Later that evening, Kyle and Patrick were back in his basement, after returning from a whirlwind odyssey that began twenty four hours earlier when they had set out in a dense fog down a curious path through an elaborate forest. The transformative journey had carried them to a place, which was very different from the one they had left. Two days ago, Kyle sat on the opposite end of the same sofa, imagining himself in Patrick's arms and now, time had transported them into that dream and made it a reality. As they cuddled on the couch and enjoyed the pleasure of being pressed together, they began to carefully test the waters and explore the other aspects of their newly discovered surroundings.

Not only had the door been opened to a world of physical intimacy for Kyle and Patrick, the doorway had opened on openness itself, making it possible to share thoughts and feelings between them which were previously kept private. This was perhaps the most thrilling and, yet frightening aspect of their newfound bond. Although, they were suddenly able to share intimate thoughts with one another, they still felt the occasional word get stuck in their throats as they continued to battle through the residual effects of fear which had prevented such candor in the weeks leading up to this period. Together, they shared revelations about themselves, including their childhood attractions to one another from afar and how each was the object of the other's desire throughout the years and the subject of many masturbation sessions. This was a time of learning and discovery, as they were both meeting for the first time on an entirely new level.

"So, all those times that I was sitting in my room and thinking about you while I was jerking off, you were sitting over here, doing the same thing and thinking about me," Patrick said, recognizing the irony.

"Yeah, if only we had known, maybe we wouldn't have wasted all that time dreaming about it when we could have actually been doing it. I guess all we can do now is try and make up for all that lost time," Kyle said as he wrapped his arms around Patrick's torso and gave him a tight squeeze.

"If that's the case, then we have got a lot of ground to cover," Patrick replied. "Because, you have no idea what kind of things I've imagined doing to you."

Kyle responded by pressing the bulge of his instantly formed erection against Patrick's thigh as a sign of his willingness to comply. The gesture was an invitation for Patrick to use him as an instrument in whatever fantasies he had in mind and Kyle expected that things were probably going to get pretty wild in the days to come.

"So, now that we have the ability to live out all of those past fantasies, why don't you tell me some of your favorites," Patrick suggested.

"You want to know my favorite fantasy?" Kyle kicked the question around in his head for a moment. "That would probably involve double penetration," he finally decided. "The thought of getting hit in both ends at the same time is one of those hidden desires that gets me there every time whenever I'm rubbing one out."

"So, your deepest desire is to be a slam pig," Patrick nodded approvingly.

"Not exactly." Kyle halfheartedly objected to the oversimplification. "I mean, it's just a fantasy. It's not like I would ever be in a position to actually do it."

"Why not," Patrick asked, unconvinced by Kyle's lack of faith.

"I don't know," he shrugged. "I don't see a lot of opportunity for it. I mean, I just don't see myself in the type of scenario that would provide the launch pad for something like that." Although he was downplaying the possibility of it, Kyle knew that he had just popped the cork and the genie was already out of the bottle. He could see the wheels turning in Patrick's eyes as a plan was hatching in the back of his mind.

"You never know," Patrick smiled deviously. "This morning you probably never pictured yourself in a foursome. To be honest, I still can't believe it myself. What do you suppose got into the girls today anyway?"

"I don't know but, it looks like while we were busy doing our thing, they were busy getting into a little thing of their own. I just don't know what prompted them to initiate an orgy. It seemed a little out of character and the whole thing was obviously planned out which makes it even more mysterious."

"Speaking of 'out'," Patrick segued, "now that they know our secret, do you think we can trust them to keep quiet?"

"Well, I can't speak to Amber but, Ally's known that I was bisexual for awhile and she's always been trustworthy although, I couldn't shake the feeling that she may have said something to Amber."

"What makes you think that," Patrick asked.

"I don't know. It's just a feeling." Kyle's suspicions were technically unfounded because Ally never actually betrayed his confidence when she and Amber discussed the possibility that the two boys had moved beyond the bounds of simple friendship since she never revealed any of his prior admissions to her in the process.

"Well, I think we can trust Amber," Patrick reassured him. "She's pretty loyal and doesn't get into the whole backstabbing and gossiping thing. So, tell me more about you coming out to Ally. How did that conversation go?"

"It wasn't some big 'coming out' moment or anything like that. Instead, we kind of started with some generic admissions about being capable of finding members of our own sex attractive, which is a long way from saying, 'I like to suck dick and take it in the ass!'"

"That's true," he nodded in agreement. "So, is Ally the only one who knows or are there others?" Patrick continued to fish. He already knew of one other person and he was curious to see if Kyle would mention Kevin.

"The list is short although it is growing," Kyle admitted. "I actually just added someone the other day when he surprised me by 'coming out' to me so I felt an obligation to reciprocate."

"It was Steven," Patrick guessed immediately.

"Steven? You mean Steven Alves," Kyle feigned bewilderment. "What makes you think it was him?"

"I just get a vibe from him and I see the way he looks at you. He seems to have a little crush on you and I noticed when we were out on the water today, you two were waving at each other like you were signaling the rescue plane and now it all makes sense."

"Well, that's interesting detective work but, you're way off," Kyle lied rather poorly.

"If you say so," Patrick rolled his eyes at the unconvincing denial. "So, is that everyone? Just Steven and Ally?"

"No! Not Steven," Kyle insisted. He was starting to feel concerned that he may have unintentionally betrayed Steven through his simple lack of a poker face and he tried desperately to steer the conversation away from Patrick's accurate suspicions. "The only others are my parents and this kid I went with in junior high."

"Whoa," Patrick said sounding surprised. "You told your parents?" Although this concept was the most difficult thing imaginable to Patrick, it was actually an unremarkable event in Kyle's life, which was an example of the stark contrast between their upbringings. "I couldn't even imagine telling my uptight, religious fanatic parents that I was bi. How did your parents react when you told them?"

"It was almost in a celebratory way," Kyle laughed. "They told me how proud they were and, basically welcomed me to the community."

"Welcomed you to which community? You mean the LGBT community? How are they part of the community," Patrick remained flabbergasted.

"Because they're both openly bisexual," Kyle explained. "That's why it wasn't really a big deal for me to come out to them. I grew up in a home where it was normalized instead of ostracized."

Finding Our Way Through the Fog
Jonathan B. Taylor

"You're so lucky," Patrick told him. "If I ever brought a guy home, my homophobe parents would probably disown me."

It was ironic for Kyle to hear someone who seemed to have every advantage in life, consider him to be the lucky one for having something so simple as understanding parents who Kyle suddenly felt he had taken for granted.

"It kills me when people use religion to justify homophobia," Patrick grumbled. "Then they talk about 'family values' but I didn't know that bigotry was considered a family value. Just because someone wants to believe in a fairytale, doesn't give them the right to be a bigot."

"A fairytale." Kyle laughed at the reference. "And, how do you think your parents would respond to your suggestion that their beloved Bible is a fairytale?"

"That's what it is!" Patrick stood by his assertion. "Think about it. As children, we're told to believe in three basic fairytales. Santa Clause, the Easter Bunny, and the Bible. Eventually, we get older and learn that two of those stories are fabrications but, for some reason, people continue to believe in the Bible and allow it to control every aspect of their lives, which is actually, why it was written in the first place. It was created as a means to control the masses, which it's done a pretty good job of for the past several thousand years if you think about it. It's really amazing how this primitive tale can function so effectively as a modern tool for those in power to manipulate such a major portion of the population. Demagogues know that it takes a certain amount of gullibility to believe in the Bible so they take that susceptibility to manipulation and exploit it. Then you have the Bible thumpers themselves who are so hypocritical in how they pick and choose what parts they want to take literally. They always love to point out that the Bible says homosexuality is wrong but, it also says that anyone who commits adultery should be stoned to death and you don't hear any of these people who like to cheat on their spouses mentioning that reference too often."

"That's true," Kyle agreed. "I also love it when they use words like 'indoctrination'. It's like, you can't indoctrinate sexuality but you can indoctrinate things like prejudice and bigotry. It always baffles me when I see members of the community who want to join up with the Bible thumpers. Talk about an oxymoron. You'd think they would see the contradiction and realize that those people are not their friends."

"You know, whenever I hear anyone reference the 'community', I feel so far removed from that term," Patrick admitted. "It seems more like tribalism to me and I'm not sure where I fit in. You have all these different factions and I'm not even sure if my group has a seat at the table. Unfortunately, there isn't a lot of kinship among the closeted bisexuals as most of us exist in our own little isolated bubbles, unaware of each other's existence. And, I know this is gonna sound messed up but, I really don't want to be lumped in with a bunch of circus freak drag queens either. I realize that's homophobic and may be hypocritical but, I can't help how I feel."

"No, you can't help how you feel and you can't control it either. But, you can control what you do or say so, you have to try to be supportive and nonjudgmental because, that's all anyone can ask," Kyle reassured him. "Trust me, I can get just as uncomfortable around circus clown drag queens and overly flamboyant gay guys as the next person and sometimes a part of me thinks, 'This is why I prefer to stay in the closet instead of standing on the platform at the public stoning with this colorful cast of characters'. But, the truth is, those are the soldiers who are out there on the front lines, fighting for the rest of us and all of the gains we've made are based on their bravery. I know that I'll be out there with them eventually but, I'm just not ready to give up my anonymity yet. And, before you feel guilty about having homophobic thoughts, you should know that this is a universal problem within the community and no group is immune. Unfortunately, we can be our own worst enemies when it comes to cannibalizing each other. For example, I saw a transgender actor who identifies as female, being interviewed on a daytime talk show and, she was complaining that straight guys didn't want to date her because they didn't want to be associated with the stigma of being seen as gay. So, this idiot was trying to distance herself from the gay community by making the highly offensive argument that any guy who was with her, shouldn't be considered gay because she had transitioned over to being a woman. Instead of speaking out against homophobia, and saying that there shouldn't be any stigma around being gay in the first place, she was feeding into the stereotype and looking for a loophole around it while throwing us under the bus in the process. I said to myself, 'This person doesn't have a clue.' and, I started to feel like some of these people who change their gender are slightly delusional and they want the rest of the world to be delusional as well. After hearing that, I decided that I didn't want to be lumped in with the trans community anymore than they want to be associated with me so, now I just see myself as part of the gay and bisexual community and consider all of the other groups to be separate entities. I still support them and see them as allies in the fight for equality but, I don't consider them a part of my community."

"To be honest," Patrick confessed, "I've never understood the attraction to trannies or super effeminate gay guys. I mean, if that's what attracts someone, why not just be with a girl?"

"Well, therein lies the problem for a lot of trannies and that's what the actress was facing. Gay guys don't want to be with them because they're girls, and straight guys can't get past the fact that they are or once were dudes so, they find themselves stuck between a rock and a hard place when, what they really want, is to be sitting on a cock with a couple of hard-ons in their face." Kyle smiled. "But, at the end of the day," he added, "there's someone for everyone, including a whole bunch of guys out there who are even into trannies. Everyone's tastes are different and we don't have any control over who or what attracts us. The funny thing is, while we sit here and imagine ourselves to be the 'normal' members of the LGBT community, the rest of the groups see us as the outliers."

"So, we're the freaks," Patrick laughed at the irony.

"It's true," Kyle laughed with him. "Despite having the largest numbers, bisexuals are the most underrepresented and least accepted members of the community. On top of that, we don't exhibit any of the stereotypical gay mannerisms and so, we're called 'straight acting' which is further frowned upon."

"I never liked that term, 'straight acting'," Patrick said. "It's like suggesting that we're pretending to be something we're not and only flouncing fairies have any legitimacy in the gay community."

"Yeah, and if you're bisexual then, the gay community treats you like some kind of a sellout for being attracted to members of the opposite sex," Kyle complained. "It's like there's no points for half-breeds."

"Alright, enough about that. Let's get back to this list." Patrick resumed his efforts to extract Kevin's name from Kyle's security files. "I know about Ally and Steven and your Parents but, what about this kid you went with in junior high?"

"Will you stop saying Steven," Kyle was growing increasingly agitated with Patrick's persistence but, the more he protested, the more that Patrick was convinced he was right.

"Okay. Okay. No Steven. But what about the other kid. Tell me more about him."

"There isn't much to tell," Kyle shook his head and shrugged. "We did a couple of sixty nines one night and that was pretty much it."

"Did he end it or did you?" Patrick continued to probe. "Or, was it a mutual ending?"

"No, he ended it," Kyle admitted. "If you want to call it that. There really wasn't much to end. It was nothing more than a slow build up to a one night stand. I would have kept it going just for the sex but, he wasn't into it."

"Why do you suppose that is?"

"I don't know. Maybe he wasn't ready or, maybe he won't ever be ready. He could just be one of those empty souls who approaches sex like a conquest and once they've accomplished their goal, they grow bored and select a new target."

Patrick thought about Kyle's words and how they were eerily describing him in his pre Kyle days. He then made one last attempt to elicit the name. "So, who is he? You have to tell me now. You can't tell me all that and then not tell me who it is."

"I'm sorry but, I can't." Kyle held his ground.

"Why not? Don't you trust me? You don't think I can keep a secret?" Patrick tried applying a little guilt as leverage.

"Well, if it's a matter of trust then, how would you ever be able to trust me if I was just blabbing other people's secrets to you," Kyle said, and with that final point, Patrick relented.

Kyle had passed the test and kept his integrity intact, making him the first boy that Patrick was unable to crack when it came to protecting the identity of a past lover. As they tightened their embrace with a reaffirming squeeze, following Kyle's denial of Patrick's attempts to elicit Kevin's name, they both heard the door to the second floor open and the sound of Kyle's mother announcing her presence at the top of the stairs before beginning her descent into the basement. Kyle immediately tried to sever their connection and scramble for the opposite end of the sofa but Patrick was holding onto him and preventing his departure. Kyle was confused by Patrick's actions and suddenly felt like he was back beneath the boat in a panic, with Patrick's legs wrapped around his neck, preventing him from reaching the surface. He came to the conclusion that Patrick enjoyed taking risks and would eventually release him at the very last moment to avoid actual exposure.

Kyle watched as his mother's feet appeared, followed by her legs as she made her way down the stairs while Patrick continued to hold him in check with his viselike grip. When she finally reached the bottom of the stairs and turned to them, Kyle saw the look of surprise on her face as she took in the image of the two of them entwined on the couch. Now he understood. Patrick wasn't just tempting fate by risking exposure after all. His intention was to come out to Claire in the most dramatic way imaginable and he had definitely scored points for theatrics by Kyle's estimation.

"Oh. I'm not interrupting anything, am I," Claire asked as she attempted to regain her composure.

"Not at all," Patrick said, nonchalantly.

"Why? What's going on," Kyle asked. "What brings you down here?"

"Nothing, I just wanted to let you know that we're leaving for New York first thing in the morning and I left a list of things I need you to do on the refrigerator where I knew you would see it."

"Okay," Kyle responded abruptly. "Well, have a safe trip and call me when you get there," he said, hurrying her along.

"Yes," she responded, taking her cue to head back upstairs as if beating a hasty retreat from a disorienting situation. "Well, I'll leave you boys to it."

"Goodnight, Mrs. Jacobs," Patrick called to her as she ascended.

"Goodnight," she smiled back at them and disappeared from view.

"Dude! What the hell was that all about," Kyle asked after they heard the door close.

"I don't know," Patrick shrugged and smiled. "You were just talking about how cool your parents are and I got inspired so, I figured, why not let them know? You're okay with that, right? I mean, I didn't think you'd mind because she already knows your bi."

"No, it's cool. It's completely cool. You just caught me by surprise," Kyle smiled and nestled his head against Patrick's chest.

"I think it's fair to say that we probably caught her by surprise as well," Patrick laughed.

"Yeah, I'm pretty sure I haven't heard the last of this," Kyle said as he mentally prepared for the can of worms that Patrick had just opened.

Finding Our Way Through the Fog
Jonathan B. Taylor

After a period of cuddling and making out on the couch, they both decided to take the night off from sex, having had their fill over the past twenty four hours but, Kyle assured Patrick that his soreness was subsiding and he would be ready for round two the following night. They enjoyed one last kiss like the one Kyle had imagined them sharing the other day when they said goodbye and, Patrick made his way out to the car and headed for home.

No sooner had Patrick's car pulled down the driveway, when Claire was back at the top of the stairs, announcing her presence before making her way down to the basement and taking a seat on the sofa beside Kyle who knew what was coming after the bombshell they had just dropped on her.

"So, how's everything going," She asked, while casually beating around the bush.

"Oh, you know, living the dream," Kyle replied coyly.

"So I see," Claire said with raised eyebrows. "Well, you know I'm not one to pry," she began, before Kyle quickly interrupted her.

"And that's something that I've always appreciated."

"Save it," she said, "and tell me what's up with you and Patrick. I'm sorry to be nosy but you two got my curiosity piqued."

"No, I understand. After all, we did just throw you for a loop," Kyle acknowledged.

That was all she needed to hear. Once the green light flashed, Claire started firing off questions. "So, how long has this been going on? Is this something new or, have you two been together for awhile?"

"Um, yes and no," Kyle answered before breaking down his response. "It's been building for awhile but, we only just recently closed the deal."

"And, does anyone else know," she asked.

"You mean Ally and Amber?" Kyle read her thoughts. "Yeah, Ally and Amber know but that's it. Nobody else does. Except for you now," he added.

"Whoa! You told Ally and Amber. How did that go down," she pressed.

"Let's just say 'it's a long story' and leave it at that." Kyle definitely wasn't interested in sharing those sordid details with her.

"Well, was it awkward," she asked.

"Surprisingly, no," Kyle said, as he thought about how comfortable they had all seemed during their afternoon orgy.

"How did they take it," she continued her line of unintentionally ambiguous questioning.

"They took it pretty well," Kyle smiled as he continued to provide his double edged answers.

"So, where do you see this going? Is it just casual or, is it something serious," Claire inquired.

"That's a good question." Kyle thought for a moment. "We're both pretty casual when it comes to relationships. I mean, neither of us does the jealous, possessive, controlling thing although, I have to admit, this is probably the closest I've ever come to being in an 'exclusive' relationship but, that's only by default, through the simple fact that I have zero interest in anyone else right now and, Patrick is all I think about. I'm not sure if that qualifies as 'serious' but, I would say that it's way beyond 'friends with benefits'."

"And what about Patrick? How do you think he sees it?"

"It's hard to say. He seems to be into me as much as I'm into him but Patrick's tough to read. He doesn't exactly broadcast his emotions and usually keeps you guessing. He's like a black hole the way he draws you in and nothing escapes him, including the inner workings of his mind which can never be seen beyond that event horizon of his."

"Wow! He sounds kind of scary."

"Yeah, but, he's the good scary. You know, the kind of scary you run to and not away from like a hair raising rollercoaster or a haunted house on Halloween."

"Well, just remember that black holes are believed to be some of the most destructive objects in the universe and should only be approached with extreme caution."

"Yeah, I think it's too late for that. Caution is already out the window along with good sense and equilibrium."

"Equilibrium? That makes it sound like there's an imbalance. Do you feel like things may be a little one-sided."

"Yes, but, the one-sided aspect is more about the relationship dynamic than the emotional connection."

"So, you feel like you're giving more than you're getting?"

"I do but, that's how we both want it and probably the only way it would ever work. Patrick's had a tough road in coming to terms with his sexuality and there are limits on what he would be able to accept of himself."

"Ah, so he's strictly a top?"

"For the most part." Kyle didn't elaborate on Patrick's ability to perform fellatio while being a hard 'no' on receiving anal.

"So, what are the difficulties he faced regarding his sexuality?"

"Basically, it was his upbringing," Kyle explained. "His right wing religious fanatic parents could have really done a number on him with their toxic homophobia but, Patrick is remarkably resilient and turned out surprisingly grounded although some emotional scarring was inevitable. I have to admit though, after hearing him talk, it has given me a newfound appreciation for you and Phil. It makes me grateful to have such young, progressive parents."

"Well, I'm glad to hear that. It's always nice to be appreciated," she smiled.

"Oh, you have no idea. Would you believe that Patrick is convinced that his parents would disown him if they ever knew he was gay? Well, in his case, bisexual but, it's the gay part that they would have a problem with. What kind of people would do that? Who would reject their own kid just because of who he is?"

"I don't know who would do that or, if Patrick's parents would ever take it that far but it sucks that he feels that way and I'm just glad that he was comfortable enough to be himself with me because, I think it's important for him to know that he has allies and doesn't have to feel like he's all alone."

"I think so too and, maybe that's what inspired him to do what he did tonight."

"So, was it Patrick's idea to reveal your relationship to me?"

"Yes. That was all Patrick and I had no idea he was going to do it. We were cuddling on the couch when you came down the stairs and I was trying to move away from him but he wouldn't let me go. Then, I realized that he wanted you to see us so, I just let it play out."

"So, now that I know about your relationship and, the girls know, do you see this trend continuing?"

Finding Our Way Through the Fog
Jonathan B. Taylor

"You mean, in terms of 'coming out'? I'm not sure how far Patrick's willing to go on that because of the whole deal with his parents. Personally, I was planning on coming out when I got to college. I just thought that with the fresh start and new faces it would be the easiest way to transition into being completely open about my bisexuality. I also figured that it would improve my dating options if I was advertising on both sides of the spectrum. But, now, the whole deal with Patrick has called my entire plan into question."

"Why is that?"

"Well, for one thing, I'm no longer looking to meet someone so, that motivating factor is off the table. Then, I have to consider what kind of effect my coming out would have on our relationship. If everyone knows that, I'm into guys and they always see me with Patrick, it would inevitably raise questions about his sexuality through the process of guilt by association. I don't know," Kyle shook his head. "Maybe I'm just looking for excuses to maintain my sexual anonymity. Did you or Phil struggle with these conflicts? How was it for you two when you told the world who you were?"

"Well, we didn't exactly go nuclear with a 'coming out' moment. It was more of a gradual process. We started with each other and slowly started telling our friends and families as it came up in conversation. Although, I think that once the information is out there, it tends to find its way around on its own. I also think that it was probably easier for us because we were doing it together and we were being shielded by a heterosexual union at the same time. People seemed to have an easier time accepting the knowledge that we were attracted to both sexes as long as it appeared that we were only acting on the straight side. But, you really shouldn't feel a need to put deadlines or commitments on coming out. It's not like you have an obligation to share your sexuality with the world. It's really nobody else's business."

"Well, actually, I do feel like I have an obligation. As more people come out, there's less stigma around it, which leads to greater acceptance. Or, as Ally puts it, more people to acknowledge that the emperor has no clothes. In that sense, I think we all have a moral obligation to help bring about change and make the world a better place for those who follow just as those who came before have done for us. Look at how much easier each generation has it as they stand on the shoulders of those who paved the way. I can't just sit back and let others fight my battle when numbers are so desperately needed. Besides, I feel like I'm only half a person with half of myself hidden and why should we hide who we are, just because others have a problem accepting who they are?"

"Well, it's good that you want to pay it forward and fight for the cause but, I still think that 'coming out' should be a spontaneous process and not something that feels forced."

"I get that. But, sometimes the process just needs a little push and setting goals can help to accomplish that."

"Well, I've got to get some sleep," she said. "We're leaving early in the morning so, I probably won't see you but, we'll call you when we arrive in New York."

After saying 'goodnight' and exchanging hugs, Claire headed back upstairs and Kyle turned in for the night as well. Lying in bed, his thoughts were consumed by Patrick and all of the things he wanted to experience with him. Despite a throbbing erection, he resisted the urge to masturbate, opting instead to save it for the following night while riding the pleasurable waves of swelling anticipation.

Finding Our Way Through the Fog
Jonathan B. Taylor

Finding Our Way Through the Fog
Jonathan B. Taylor

152

CHAPTER 14,
'MEASURING UP'

For Kyle and Patrick, the following day was largely uneventful and was all about the buildup to the coming evening. It began with a morning workout at Kyle's which they somehow managed to get through without ripping each other's clothes off and going at it right there on the rubber floor mats. Patrick was all business and it helped that they were working their backs and biceps, which didn't involve any provocative spotting like their bench press and squat routines.

After completing their sets and downing a couple of chocolate protein shakes, they reported for duty at West Beach where they took up position on their lifeguard chairs and spent the day dreaming about their plans for the evening. At one point, Ally and Amber stopped by to see Kyle before making their way down the beach to Patrick's perch where they showed him the same courtesy. Kyle had a much lengthier visit from Steven who hung out with him for a couple of hours. He knew that this would probably add to Patrick's suspicions that Steven was the one who had come out to him but, he was enjoying his company in light of their newfound bond and didn't want to disturb that connection in spite of appearances. He just hoped that Patrick wouldn't do or say something to give Steven the false impression that Kyle had somehow betrayed him.

Kyle and Patrick finished out their shift at the beach and returned to Kyle's house where they enjoyed a brief make out session on Kyle's doorstep before peeling themselves apart and reluctantly agreeing to 'save it for later'. Kyle went inside to prepare for the evening with his predate ritual of showering, shaving, and douching while Patrick made his way home through the woods to get cleaned up and retrieve some things that he needed to carry out the night's intended activities.

Once he had finished cleaning himself inside and out, Kyle found his way upstairs to his parents' kitchen to forage for food, where he discovered the note that his mother had mentioned leaving him on the refrigerator with a list of things she wanted him to do. He saw that it only had one sentence on it, which, was written entirely in capital letters and read, 'CLEAN UP AFTER YOURSELF!' "That's cute Claire," he said aloud as he crumpled the note and dropped it in the receptacle beneath the counter. He then proceeded to put together an oversized ham and cheese sandwich that he ate with some pickle wedges and low salt potato chips before making his way back downstairs where he planted himself on the sofa to wait for Patrick's return. At around six o'clock, he heard the familiar sound of Patrick's Challenger pulling up the driveway and instantly felt his heart rate quicken as the butterflies once again began to flutter.

Kyle was wearing his gossamer, grey, gym shorts again with no underwear, which left little to the imagination and even allowed him to make out the pinkness of his genitals through their timeworn translucence. He figured that he may just as well have been sitting there naked but it was only a matter of time before that would be the case. As he listened for the next familiar sound of Patrick's sharp knock, he was pleasantly surprised to see him walk right in without knocking as if he owned the place. Kyle saw this as a symbolic gesture of the latest phase in their relationship, where there was no need for Patrick to be knocking at Kyle's backdoor when he could simply enter at will.

Patrick crossed the floor in his catlike mode and approached the couch with a purpose that told Kyle not to expect much foreplay or small talk from him tonight as he was obviously ready to get right down to business. He was wearing an all white ensemble of chino style shorts with a short sleeve, collared, pullover, which made it appear as though he had just stepped out of an ad for men's tennis wear. Patrick's attractiveness was amplified by Kyle's anticipation as he enjoyed the freedom of forming an erection upon seeing him, without the hassle of having to conceal it.

"I see you're wearing my favorite shorts," Patrick said, as he dropped his backpack on the coffee table. "Now, lose them," he ordered sternly to which Kyle immediately complied.

He slipped out of his shorts hurriedly and tossed them on the floor so, that he was sitting naked on the sofa with his erection standing at full attention and ready for action. Patrick stood for a moment and took in the scene before him. Here was Kyle Jacobs, the subject of his fantasies for so many years, sitting before him with his clothes off and willing to do whatever Patrick said. It was as if his deepest desires had come to life and were manifested right there on that sofa. Patrick dropped to his knees and took Kyle in his mouth to begin sucking on his dick while moaning with pleasure in the process.

"Why does it sound like you're enjoying this more that I am," Kyle asked as he put his hands on the top of Patrick's head while closing his eyes and tilting his own head back, which seemed to drain the blood from the front of his brain and send it directly to his pulsating erection.

Finding Our Way Through the Fog
Jonathan B. Taylor

Patrick felt Kyle swell in his mouth and grow noticeably more rigid, indicating that ejaculation was imminent, which caused him to stop the blowjob abruptly and deprive Kyle of his orgasm.

"Why'd you stop," Kyle asked, unable to conceal his disappointment. "I was just about to come."

"I know," Patrick replied. "That's why I stopped. Because, that's not how I want to make you come." He then stood up and reached for his backpack on top of the coffee table.

"We're not going back in the woods, are we," Kyle asked, with fresh disappointment.

"Why? Didn't you enjoy it the last time," Patrick asked.

"No, I definitely did," he responded. "But, we have the whole house to ourselves so; I was hoping we would take advantage."

"Well, don't worry," Patrick said. "We're not going anywhere."

"So, what's in the bag," Kyle asked curiously.

Patrick reached into the backpack and retrieved two items, which he held up for Kyle's viewing. In his right hand, he had a coil of half inch thick, soft, black, nylon rope that looked like something a mountain climber may use and in his left hand, he had a black, satin blindfold with an elastic headband which was one of several that his mother would use to sleep the day away after popping a bunch of pills from her own personal pharmacy.

"Okay. I see you brought some props," Kyle laughed nervously as he watched Patrick uncoil the rope with a menacing look on his face. "What are you planning on doing with those?"

Finding Our Way Through the Fog
Jonathan B. Taylor

"Hold out your hands," Patrick instructed, without providing an explanation. He then snapped the rope as if testing its strength between his own outstretched hands.

Kyle reluctantly obeyed and, while Patrick methodically bound his wrists together, he suddenly found himself feeling slightly fearful and extremely vulnerable. He was putting his trust in someone who was already proven to be careless with his safety and wellbeing as his mind flashed to the image of nearly drowning beneath the boat with Patrick's legs clamped around him in a viselike grip. Kyle's feelings of helplessness were intensified when Patrick lowered the blindfold over his eyes and he felt himself back on the rollercoaster, experiencing those alternating waves of arousal, excitement and, dread to, which he was quickly becoming addicted.

With Kyle's hands securely fastened, Patrick took the ten feet of excess rope that ran from his binds and looped it into coils before pulling on the tether and bringing Kyle to his feet off the sofa. He then proceeded to lead him by his reins toward the workout area where the stage was set for a devious act of deception in, which Kyle would unwittingly be starring. Kyle stepped cautiously while being jerked and tugged by his leash as though he were back at South Point, following Patrick through a minefield of obstacles in the water, only this time, he was expecting his shin to collide with an unseen object as opposed to his bare feet.

Bound and blindfolded, Kyle journeyed through a kaleidoscope of visions that rolled through his mind, behind a black, satin curtain. As he revisited the random memories of being held beneath the boat or stumbling over rocks, Kyle recalled his conversation with Patrick in which he revealed his desire to be double penetrated and, which Patrick referred to as his wanting to be a 'slam pig'. Now, he began to wonder if this was Patrick's way of introducing the third member, which was required to make that fantasy become a reality. He pictured a faceless mystery guest entering the room and violating him from one end while Patrick decimated him from the other. This unknown individual would then leave, without Kyle ever knowing his identity, only to be seen lurking behind every stranger's smirk in the future.

With his twisted imagination in full contortion, Kyle then began to wonder what would happen if it didn't stop there? What would happen if Patrick decided to bring in a trainload of potential partners and allow each one to take a turn on him while he was powerless to prevent the onslaught? It occurred to Kyle that his entire image of Patrick being inexperienced with other boys had turned out to be erroneous and he actually knew nothing about his sexual past or how many previous lovers he could muster for such a task.

When they reached their destination, Patrick left Kyle in a holding pattern by the weight bench while he unhooked the heavy bag from its chain, which hung from a bracket on the ceiling and, leaned it against the wall in the corner. He then grabbed the rope and yanked it aggressively as he would with a stubborn plow horse, causing Kyle to lurch forward and nearly lose his balance while Patrick shifted him into position beneath the chain. Next Patrick slung the line over the hook and pulled it through the makeshift tackle, hoisting Kyle's hands above his head in the process. He tied off the fetter and wrapped the excess rope around Kyle's wrists for added restraint before stepping back to admire his handiwork. Kyle looked exquisite in bondage and Patrick's erection formed quickly in response to the sight. He removed his own clothing and approached Kyle from the front, placing his hands on

Finding Our Way Through the Fog
Jonathan B. Taylor

Kyle's hips while pressing his mouth against his lips. They then proceeded to probe each other's orifices with their tongues as if attempting to see who could penetrate the deepest while their erections clashed in an epic swordfight below their waists.

After a few minutes of tongue wrestling and sword fighting, Patrick pulled back and told Kyle, "I need another fix." He then went to his knees and took Kyle in his mouth, savoring the taste of his hard dick as he sucked and swallowed, creating an intense vacuum, which brought Kyle back to the brink of climax before Patrick once again abruptly stopped. "What is it about your dick that makes it taste so much better than the rest," Patrick asked as he got to his feet although he already knew the answer. It was his intense feelings for Kyle that made his dick taste so good.

Patrick retrieved his backpack from the coffee table and placed it on the weight bench where he removed the other items that would play a part in the rest of his plan. First, he took out the tube of lubricant and removed the cap so that it was ready to be applied when the moment arrived. Next, he removed a thin, leather belt and placed it on the bench beside the lube. Finally, he pulled out a balled up terrycloth towel, which he unrolled to reveal three small compact digital video recorders hidden inside. Patrick had a bad habit of secretly videotaping his sexual encounters, unbeknownst to his partners and Kyle's submissiveness was too enticing an opportunity for him to pass up. He realized that he likely could have done this with Kyle's consent but Patrick didn't see much fun in that and saw no reason to risk a denial.

As Patrick strategically placed one camera on top of the heavy bag in the corner to capture the front facing view and another on a shelf to the right for the side angle shot, he thought to himself, "This is why you should never trust anyone with the words 'trick' or 'con' in his name." The third camera he kept within reach on the weight bench for close-up shots. At one point, Kyle asked what he was doing as he heard Patrick moving around the room but Patrick told him that there wouldn't be much point in blindfolding him if he was going to tell him everything that was going on anyway and that did the trick because Kyle stopped asking.

Finally, with everything in place and the cameras rolling, Patrick was ready to start the show. He approached Kyle from behind and said, "Now, before we begin, the safety word is, 'bumblebee'."

"Wait! What?" Kyle sounded both confused and concerned. "What do you mean 'safety word'? Why do we need one of those," he asked with nervous laughter as he hoped that Patrick was only making a joke.

"Because," Patrick explained, "sometimes words like 'no' and 'stop' aren't enough in this type of sex play."

"Yeah, I understand the concept of 'safety words' but I'm wondering what you're planning on doing that requires one," Kyle said as his concern slowly intensified. "You didn't say anything about doing fifty shades of gay."

"Don't worry. You're in good hands," Patrick said as he caressed Kyle's ass cheeks and pressed his erection between them once again like placing a hot dog in a bun.

"So, does all this mean that you're already getting bored and feel the need to spice things up," Kyle asked as his concern took a new turn.

"Not at all," Patrick replied. "I just want to put my dick in your ass and I don't care when, where or how we do it as long as it gets done. This was just a way to keep things interesting and have a little fun but if you're not into it, we can just keep alternating between doggie style and missionary."

"No, I'm definitely into it," Kyle quickly responded. "You can see how hard my dick is ever since you tied my wrists together."

"Okay, then; that's what I like to hear," Patrick said, slapping Kyle's ass hard before rubbing it vigorously and slapping it again causing Kyle to arch his back slightly and thrust his ass toward Patrick indicating an eagerness for more. A sinister smile appeared on Patrick's face as he picked up his leather belt off the weight bench and slowly ran it over Kyle's shoulders and across his back before folding it in half and pulling the two ends apart to create a sharp crack, which caused Kyle to flinch slightly from the jarring sound. "It's time for your punishment," Patrick declared as he thrashed Kyle harshly across the buttocks with the leather strap, causing a flaming pink stripe to appear on the flesh of Kyle's right ass cheek. He then gave him a matching stripe on the left cheek. Kyle winced from the pain but refrained from invoking the safety word, allowing Patrick to deliver several more lashings before finally stopping. "That was for biting my dick," he explained as he placed the belt back on the bench and picked up the tube of lubricant, which he applied generously to his rigid penis while coating his fingers in the process. Patrick spread Kyle's exquisite ass cheeks apart to reveal his tender pink asshole, which was offered up willingly with a wink. He inserted his middle finger, causing Kyle to arch his back even more and thrust his ass out further while moaning with pleasure at Patrick's pleasant intrusion. Patrick found Kyle's ass to be far more accommodating on this second go around as he easily inserted the next two digits and effortlessly spread them apart while once again boring Kyle out with a twisting and turning motion.

"Did you get nice and clean for me," Patrick asked in his stern voice.

Kyle nodded eagerly. "I even triple douched," he said proudly. "The first one felt so good, I decided to treat myself to a couple more."

"That's awesome," Patrick said approvingly as he removed his fingers from Kyle's anus and thrust his erection into him, causing Kyle's muscles to clench from the initial pain but he adjusted immediately and found the experience to be overwhelmingly pleasurable compared to their previous encounter, which had been overwhelmingly painful. Patrick watched as the shaft of his erection slid in and out of Kyle's ass like a well-oiled piston while the glistening coating of lubricant shimmered in the soft light. As he mechanically pumped his piston into Kyle's silky smooth chamber, Patrick caught sight of the coveted 'pink sock', which appeared on the recoils while Kyle's ass was turned slightly inside out like a latex glove being peeled off of a finger only to see the quarter inch phenomena disappear back inside of him on the relentless forward thrusts.

Patrick decided that he wanted to capture the image on video but first he needed to clean his hands off so, he reached down to grab the towel, which was lying in a pile on the weight bench. Once he had sufficiently removed the slippery traces of lubricant from his fingers while continuing his persistent pounding, Patrick picked up the compact digital video recorder and zoomed in on the close up image of his achievement, capturing it from a variety of angles. First, he took the aerial shot from above, before holding the camera out to the side briefly Jand then finishing up with the underneath shot, which viewed the action from below. He only needed about twenty seconds worth of footage for each shot, which could be edited in with the wide angles later when he put the whole thing together on his laptop. Patrick then placed the camera back on the bench while leaving it trained on them and continuing to record from the awkward vantage point on the outside chance that it may capture some additional usable footage.

With his close-ups completed, Patrick was able to refocus his attention on the task of fucking Kyle while engaging his newly freed up hands in the process. First, he placed them on Kyle's waist and softly caressed his sides before migrating around to his abs in a slow, circular, massaging motion as he continued his rhythmic thrusting into Kyle's tight ass with his monster size erection. Each forceful plunge lifted Kyle off his heals slightly as if he were being hoisted on a meat hook from behind. Patrick then slid his hands up to Kyle's chest and cupped his pectorals while running his fingertips softly around Kyle's erect nipples before hooking his hands over Kyle's shoulders and pulling their bodies closer together as he turned his head against Kyle's neck and pressed his face to his back. Now his entire body was riding against Kyle's in rhythmic waves while his hard dick continued to probe the walls of Kyle's rectum and massage his prostate in the process. Patrick could feel that Kyle was about to climax as all of his muscles began to tense and spasm, followed by a soft whimper as Kyle enjoyed another one of his full body orgasms.

In the wake of his convulsive climax, Kyle was no longer experiencing the intense pleasure that overrode the stinging pain from Patrick's intrusive penetration but he was pleased to find that the level of discomfort he felt was significantly less than what he had endured during their previous encounter. Aroused by the thrill of making Kyle come from behind, Patrick achieved his orgasm moments later and once again, Kyle could feel Patrick's warm discharge squirting inside him.

With their latest encounter concluded, Patrick worked quickly to retrieve his cameras and wrap them back up in the towel, knowing that Kyle would want to be released from his restraints now that his erection was subsiding and the fun was over. Once the recording devices were safely tucked away in his backpack, Patrick proceeded to unhook Kyle from the chain and untie the rope from his wrists. Kyle shook the numbness out of his hands and wriggled his fingers in an attempt to get the blood back into his arms.

"I have to admit, that was pretty fucking awesome," Kyle said as he peeled off the blindfold and squinted while his eyes adjusted to the light.

Looking down at the floor, he saw the puddle of come, which had just shot out of him moments ago so, he went to retrieve some napkins for the cleanup while Patrick finished winding his rope and stuffing it into the backpack along with the belt and blindfold. He held the tube of lubricant in his hand for a second before saying to Kyle, "We should probably just keep this here."

"Definitely," Kyle agreed as he returned to the crime scene and wiped up the evidence from the floor.

When he finished his task, Patrick tossed him the bottle, which he carried over to the bed and placed in the drawer of his nightstand while Patrick headed for the bathroom to take a shower. Kyle had been dreaming of sharing a shower with Patrick for what seemed like forever and he wasted no time in joining him. Once inside the glass enclosure, they took turns lathering each other up and exchanging kisses while the warm water poured over them like a cascading waterfall. As it ran down their faces and found its way into their open mouths, they sucked and licked the liquid from each other's tongues in an effort to quench their insatiable thirst for one another. Despite their arousal, they managed to get through the shower without a second sexual encounter and when they were finished toweling off; they made their way to Kyle's bed where they fell into a passionate kiss while rolling around on the mattress with their naked bodies entwined.

Patrick paused for a moment and looked down at his erection, which prompted Kyle to immediately respond to the nonverbal command and begin performing his oral obligations. He took Patrick's rigid member in his mouth and began sucking on it while stroking the shaft with his right hand and caressing his balls with the fingertips of his left. Patrick propped himself up on his elbows and took in the exquisite sight of his dick sliding in and out of Kyle's luscious lips. He had always found the image of a guy sucking his dick to be intensely more arousing than watching a girl do it but seeing Kyle in action had taken the experience to a whole new level and was far more thrilling than anything he had ever known before. As he took in the scene, Patrick could see that Kyle was really enjoying himself, judging by the steady drone of 'mmmms' that resonated in his mouth and throat like a purring kitten and provided gentle vibrations, which flowed with the waves of pleasure that rolled through his body.

For Kyle, the task of sucking on Patrick's monster size erection required an extra bit of effort as he found that his jaw was cramping up from having to hold his mouth open so wide. He also noticed that his fingers didn't even touch his thumb when he was wrapping his hand around the base. When Kyle had to pause for a moment to give his sore jaw a rest, he inspected the distance between those digits.

Finding Our Way Through the Fog
Jonathan B. Taylor

"Why'd you stop," Patrick asked, looking down with disappointment.

"We gotta measure this thing," Kyle announced, as he got up from the bed and walked over to the dresser to dig through his 'junk' drawer and retrieve the small travel sew kit that he had thrown in with all of the other odds and ends for just such an occasion.

"Now," Patrick exclaimed. "You have to do this right now?" It was obvious that he would have preferred Kyle to get back to his blowjob.

"We gotta strike while the iron's hot," Kyle explained as he returned with his trophy and pulled out the roll of vinyl measuring tape that was tucked in the plastic case along with some needles and small spools of multi colored thread. He took the measuring tape and stretched it along the length of Patrick's erection.

"Oh, shit," he exclaimed as he observed the reading. "Nine and a half inches! That's insane! Now, let's check the girth," Kyle said, wrapping the tape around the base of Patrick's shaft where his fingers had been unable to reach around. "Oh, man. We got a circumference of six inches! Well, blow my ass out! That is one fat cock! It's like a fucking beer can," Kyle declared as Patrick beamed with pride over the numbers.

"Okay, now it's your turn," Patrick announced as he took the roll of measuring tape in one hand and Kyle's erection in the other. "First, we have to get it to optimum size," he said, taking it in his mouth and sucking hard while bobbing his head up and down in slow, methodical strokes. He then did his signature swirl around the tip with his tongue before sliding it all the way down to the back of his throat.

"Okay, stop," Kyle said reluctantly. "I'm gonna come."

Patrick pulled his mouth off Kyle's fully engorged erection and said, "That was fast." He then held the tape to the top side of the base to get his measurement. As he stretched it toward the head, Kyle spoke up.

"You know, technically they say you should measure from the underside of the base."

"No problem," Patrick said obligingly. "We can measure from wherever you want. I can even measure from your asshole if you like. That's one way to come up with a foot long hog."

"Alright, alright. Very funny. So, what's the damage," Kyle asked dryly.

"Six and three quarter inches," Patrick announced. "And, around the base," he said, wrapping the tape around the bottom of Kyle's shaft, "we got five and a quarter. That's respectable. They say the average length is about six inches so you're above average."

Kyle curled the corner of his mouth up and shot Patrick a sideways look. "You're such a dick," he said, shaking his head in exasperation.

"What," Patrick asked, as a burst of laughter escaped with the words. "What did I do?"

"Six and three quarters. That's respectable." Kyle repeated Patrick's words mockingly, in an overly cajoling voice. "It's like saying what a good job I did for coming in fourth place."

"Well, you didn't come in fourth. You came is second and even if it had been fourth, there's nothing wrong with that," Patrick pointed out encouragingly. "It's better than last."

"That's easy for you to say." Kyle grumbled. "You won the race. And, for the record asshole, when there's only two people racing, second place is last place."

Finding Our Way Through the Fog
Jonathan B. Taylor

"I don't know why you're making a big deal out of this and, wasn't it was your idea to measure these things in the first place," Patrick pointed out. "Look, at it this way. You're six and three quarters. That's almost seven inches and, I'm just over nine so, that's only a couple of inches more. It's not that much of a difference." Patrick lied but Kyle wasn't buying it.

"It's closer to three inches and in this case, it makes a huge difference. And, not only is your hard on so much bigger, but your dick looks just as big when it's soft and swinging, which means, if we were taking flaccid measurements, the numbers would be even further off the chart," Kyle said as he lowered his head to resume Patrick's blowjob. However, once he had Patrick's dick back in his mouth, all of the residual resentment over its size was washed away by its splendor and Kyle found himself completely captivated by it once again. The blowjob was short lived as Patrick was already close to climaxing when Kyle had stopped to measure him so it was only a matter of moments before Kyle brought him back to the brink and pushed him over the edge where he reached his climax. Once the floodgates were open, Patrick began pumping his load into Kyle's mouth, which he swallowed greedily as a reward for his efforts. After sucking every last drop from Patrick's dick, Kyle looked up at him with a smile and said, "Forget everything I just said. I love your big dick and I don't care that it's so much bigger than mine. I love getting all my muscles stretched to the point of rupture by it and I love you!"

Patrick's face lit up with a smile at the sound of those words as he stared into Kyle's eyes and said, "I love you too!"

It was another first for the two who had never uttered the phrase to a lover before and they were both surprised at how easily the words had rolled off their tongues. In the spirit of rolling tongues, it was now Patrick's turn to take care of Kyle so they both adjusted their positions with Kyle laying back and resting his head on the pillow as Patrick rested his head on Kyle's lower abdomen. With the side of his face pressed against Kyle's soft flesh, Patrick began sucking on his dick in a sideways motion. Despite the awkward angle, Patrick managed to continue his medley of sword swallowing and tongue twirling while softly stroking the inside of Kyle's thigh with his hand, which coaxed a couple of whimpers from him the moment before he climaxed. As he ejaculated, Patrick let Kyle's come fill his mouth, where he held it for a moment to savor the taste before swallowing it with a smile.

With both of them satiated, Patrick repositioned himself beside Kyle where they lay looking at one another with their faces nearly touching on the pillow. They each took in the sight of the other's naked body before them with their slowly subsiding erections beginning to drape down toward the mattress. Patrick reached out his hand and ran his fingertips along the exquisite lines of Kyle's angelic face before pressing his soft pink lips against Kyle's deep red ones as they bathed in the warm breath from their rubbing noses. Eventually, they found their way back into each other's mouths and enjoyed a sensual kiss with the taste of semen still fresh on their tongues.

"Now, that was pretty fucking awesome," Patrick said, in reference to their pleasant exchange of blowjobs. "I only wish that you didn't come so fast. Then I could spend hours sucking on your dick, instead of just a few minutes."

"I wish I didn't come so fast either," Kyle agreed, "because, your blowjobs are so good that I would like them to last forever."

Patrick smiled. "I feel so lucky to be lying here with you right now," Patrick said as he slid his hand around Kyle's waist. "It's like having everything I've ever wanted. It almost doesn't seem fair to have so much."

"What do you mean," Kyle asked as he wondered where this was coming from.

"Do you ever feel guilty when you see images of people struggling or suffering in the world," Patrick asked.

"You mean, like in those commercials with the starving children?"

"Yes," Patrick replied. "Exactly."

"I don't know if I feel guilty but I definitely feel empathy," Kyle reasoned.

"I do," Patrick admitted. "I always feel guilty and I wonder why do I have it so easy while others have it so hard?"

"Whenever I see those commercials, I can never understand why people are bringing children into this world to suffer like that under such horrible conditions. It's like, why would someone have kids when they can't even feed themselves? Isn't the world overpopulated enough without bringing more people into unsustainable surroundings? I get the whole unplanned pregnancy thing but don't these people know about birth control or the simple art of pulling out? You'd think that after the third or fourth kid, they would catch on," Kyle said while furrowing his brow as he searched for an answer.

"That's what's great about gay sex," Patrick explained. "There's never a risk of accidental pregnancy and you never have to pull out. You can just fire at will when it comes to unloading in your partner."

"That's true," Kyle concurred. "We're the answer to the population explosion. Everybody needs to pair up with a same sex partner and stop these senseless acts of reproduction."

Finding Our Way Through the Fog
Jonathan B. Taylor

They both nodded in agreement, as they continued to lie on their sides and gently run their fingers over one another's bodies while staring into each other's eyes with their faces inches apart on the pillow.

"So, what's the plan for tomorrow," Kyle asked. "We have the day off and the house to ourselves so we could do this all day if we wanted."

"Actually, I was thinking about taking us on a little road trip," Patrick revealed.

"Where to," Kyle asked with sudden intrigue.

"It's a surprise," Patrick smiled.

"Ooh, another surprise," Kyle said approvingly and with their next adventure cued up, they both drifted off to sleep with the thrill of the day and the excitement of tomorrow providing a prelude to a pleasant night of dreams.

CHAPTER 15, 'FIFTY SHADES'

Patrick sat at the antique, mahogany desk that was situated in front of the large picture window, which looked out over the East Side Marina from his second floor bedroom in the Connor family estate. He had dropped Kyle off at his house earlier, after spending the day in Boston together and instructed him to be ready for another ass pounding when he returned that evening to, which Kyle smiled and nodded excitedly at the news. Now, Patrick was finally sitting at his computer, performing the task, which he had been working on in the back of his mind throughout the day. He was taking the images of last night's sexual encounter with Kyle from the digital recorders and turning them into one of his underhanded 'adults only' videos for the latest edition to his private library.

First, he loaded the footage from the three recorders onto his computer where he could begin the editing process. Next, he took the images from the three different angles and turned them into a single continuous shot by layering the close-ups and wide-angle views in a steady progression, which provided a pleasant build up to the explosive climax. When Patrick was finishing up with the final scenes that included Kyle's orgasm, he was pleased with the clarity of those images, which depicted Kyle's semen erupting in multiple streams from the head of his dick while all of the muscles in his body were visibly convulsing and contorting. He pasted the different angles of those shots, one after the other and used the magnifier to zoom in, adding multiple clips of the same action. The end result had Kyle appearing to ejaculate nonstop for about thirty seconds while spewing about thirty shots of come out of his pulsating erection. For the final touch, Patrick added a soundtrack of seventies style porn music that he downloaded from a ring tone app.

He was extremely pleased with the end result and saw this video as a work of art compared to his other secretly recorded sex tapes, which had been shot with a single hidden camera and had a voyeuristic feel that made it seem like you were watching the action through a peephole. However, Kyle's submissiveness had provided Patrick with the perfect opportunity to implement the blindfolded bondage technique, which allowed him to place multiple cameras in plain view and capture clear images from various angles including close-ups while his costar remained clueless. Despite having violated Kyle's trust in the worst way imaginable, Patrick's conscience remained clear and he felt only excitement and a sense of accomplishment over what he considered to be his greatest achievement and a cinematic masterpiece. He had captured their exquisite encounter in a jar and added it to his collection where it could be taken out for viewing whenever he had the desire. On top of that, he figured what Kyle didn't know, wouldn't hurt him.

Patrick leaned back in his leather upholstered office chair and enjoyed the fruits of his labor by replaying the final product on a continuous loop while stroking himself lightly through the soft material of his new silk boxer shorts. Just as he was about to pull out his dick and begin masturbating, he caught himself and realized that there wasn't much sense in jerking off to the image of him fucking Kyle when the real thing was waiting for him in his basement across town.

Finding Our Way Through the Fog
Jonathan B. Taylor

"Oh, shit," Patrick said, as he suddenly remembered that Kyle was waiting for him and realized that he had completely lost track of time. He also realized that he still had a stop to make on his way to Kyle's and he was already running late for that important pickup.

Patrick worked quickly to close out his open files and put everything in its proper place before shutting down his computer. He named the new file containing his latest video, 'Fifty Shades of Gay' in reference to a comment that Kyle made during the encounter. He then placed that file inside another folder named, 'Danger: Virus Inside, Do Not Open!' before making two additional backup copies to be stored in separate locations within the software and on a flash drive. As he placed the cursor on the file folder icon, he held the left clicker of the mouse and dragged the image to the desired location to be placed in another existing folder as he attempted to bury his cache within the system. Unfortunately, in his haste, he released the clicker prematurely while attempting to place one of the copies in a folder titled, 'XXX' and accidentally dropped it in an adjacent folder named, 'Epic Fails', which was ironic considering the magnitude of the mistake he had just made.

The 'Epic Fails' folder contained a compilation of videos that Patrick had found online, which depicted crashes and wipeouts from a variety of different sporting activities that were intended to be shared with a group of likeminded individuals through a reciprocal email exchange. With one wrong click of the mouse, Patrick had unwittingly teed up a copy of his sadomasochistic sex tape for a potential cataclysmic email blast to a bunch of video sharing strangers. After closing out his remaining files, Patrick shut down his computer and headed for Kyle's place, oblivious to the disaster that was now on deck.

Finding Our Way Through the Fog
Jonathan B. Taylor

CHAPTER 16, 'SEBASTIAN'

With Patrick on his way, Kyle found himself back in position on the couch once again, waiting for him to arrive just as he was on their previous two date nights. He had completed his deep cleansing ritual, which was preceded this evening by a quick leg workout that focused on his glutes with the intention of putting an extra pump on his ass for Patrick's added pleasure. Despite his inclination to make the squats, lunges, and hip thrusters a regular part of his predate routine, he decided that they were best kept in moderation to avoid overtraining and creating a disproportionately large ass like some kind of a caricature. The only other thing that distinguished this date night from the previous ones was the fact that Kyle had swapped out his timeworn grey gym shorts for the black and green paisley pattern silk boxer shorts that were one of a half dozen pairs, which Patrick had purchased for him on their little excursion earlier that day.

Patrick's surprise road trip had taken them into Boston that morning to check out their new apartment, which was located in the Fenway District. There was no working elevator in the century old brick building so, they had to climb four flights up a narrow staircase to reach the two bedroom unit, which smelled of old wood and antique varnish. The appliances and furniture looked like throwbacks from the seventies and the squeaky bedsprings sounded like they were in need of some oil. However, the place was perfect from their perspective because they would be sharing it together and what it lacked in décor, it made up for in location. It was within convenient walking distance to the bus and train stops as well as a nearby parking garage where Patrick could keep his Challenger. Patrick told Kyle that he didn't have to worry about rent or any other expenses because he had already paid everything for the entire year but Kyle insisted on putting up his housing allowance so that he could at least feel like he was contributing even though Patrick would still be footing the bulk of the bill.

After checking out the apartment, they visited the Museum of Science and the Aquarium before hitting some stores to do a little shopping. Everything was out of Kyle's price range but it didn't stop Patrick from pulling out the plastic when Kyle commented on the luxuriousness of some silk boxer shorts, which prompted Patrick to purchase a dozen pairs before handing half to him. Following their upscale shopping spree, they enjoyed lunch at a posh restaurant with spectacular views of the harbor before making their final stop at a private clinic, which specialized in testing for venereal diseases. This move by Patrick caught Kyle a little off guard and after a bit of nail biting, they were each given a clean bill of health in rapid results, which could be viewed discretely within a couple of hours on the company's website. Kyle thought it seemed a little late to be doing this now, considering the amount of sex they already had but at least, they could put their minds at ease by knowing that neither was putting the other at risk of contracting a sexually transmitted disease. In order to protect the integrity of their newly created safe zone, Kyle and Patrick agreed to be retested and update those results if at any time they were to engage in extracurricular sexual activity with outside partners moving forward.

Finding Our Way Through the Fog
Jonathan B. Taylor

Back in his basement now, Kyle rode a rollercoaster of desire, excitement and anticipation from the comfort of his sofa, as he scrolled pleasantly through his memories of the day's events until those fulfilling reflections were suddenly interrupted by the sound of Patrick's car rolling up the driveway. Once again, his heart began to race while his palms began to sweat and his mouth began to water. Like a cat with a can opener, the thumping of Patrick's motor triggered a Pavlovian response in Kyle, which was capped off by an instantly formed erection. He was able to track Patrick's movements as he heard the sound of a car door closing, followed by a second, which caused him to suspect that Patrick may have retrieved something from his trunk and he wondered what type of sadomasochistic sex toy he would be introducing tonight.

When the door opened and Patrick entered the basement, Kyle was both surprised and confused by what he saw. Patrick had brought a person with him in the form of a stunningly handsome individual who moved with a similar catlike prowess to Patrick as he followed him across the room. While Kyle worked to process the information in these latest developments, he instinctively grabbed the small throw pillow that sat on the couch beside him to cover up his noticeable erection, which was pitching a tent in his new boxers.

Patrick caught the move as he was making the introductions. "This is Sebastian," he said to Kyle, "and he'll be joining us this evening." He then turned to Sebastian and said, "Sebastian, meet Kyle." Sebastian and Kyle smiled at each other while Kyle's cheeks flushed with pink in light of what this meant for him. The genie was working his magic and making Kyle's double penetration fantasy become a reality. "And, relax," Patrick said, pointing to the pillow. "There's no need to cover up considering that none of us will be wearing clothes for much longer."

Patrick and Sebastian stood a few feet in front of Kyle and slowly came together for a kiss, slipping their hands around each other's waists and their tongues into each other's mouths as Kyle enjoyed the show from his front row seat on the sofa. Tossing the small throw pillow aside, he slid his hand through the waistband of his silk boxer shorts and began to stroke himself softly while the shape of his knuckles glided visibly back and forth beneath the delicate material. Kyle was enthralled by the image of Patrick and Sebastian's steamy make out session and quickly ranked it as one of the hottest scenes he had ever witnessed because they were two of the hottest guys he had ever seen going at it like this.

Although Patrick was still the best-looking boy that Kyle had known, Sebastian was currently running a close second. He was tall and lean at six foot two and one hundred eighty pounds with well-developed shoulders and arms that appeared to be the focus of many workouts in the weight room with sinewy muscle striations that were similar to Kyle's but appeared more pronounced beneath his bronzed skin. He had slightly curly auburn hair that was short on the sides and longer on the top, which he would comb back with his fingers to keep it from falling over his bright green eyes that were closer in color to Amber's emerald green than to Kyle's hazel color. His prominent cheekbones and square jaw line were comparable to Patrick's although Sebastian appeared older and Kyle accurately estimated his age to be around twenty-five. Kyle wasn't sure where Patrick had found him but he liked what he saw and was really looking forward to making this sandwich. Under normal circumstances, Kyle would have expected to feel some apprehension over the prospect of having sex with a complete stranger but Sebastian was so incredibly handsome that he felt only desire for the sexy player and saw him as merely an extension of Patrick this evening to serve as just another prop in their latest drill at 'sexual encounter fantasy camp'.

While Patrick and Sebastian continued performing their lingual endoscopy, they slowly began to undress one another in the process. Sebastian unbuttoned Patrick's short sleeve oxford shirt, which was teal colored to match his eyes and slid it off his shoulders while letting it slide down his arms to drop on the floor. Patrick then pulled Sebastian's shimmery, silver t-shirt over his head, which momentarily interrupted their kiss before they reconnected and resumed pulling at each other's lips and sucking on each other's tongues with their overly sensual mouths. Sebastian slipped his fingers into the waistband of Patrick's tan cargo pants and pulled him close before unbuttoning and unzipping the relaxed fit trousers and letting them slide down Patrick's legs where they were kicked off his feet along with his white, nylon mesh, running shoes. Kyle saw that Patrick was also wearing his new silk boxer shorts and he laughed to himself at how they were once again dressed like twins while wondering if Sebastian would take notice.

Proceeding with their choreographic disrobing, Patrick unfastened Sebastian's thin leather belt like the one he had used to lash Kyle with the previous night and yanked it from its loops before cracking it like a whip and tossing it on the floor. He then unbuttoned and unzipped Sebastian's navy blue chinos and let them slide to the floor where they were kicked off along with his black suede loafers in a similar move to the one Patrick had performed moments ago. Sebastian then pulled down Patrick's luxurious boxers to reveal his protruding erection, which pointed straight out like a trumpeting baby elephant's trunk. Finally, Patrick slid Sebastian's black boxer briefs down to his thighs, where Sebastian lifted each knee and worked them off the rest of the way, giving Kyle his first glimpse of Sebastian's magnificent member, which was fully erect and lined up for comparison with Patrick's menacing marvel. He was pleased with its overall size, which appeared to be around seven and a half to eight inches, placing it in the 'Goldie Locks zone' of big dicks and making it just big enough without having Patrick's problem of being 'too big'. While Kyle fixated on Sebastian's erection, he caught himself wishing that he could put that dick on Patrick's body as he mentally assembled the perfect Patrick in the back of his mind.

With each article of clothing that was shed, the level of passion intensified between Patrick and Sebastian, reaching its peak when they were both fully naked and caressing one another's backs and asses in a half embrace while using their free hands to stroke each other's erections as their kissing became more urgent. Kyle removed his own boxer shorts and began openly stroking himself on the sofa while watching Patrick and Sebastian come closer to fucking each other in front of him. As he salivated over the sight of their hard dicks, Kyle was once again frustrated over the size of his own erection in comparison to those larger versions.

"Fuck," Kyle suddenly blurted out. "Why does it seem like every guy I'm with has a bigger dick than me? Where are all of the average guys who I'm supposedly bigger than? Just once I would like to be the one who gets to gloat."

Patrick and Sebastian began to laugh at Kyle's endearing outburst, which interrupted their moment and finally broke the spell they had fallen under, prompting Patrick to get back on track with the task at hand. He instructed Kyle to grab his phone, which was sitting next to him on the end table beside the sofa and told him to bring up his test results on the website of the clinic they had visited earlier in the day. While Kyle carried out this assignment, Patrick and Sebastian retrieved their own phones from their pants' pockets and did the same.

"Once everyone has their test results on screen, we show them to each other as proof that we're all safe and clean," Patrick explained, holding out his phone for their viewing while Kyle and Sebastian followed suit. Patrick observed Sebastian's results while Sebastian scrutinized his and Kyle's. "Those are almost a week old," Patrick remarked in reference to the date of Sebastian's test results.

"That's within the policy parameters," Sebastian pointed out.

"Yeah, but how many people have you fucked in that time," Patrick questioned.

"What is all this," Kyle asked as Sebastian studied his phone's screen.

"You see," Patrick explained, "Sebastian belongs to a very exclusive club and this is the price of admission."

"Well, this and five hundred dollars," Sebastian added with a smile.

"Okay, I think I get it now," Kyle said as Sebastian's statement sank in and shined a light on the situation. He wasn't just some random dude that Patrick had met on the street. Sebastian was a prostitute who definitely didn't come cheap and obviously had a history of servicing Patrick in the past.

"Well, I gotta use the bathroom," Patrick said as he suddenly broke off and headed in that direction. "Why don't you two get acquainted and I'll be back in a minute."

Finding Our Way Through the Fog
Jonathan B. Taylor

With Patrick no longer providing the buffer, Kyle instantly felt a little awkward sitting naked on the sofa with a total stranger standing naked in front of him. Sebastian being the professional sensed Kyle's discomfort and proceeded to break the ice.

"Do you mind if I sit down," he asked as he made his way to the sofa.

"No, of course not," Kyle replied. "Make yourself at home."

He sat down next to Kyle who was trying not to be obvious about the fact that he couldn't stop staring at Sebastian's erection by attempting to observe it only from the corner of his eye.

"So, Patrick wasn't kidding when he said that you were the most beautiful person he'd ever seen," Sebastian commented in a deep voice that seemingly had too much bass for his body size.

"Patrick said that," Kyle smiled as his cheeks turned pink around his deep dimples. "Are you sure he wasn't looking in a mirror?"

"What are you saying," Sebastian laughed. "That he's a narcissist?"

"Patrick a narcissist. No," Kyle replied sarcastically. "Lots of people reverse the lenses on their mirrored sunglasses."

"Oh, shit," Sebastian said while continuing to laugh. "Shots fired," he announced as if the call had come in over a police radio.

"I'm just kidding," Kyle laughed with him. "What I mean is Patrick is the best looking person here. But, don't worry, you are definitely running a close second."

Finding Our Way Through the Fog
Jonathan B. Taylor

"You see," Sebastian responded, "the fact that you don't know how attractive you are, only adds to your appeal because let's face it; there is nothing worse than someone who is really good looking and knows it."

"What about someone who thinks they're really good looking but isn't," Kyle suggested.

"Well, that's just sad," Sebastian said while lowering his head and shaking it in the negative.

Kyle wasn't sure if Sebastian was only saying these things because he was being paid to but he enjoyed hearing them and along with the laughs they shared, the compliments were able to cut through the tension allowing them to relax and feel at ease with one another.

"So, what do you do," Kyle asked boldly as he looked Sebastian up and down and in the eyes before finally zeroing in on his erection.

"Basically, I make dreams come true," Sebastian said as he followed Kyle's line of vision to his hard on, which he began to wave enticingly with his hand like a tempting lure.

"See anything you like," he asked, while watching Kyle's eyes dance around in pursuit of his swaying erection.

Kyle licked his lips and nodded eagerly. "You've got a nice dick," he said with a smile as though he were looking at the tantalizing appetizer before a mouthwatering main course.

"You want to suck it?" Sebastian offered his hard dick up to Kyle who wasted no time in going to his knees on the floor in front of him and swallowing his erection as far down his throat as he could possibly get it.

Just then, Patrick came out of the bathroom and observed the scene that was unfolding on the sofa as he made his way toward the nightstand and retrieved the tube of lube from the drawer. "Now, that's what I call getting acquainted," he said approvingly as he walked over to join them.

Patrick dropped the lubricant on the coffee table and got down on his knees beside Kyle where he began to lick and suck on Sebastian's shaft and balls while Kyle concentrated on the head. This was their fist time working as a team and they each put an arm around one another with Kyle resting his hand on Patrick's shoulder and Patrick curling his hand around Kyle's waist. Next, they took a page from Ally and Amber's playbook when their mouths met up on the helmet of Sebastian's hard on and they began swirling their tongues around it while French kissing on the tip.

Sebastian let out a pleasurable moan and said, "There's got to be an easier way to make money," while they all snickered at his quivering sarcasm.

As Kyle and Patrick took turns alternating between sucking on Sebastian's helmet and licking his shaft and balls while periodically exchanging kisses, Patrick began to caress Kyle's ass cheeks and slide his finger between them before gently circling his puckering hole. This prompted Kyle to arch his back and thrust his ass out in his customary invitation to be penetrated and probed. Patrick took his cue and moved into position behind Kyle where he grabbed the tube of lubricant from the coffee table and squirted a glob onto his fingers. As Kyle continued to suck on Sebastian's dick, Patrick began to explore him with his fingers and work him open until he was sufficiently dilated. However, Patrick wasn't planning on fucking Kyle just yet. He was actually preparing him to get fucked by Sebastian. With his asshole ready for action, Patrick stood behind Kyle and hoisted him by his underarms onto the sofa so that he was straddling Sebastian on his knees and hovering over his waiting erection. Patrick then slathered

Sebastian's dick with lubricant before instructing Kyle to lower himself onto the greased pole and he watched the plunger depress as Sebastian's dick slowly disappeared into Kyle's plump white ass. Sebastian and Kyle both moaned pleasurably as Sebastian's dick slid inside of him and Kyle found himself wishing that Patrick's dick felt more like Sebastian's.

"Is he clean," Sebastian asked Patrick as if Kyle's preparedness was somehow his responsibility.

"Oh, yeah," Patrick assured him. "Trust me, he's completely simonized. You could eat off that asshole. Or, should I say, 'eat out' that asshole?"

Kyle smiled at Patrick's praise as he rode up and down on Sebastian's hard dick while his own erection brushed against the soft ripples of Sebastian's velvety six-pack, sending waves of ecstasy through both their bodies. Patrick was also smiling as he stroked himself on the sidelines while watching Sebastian's balls clench and jiggle as his glistening dick slid in and out of Kyle's ass. However, the scene was too enticing for Patrick to remain a spectator so he got back down on his knees and stuck his face in the action between Sebastian's legs to resume licking and sucking his balls with Kyle's ass repeatedly slapping him on the forehead.

This prompted an enthusiastic, "Yes!" from Sebastian who declared, "This is the best gig ever! You guys are great!"

Patrick then climbed onto the sofa and stood beside Kyle and Sebastian with his feet pressing deep into the cushions and his erection looming between their smiling faces. They both began to lick and suck their way up his shaft as their mouths slowly came to a head and their tongues entwined on the tip before Kyle engulfed Patrick's erection in his mouth and began sucking it hard as Patrick placed his hands on Kyle's head and forced himself to the back of Kyle's throat. This was exactly what he was waiting for and the moment had finally arrived. Patrick had made Kyle's fantasy become a reality and he was taking it decisively in both ends.

"If we're gonna do this, we should do it right," Patrick said to Sebastian. "I think we should get him on his back."

"Where," Sebastian asked. "Right here on the couch?"

"Actually, I was thinking of laying him out on the coffee table," Patrick suggested.

"But, won't that be uncomfortable for him," Sebastian asked with a serious face before they both burst with laughter at the absurdity that either of them would be concerned with Kyle's comfort.

Patrick stepped down off the sofa and stood behind Kyle where he once again took him by the underarms while Sebastian held him by his thighs and together they transferred Kyle onto the coffee table where they laid him crosswise in the middle of the platform. Sebastian got down on his knees in front of the table and folded Kyle's legs back before sliding his dick back into Kyle's ass while on the other end; Patrick folded Kyle's head back so that it was hanging off the edge of the coffee table and slid his own dick back into Kyle's gaping mouth. As predicted, Kyle was extremely uncomfortable being perched on the two foot wide narrow strip of table with the hard wooden edges digging into his neck and lower back where they hung off the sides while Sebastian's dick was burning a hole in his ass and Patrick's dick was throttling him in his throat.

"Watch," Patrick, said to Sebastian, "when I fold his head back like this it lines up his mouth with his throat and gives me a straight shot so that I can go all the way in up to my balls." Patrick then demonstrated by making his entire erection disappear down Kyle's throat, causing him to spasmodically gag and choke.

"Whoa! That's wild," Sebastian said as he watched Patrick's monster size erection being consumed by Kyle's gaping mouth. "I can even see where your dick is by the way his throat bulges out."

The two of them laughed and high fived each other as they pumped and thrust themselves into Kyle whose head was swimming in ecstasy from their intrusions.

"You know what's funny," Sebastian said as his balls smacked against Kyle's soft ass cheeks, "This is supposed to be his fantasy and yet, he's doing all the work and we're having all the fun."

"I know it certainly seems that way but trust me, he's enjoying this," Patrick said and then added, "In life, you have guys who like to fuck and then there are guys who like to be fucked. That's what makes the world go round and Kyle here is one of those guys who likes to get fucked, which works out just fine for me," Patrick smiled and shrugged.

"Me too," Sebastian seconded.

"Just wait, any minute now, you're gonna see how much he likes it when he shoots his load all over the place." Patrick nodded with his classic smug smirk on his face.

Hearing Patrick and Sebastian referring to him as if he were an object whose sole purpose was to provide them with pleasure was intensely arousing for Kyle. The combination of their callousness and relentless thrusting brought him quickly to the brink and seemingly, on cue from Patrick's careless comments, Kyle began to ejaculate, launching several spurts of come from the head of his pulsating dick onto his convulsing belly.

"You see," Patrick said excitedly as he lowered his face to Kyle's stomach and began swirling his tongue around to lick up the freshly shot load.

"Dude, I'm about to bust. Do you want it," Sebastian said to Patrick, as he was close to climaxing himself and knew how much Patrick loved to swallow.

"No, it's cool," Patrick said reluctantly. "You can blow it in his ass. He likes it when you do that," Patrick said as he sucked and licked the remnants of Kyle's orgasm from the tip of his dick in what had essentially become a sixty-nine with a bonus round on Kyle's other end.

"Alright then, in the ass it is," Sebastian said as his body started to shake and quiver and his dick began to pulsate as he pumped his warm load into Kyle's welcoming rectum.

When he finished ejaculating, Sebastian pulled out and watched as Patrick continued to suck Kyle's dick while continuing to thrust his own deep into Kyle's throat. Within moments, Patrick reached his climax and began to ejaculate in Kyle's mouth where his load was gulped and swallowed by its eager recipient.

"We're not done yet," Patrick declared as he pulled out and stood over Kyle who was slowly unfolding and climbing down from his perch on the coffee table. Patrick picked up the tube of lubricant and instructed Kyle to head over to the bed. "Now, we're gonna take turns fucking you in the ass," he said as they followed Kyle to the next staging area.

"Dude, you weren't kidding," Sebastian said as they both locked onto the tantalizing sight of Kyle's ass making its way to the bed. "He really does have a perfect ass! But, what's with those red marks?"

"Oh, that," Patrick said as he observed the flaming pink stripes that decorated Kyle's creamy white ass cheeks, "I had to dole out a little punishment with the belt," he explained nonchalantly.

"Nice," Sebastian responded approvingly.

When they reached the bed, Kyle waited for Patrick to deliver the customary shove onto the mattress where he landed with a thud before clamoring onto his hands and knees to 'assume the doggy style position' as Patrick had instructed while he and Sebastian climbed onto the bed and assumed their pitcher's positions on their own knees behind him. They then exchanged another sensual kiss while Patrick applied a generous coating of lubricant to their throbbing erections before tossing the tube onto the nightstand and beginning his assault on Kyle's ass. Patrick thrust himself forcefully into Kyle with the full intention of causing him pain, which he accomplished quite successfully judging by Kyle's gasps and whimpers. Patrick was punishing Kyle for enjoying another man's dick in his ass, despite the fact that he was responsible for putting it there in the first place. Kyle grunted and winced from the merciless intrusion while developing a new appreciation for Sebastian's more user friendly hard on as opposed to Patrick's marauding member. While Patrick stuffed his oversized erection into Kyle's overly tight ass, he and Sebastian's mouth's found each other once again and reignited the passionate make out session, which had kicked things off earlier in the evening. When Patrick was close to climaxing, he pulled his dick out of Kyle's ass and let the moment pass while swapping out with Sebastian who thrust his own dick into Kyle and picked up the ass pounding where Patrick had left off.

"Let's see how long we can keep this going," Patrick said to Sebastian in spurts as their tongues swirled around in each other's mouths.

"What do you mean," Sebastian asked in the same broken tone.

"Let's see who can last the longest without coming," Patrick replied.

"You're on," Sebastian accepted his challenge. "But, what are we playing for?"

"Nothing," Patrick shrugged. "Just bragging rights."

Sebastian agreed to Patrick's terms as they continued kissing and caressing one another while sharing in the pleasure that was provided by Kyle's sweet and supple ass. The tag team went back and forth like this, with each of them pulling out the moment before they were about to ejaculate and passing Kyle off to the other while Kyle's ass continued to burn in agony. As Patrick and Sebastian each came closer to climaxing, the duration of those turns behind Kyle grew shorter until finally, on his fifth turn, Patrick couldn't hold it any longer and accidentally allowed his load to explode into Kyle's ass. Sebastian celebrated his win with a victory lap inside of Kyle where he was finally able to shoot his load in another convulsive orgasm that looked more like a seizure. "I win," Sebastian gloated as he and Patrick came together for a congratulatory kiss with their semi hard erections jostling between them.

"Well, that's what happens when an amateur goes up against a pro," Patrick said, offering up an excuse for his lack of staying power.

"That's right," Sebastian said. "Let that be a lesson to you."

"Come on," Patrick said, slapping him on the ass and climbing off the bed, "let's take a shower."

As the two of them headed toward the bathroom, they seemed to disregard Kyle completely while he lay in a crumpled heap on the bed with his asshole burning and having served his purpose. Kyle couldn't help feeling a little left out as he watched Sebastian knead Patrick's shoulders and traps while he walked behind him on their way to the bathroom. They appeared to be bonding over the shared experience of double teaming Kyle and he wondered if this was how those girls felt who were threatened by the concept of male bonding as Ally had suggested on the boat the other day. This was the closest that Kyle had ever come to feeling jealousy although, he didn't want Patrick and Sebastian to stop what they were doing but he would have liked to join them. As he watched Patrick and Sebastian kissing and lathering each other up from his vantage point on the bed, he contemplated making the trip to the bathroom and getting in between them once again but the pain that he was already feeling in his ass, prevented him from seeking that added abuse. He also resisted the urge to masturbate in order to maintain his erection, which kept the steady waves of pleasure rolling through his body to override the pain and ensure that he continued to feel good about the overall experience, which wasn't guaranteed in a post orgasm atmosphere.

After their shower, Patrick and Sebastian got dressed in the middle of the room where they had performed their seductive striptease for Kyle a short time ago. The act of putting their clothes back on was far less erotic than when they were taking them off but Kyle figured that the two of them were so hot that he could watch them doing just about anything and be completely captivated by it. Once they were fully clothed, Patrick reached in his pants pocket and retrieved five crisp new one hundred dollar bills, which he fanned out in front of Sebastian before folding them up and stuffing them into the pocket of his T-shirt while they exchanged another kiss for the road. As they made their way out the door, Patrick said to Kyle, "I'm just gonna drop him off in town. I'll be back in like ten minutes."

"It was nice meeting you," Kyle waved as he lay naked on the bed with his asshole in tatters while Patrick and Sebastian laughed together at the levity of his statement as if sharing an inside joke at Kyle's expense.

With both the starting and relief pitchers gone, Kyle was able to limp toward the shower without the added humiliation of having them admire their handiwork on his way there. As he washed himself, the soapy water stung his raw and tender asshole, making the showering process painfully more complicated. When he was finished, he grabbed the tube of hemorrhoid cream from his medicine cabinet, which he had acquired from his parent's medicine chest upstairs, following his previous painful encounter with Patrick's monstrous erection. He hoped they wouldn't notice that it was missing as he went to the bed and laid on his back with his knees pulled to his chest. Once he was in position, he inserted the applicator tip, which felt like a razor blade going into his sore asshole. Fortunately, it was a brand new tube, as Kyle didn't want to be doing sloppy seconds on an ass cream applicator tip. After injecting a healthy dose of the soothing balm, he was too sore for a trip back to the medicine cabinet so he cleaned the tip with some tissues and replaced the cap before tossing it in the drawer of his nightstand along with Patrick's tube of butt lube. "Nice collection I'm accumulating here," he thought to himself as he sat back and reflected on the latest chapter in their twisted drama. He still wasn't sure how he felt about the evening's adventure. Although the experience was undoubtedly enjoyable, he found himself battling through waves of regret that repeatedly crept up on him and threatened to overtake his entire thought process. The idea of being used and discarded, which had seemed so thrilling in the heat of passion, was far less pleasurable in the wake of a subsiding erection. Now, Kyle cringed as he considered the many drawbacks to being Patrick's bitch with pain and regret being the two top contenders. He figured that maybe certain fantasies were best left to the imagination and it probably wasn't necessary to act out every depraved thought that went through the back of his mind. He supposed that one day he would look back on this future masturbation fodder and reminisce about it in a purely favorable light but for the moment, he just wished that his ass would stop burning.

One thing that Kyle wasn't complaining about was Patrick's choice for a doubles partner. Sebastian was the perfect person to bring in for their three way. Not only was he incredibly handsome with a nice body and dick to match but he was also a professional who was there to provide a service, which was exactly what this occasion called for. Now, that the job was done, there were no strings attached and they could count on his discretion because that was the nature of his trade. Although Kyle was curious to know how Patrick and Sebastian had ever gotten together in the first place, he didn't like to pry so he would keep his questions to himself and let the curiosity eat away at him. However, if Kyle had asked, Patrick would have told him the story of how he first saw Sebastian at a neighbor's house on the East Side about a year ago and was instantly struck by his good looks. Eventually, he began to notice Sebastian turning up at the homes of other bored, rich, housewives while their husbands were known to be at work and he quickly concluded that Sebastian probably wasn't giving these ladies tennis lessons. However, it wasn't until Patrick saw him leaving the home of Mr. Thompson, who is known to be gay, that Patrick finally approached Sebastian in a client's driveway one morning and propositioned him for his services. At the time, Patrick was only seventeen but he lied and said he was eighteen, which didn't really matter because Sebastian wasn't exactly checking I.D.'s. Following that encounter, the two hooked up and Patrick had been a steady customer ever since.

Patrick returned to Kyle's house about a half hour later and found him lying on his side in the fetal position, which had proven to be less painful than lying on his back. After undressing, Patrick climbed into the bed and curled up behind Kyle as the big spoon while Kyle turned his head around for a kiss. He could smell fresh come on Patrick's breath and taste it on his tongue, which told Kyle that Patrick must have sucked off Sebastian in the car and explained what had taken him so long to return.

"So," Patrick said, "now that we checked off the three way fantasy box, what's next?"

"I don't know," Kyle answered. "What did you have in mind?"

"Why don't you tell me another one of your fantasies," Patrick suggested.

"Well, what about you," Kyle asked, turning the tables on Patrick as he wasn't exactly feeling the idea of exploring anymore of his own wild fantasies at the moment. "What's your number one fantasy?"

"You're looking at it," Patrick replied.

"I don't understand," Kyle said, puzzled. "Spooning? That's your fantasy?"

"No," Patrick said, smiling. "You're my fantasy. You're everyone's fantasy." He pressed up tightly against Kyle and placed his lips on the back of his neck. "Don't you know that it's every guy's fantasy to have someone who looks like you for their submissive lover?"

Kyle's cheeks turned hot pink as he blushed from Patrick's words. He knew that Patrick wasn't above telling someone what they wanted to hear as a diversion in order to avoid answering a question but Kyle ate it up anyway, regardless of his motives. Patrick wrapped his arms around Kyle and held him tight while nestling his dick between Kyle's ass cheeks. They both drifted off peacefully down a tranquil river of dreams, unaware of the impending plunge over a waterfall that was quickly approaching.

Finding Our Way Through the Fog
Jonathan B. Taylor

CHAPTER 17, 'ARMAGEDDON'

Kyle awoke the next morning to find himself alone with no sign of Patrick in the bed or anywhere else around the basement. He noticed that Patrick's clothes were gone from the wooden armchair beside the dresser where he had left them after getting undressed the night before and Kyle quickly concluded that Patrick must have quietly slipped out sometime in the morning without waking him. He reached for his phone on the nightstand and saw that he had one message from Patrick, which read, 'Didn't want to wake you. Be back later. I love you! – P'. Kyle felt a burst of elation upon reading the words and quickly typed out a response. 'Can't wait! I love you too!' He then signed it, 'KY' as a sly nod to the tube of lubricant that sat in the drawer of his nightstand. With his message sent, Kyle grabbed the pillow from the other side of the bed and wrapped his arms and legs around it as he lay on his side and imagined it was Patrick he was holding. Being in love was a new experience for both of them and the longing and aching that they felt when they were apart seemed to intensify the joy and pleasure they felt when they were together. As Kyle squeezed his pleasant substitute for Patrick, he found himself reliving the memories from the previous night's exploits, which was becoming a standard part of the routine in the wake of their sexual encounters. Those erotic recollections would then trigger pulse pounding erections, which sent pleasurable waves of ecstasy through his body and made the memories seem almost magical. Kyle fought back the urge to masturbate, knowing how the enjoyable flashbacks would lose their luster if he were to consume them in a sudden orgasm.

Although his ass was feeling better, Kyle still had some residual discomfort so he injected a fresh shot of hemorrhoid cream to soothe the pain and reap the benefits from the healing properties of the butt balm. Eventually, he dragged himself out of bed and made his way upstairs to his parents' kitchen where he had an oversized bowl of bran flakes with sliced banana and strawberries for breakfast. After running a load in the dishwasher, Kyle returned to the basement and spent the rest of the morning on the sofa, catching up on some reading with his latest science magazines, which he had been neglecting and were now piling up on the end table. It was around noontime when Kyle was about to begin a cardio workout, that his phone started buzzing and the messages began pouring in. The first was from Steven and read, 'There's something you need to see. This video is being circulated online by some kids from school. Don't worry about the name. It's not a virus although you may get sick when you see it.' Kyle observed the folder icon and saw the caption, 'Danger: Virus Inside: Do Not Open!'

"What is this," he wondered aloud as Steven's ominous words sent a chill down his spine. Kyle reluctantly pressed the folder icon and opened the file, which revealed another file folder inside with the caption, 'Fifty Shades of Gay'. Kyle immediately recognized this reference as one he had made to Patrick the other night and he suddenly felt that sick feeling, which Steven had warned him to expect. Kyle wasn't sure what was hiding around the next corner but nothing could have prepared him for the worst case scenario, which appeared on his screen when he opened the 'Fifty Shades' folder and the bombshell exploded to reveal its contents. Kyle watched in disbelief as he saw the image of himself standing naked and blindfolded with his wrists tethered over his head while Patrick whipped him mercilessly from behind with a leather belt as his rock hard erection provided a clear indication that he was enjoying the abuse. Kyle fast forwarded through the video and discovered the different camera angles, which seemed to capture the action from a variety of vantage points including close-ups and he began to wonder who else had been in the room with them that night.

The whole thing was so inconceivable that Kyle couldn't even wrap his head around it initially and felt as if he were watching it all happen to someone else. However, the reality of the situation eventually sank in and Kyle was overcome with a cyclone of emotions as betrayal, humiliation, anger, and heartache swirled around his head like a dizzying flock of tweeting birds. It was as though the rollercoaster had come free from the tracks and was careening off the edge of the highest hill with an unforgiving landscape below. This went way beyond a simple act of being outed as Kyle saw his most private and intimate moments playing out in a public arena where anyone could see them.

"What the fuck," Kyle said aloud as he watched his extended ejaculation sequence roll out with the help of some cinematography. "What kind of sick fuck does something like this," Kyle wondered. "What kind of sick fucking game is he playing?"

None of it made any sense as Kyle tried to contemplate Patrick's endgame. It was obvious he wanted to end things between them because there was no way of ever coming back from something like this but Kyle didn't understand why Patrick would choose to do it in such a cruel and dramatic way. He wasn't only hurting and humiliating Kyle with his twisted stunt. By publicizing the video, Patrick was putting himself out there as well and running the risk of exposing his own sexuality to his Bible crazed parents in the process. Kyle thought about Patrick's coming out to Claire the other night and wondered if he was just following through on that dramatic gesture with an over the top grand finale. Then he remembered Patrick's feelings of guilt over his charmed life and wondered if this was his way of paying penance and leveling the playing field. By running his life through a wood chipper, Patrick wouldn't seem so blessed when standing beside those less fortunate. That was assuming that anything Patrick had told him was true.

As Kyle searched for an explanation of why his life was falling apart, he knew that Patrick was the only person who could provide the answers to those questions but he couldn't even think of talking to him right then. If Patrick was cold blooded enough to do something this caustic, there was no telling what type of sadistic venom could spew from his mouth at an eventual confrontation and Kyle wasn't looking forward to that sickening scenario. Rather than trying to solve the puzzle with pieces he didn't have, Kyle looked inward for answers and wondered how he had put himself in such a precarious position in the first place. He knew that it was his unrelenting submissiveness, which had created the monster with the power to perform this treacherous act of treason. This realization led Kyle to do some soul searching as he tried to understand why he found it so alluring to be on the bottom and he wondered why his dick got so hard whenever Patrick asserted his dominance over him. He remembered Patrick saying that it was every guy's fantasy to have a submissive lover like him and he thought of how thrilling it was to hear those words. This made him wonder if perhaps he had some overwhelming need to feel desirable to others, which was the driving force behind his self destructive behavior. If it was in his nature to be submissive, then Kyle didn't see much chance of changing that. It wasn't like he could go to a warped version of some creepy conversion camp and be transformed from a bottom to a top. His only recourse was to try making better choices when it came to picking partners and start thinking with the big head instead of the little one.

Despite having a stomach full of knots and suffering from a severe anxiety attack, Kyle attempted to take his mind off things by getting on with his planned cardio workout. He began by jumping rope, which he alternated with five minute intervals on the heavy bag. As Kyle landed his well placed punches and kicks, he imagined that the bag was Patrick, just as he had done with his pillow a few hours ago only now, he was hitting him instead of hugging him. It was jarring for Kyle to see how quickly love turned to hate but he knew that Patrick was still in his system and his feelings for him weren't so easily overturned in spite of those unforgivable actions.

One of the things that angered Kyle the most as he took out his aggression on the heavy bag, was how Patrick's underhanded video had conveniently featured him as the bitch in their sadomasochistic encounter while Patrick appeared in the less awkward position of being on top. There was generally less stigma surrounding pitchers than there was around catchers when it came to gay male intercourse because people tended to be more accepting of guys who did the fucking as opposed to those who liked getting fucked. Tops were viewed as somewhat normal dudes that were doing typical guy stuff who just happened to have different tastes in partners. It wasn't that simple for catchers who were usually seen as freaks and thought to be doing things that were considered unnatural with some even viewing them as culprits who were corrupting their otherwise normal cohorts.

These thoughts only enraged Kyle further as he launched a barrage of haymakers at the heavy bag. "How about if I told everyone how much you love to suck dick," Kyle growled through clenched teeth as he continued his volley on imaginary Patrick. "Then you can have a little taste of your own medicine you fucking piece of shit!"

As Kyle blew off steam in his workout, he was able to vent some of that anger through his fists and feet but it came at a cost because the anger had been overriding the pain from his broken heart and whenever the anger subsided, the heartache would instantly fill the void. The emptiness Kyle felt, would then trigger his consistent longing for Patrick, which was a typical symptom of the broken hearted. In spite of everything, Kyle still wasn't ready to let go as happier times with Patrick played tricks with his mind by flashing in his head like a strobe light against the darkness of the day. It felt like there was a battle brewing between Kyle's head and his heart in, which only one would emerge victorious.

After his workout, which lasted close to an hour, Kyle was exhausted so he drank a chocolate protein shake and took a shower before settling down on the sofa to lick his wounds and try to take his mind off things but those efforts proved futile in light of the current catastrophe. He was still experiencing some residual pain from last night's three-way, which made it more difficult to block those images from his mind as the memories were now tainted by an overwhelming feeling of regret. Kyle could see that the sun was shining brightly outside through the bunker style, basement windows, which sat high on the walls around the room but his mood matched one of a dreary, dismal day in the fall rather than one of a bright, sunny day in the summer. He felt as though life had played the cruelest of jokes on him by tricking him into falling in love with the most despicable person on the planet. Kyle eventually gave up on the idea of trying to take his mind off things and surrendered to the storm of thoughts that swirled around his head, allowing them to flood his brain.

He reluctantly picked up his phone to check his messages and was shocked to see that he had been inundated by emails from a number of unknown sources. It appeared that both the video and his email address were being passed around at an alarming rate and the video, which had been titled, 'Virus Inside' was living up to its name by actually going viral. He remembered his mother's words when she said, 'We didn't exactly go nuclear with our coming out.' "Did this qualify as 'going nuclear'," Kyle wondered as he pictured the story spreading like a mushroom cloud over the masses.

As Kyle looked at all of the messages, he wondered what could possibly make people think that he wanted to talk to anyone right now. "Fuck! Is there anybody who hasn't heard about this," he said as he combed through the endless array of emails. Most appeared to be from well-wishers with captions like, 'Supporting You!' or 'Team Kyle' while a handful of hateful texts were peppered in by the inevitable trolls. 'Die Queer!' and 'Kill Yourself!' were common themes but Kyle's favorite was definitely, 'God Hates Fags!'. "That one must be from Patrick's parents," Kyle thought while wondering, which bible passage they were quoting. Then there were the apparent propositions with captions like, 'Call Me!' and 'Let's Meat!' with emphasis on the spelling of 'Meat'. Never had Kyle felt so reviled and desired at the same time.

Finding Our Way Through the Fog
Jonathan B. Taylor

He was no more interested in reading any of those messages than he was in actually responding to them but there was one message he was looking for, which was noticeably absent. He was hoping to find a text from Patrick in the mix, which could provide some type of explanation for why his dream world had suddenly turned into a nightmare but all he got was radio silence from the architect of this disaster. However, there was one message that caught his eye as he scrolled through the lot. It was from Kevin McCoy and the caption read, 'Sorry! All My Fault!'

"How was this all Kevin's fault," Kyle wondered, as he opened the mysterious clue and began to read.

'Kyle, I'm so sorry this happened to you and I feel like I may have played a role. Sometime over this past winter, I hooked up with Patrick and during that time, I told him about some of my past hookups with other guys including that time with you. Looking back now, I'm afraid that I may have set this whole thing in motion with my big mouth and led him straight to you. If that is the case then, I'm sorry. I never should have done that and I hope you'll forgive me. – Kevin/ P.S., I've always regretted how I handled things with us and if you ever want to give me another chance, I promise not to disappoint you.'

Kyle rolled his eyes at Kevin's lame attempt to reignite their flash in the pan bromance as the startling revelation that Patrick had been fully aware of it, slowly sank in. Next, Kyle's memory flashed to the image of Patrick emerging from the woods and approaching him at the picnic table on that warm spring day in March and suddenly, their chance meeting was beginning to look more like a calculated encounter. "Had Patrick been planning this from the start," Kyle wondered as the endless possibilities began to run wild in his head once again. Then he remembered Patrick's persistent prodding to try and make him reveal Kevin's name as the boy he hooked up with in junior high, when it turns out Patrick had known about Kevin all along. Apparently, one of Patrick's tactics involved eliciting the names of previous lovers to gain intel on potential partners. "So, all this time that I thought I was getting laid, it looks like I was really getting played," Kyle thought to himself as he was suddenly startled by a knock at the door. His heart began to pound in his chest so hard that his teeth chattered and his hands began to shake uncontrollably as he pictured Patrick standing on the other side of that door, ready to set it off with a stick of dynamite clenched in each fist. The explosive confrontation that he had been dreading was at his doorstep and he sat frozen in the headlights, unable to say a word. By staying silent and motionless, he hoped the threat would pass until he heard the sound of Steven's voice calling to him from outside, which allowed him to relax and begin to breathe normally again following the initial sigh of relief.

Kyle wasn't really interested in seeing anyone at the moment but Steven was one of the few people he could deal with and someone who actually had a chance at lifting his spirits. Kyle walked over to the door and opened it to find Steven standing on the small concrete landing with his mountain bike leaning on its kickstand a few feet away.

"Come on in," Kyle invited as he moved aside to let Steven through.

When he stepped inside, Steven looked around the room and took in his surroundings. This was his first time being in Kyle's basement and he nodded approvingly at the layout. "So, this is the famous gym," Steven said, as he scoped out Kyle's workout area.

Finding Our Way Through the Fog
Jonathan B. Taylor

"Well, I don't know how famous it is," Kyle said, forgetting about the fact that it was the setting for the sex tape, "but, yeah, this is where I get it in." That phrase reminded him of the significance of the site and he thought of the possible punch lines he would have heard from Nick or Ally if he had made such a slip in front of them. 'Well, it's where Patrick certainly got it in,' Ally may have said. 'Or, where it gets into you,' Nick would have added. As Kyle looked at Steven, he noticed that he was wearing his lifeguard shorts with a faded red tank top that was close to being pink. "Did you work today," he asked, slightly confused by the time. Their shifts usually ended at four and it was barely one o'clock.

"Just the morning. I covered for Ally while she went to her dentist appointment," Steven explained, before adding, "You can probably expect a visit from her and Amber later." Steven paused, as he searched for something else to say. "So, you and Patrick?"

"Yeah," Kyle nodded disgustedly, "me and Patrick. Or, so I thought. I don't even know what to think anymore," Kyle growled through clenched teeth with fists to match.

"This whole thing sucks," Steven said as he slammed his own fist into his palm. "I couldn't believe that shit when I saw it."

"How much did you see," Kyle asked while his cheeks turned hot pink over the thought of Steven seeing his humiliating performance. "Did you watch the whole thing?"

"No," Steven lied. "I hardly saw anything and I shut it off as soon as I realized what I was watching." He had a sincere look in his eye that made Kyle almost believe him but he was unable to hold it and quickly shifted his gaze to the floor, which gave away the deception. However, Kyle appreciated the effort and it was enough to let his face return to its normal flesh tone.

"I still can't believe Patrick would do something like this," Kyle fumed.

"So, did you even know he was filming you," Steven asked as if he already had a pretty good idea of the answer.

"Not a clue," Kyle answered.

"That's what I figured." He gave an affirming nod.

"What gave it away," Kyle asked curiously.

"Just by the way you were blindfolded the whole time. It made it seem like there was a good chance that you didn't know about the cameras if you were unable to see them."

"I thought you didn't see the whole thing," Kyle pointed out the discrepancy in his story.

"Oh, what I mean or, what I meant was," Steven stammered as a guilty smile appeared on his face, "I didn't watch it all the way through but I may have skipped through it to the end and it looked like you had the blindfold on the whole time."

Steven's explanation wasn't working and Kyle's cheeks went right back to bright pink.

"I just can't understand how he could put something like this out there like that," Kyle said with a dumbfounded look on his face. "If he wanted to hurt me, then he went to an awful lot of trouble and hurt himself in the process and that's the part that I really don't understand."

"You think he leaked it on purpose," Steven asked doubtfully.

"I have no idea," Kyle replied with frustration.

"You haven't talked to him then?" He sounded surprised.

"Not a word," Kyle replied.

"That's fucked up," Steven said. "Maybe he's afraid to face you because of how bad he messed up?"

"Yeah, or maybe he's accomplished everything he set out to do and now he doesn't have any reason to ever talk to me again," Kyle countered.

"Well, it's completely fucked up that he made that video but I don't think he planned for anyone to see it," Steven assured him.

"What makes you say that," Kyle asked curiously.

"Just the way it came out," Steven explained. "Supposedly, it was sent out with a bunch of 'crash and burn' videos like it was done by accident."

This was the closest thing to good news that Kyle had heard all day and the first bit of hope to suggest that Patrick hadn't maliciously released the video. It didn't change the fact that he made it in the first place but it hurt a lot less than the thought of him putting it out there intentionally.

"That's my opinion," Steven concluded. "And now, I gotta go. I got a hot date tonight."

"With Billy," Kyle asked?

"Yeah," Steven answered with smile.

"I'd ask how it's going but judging by that smile, I'd say that it's going pretty good."

"It's pretty sweet," Steven nodded happily.

"That's great," Kyle said. "I just hope you never get the rug pulled out from under you like I did."

"Well, I'm gone," Steven said as he moved toward the door. "I just wanted to stop by to see you and let you know that I'm here if you need me."

"Actually, there is something you can do for me," Kyle said.

"Name it," Steven responded without hesitation.

"Could you cover my shift tomorrow? I'm just not ready to deal with people right now."

"Of course," Steven said. "For as long as you need." He then put his arms around Kyle in a reassuring embrace that left Kyle feeling empty and missing Patrick more than ever.

After Steven left, Kyle returned to the sofa with his spirits slightly buoyed by the visit, which provided a reprieve from the twisted knots in his stomach that plagued him throughout the day. However, the crushing weight of reality continued to loom over him and threaten to draw him back into that dark place if he should dare to dwell on it once again. At shortly after four o'clock, Kyle heard a car rolling up the driveway, which was too quiet for Patrick's and he assumed was probably Ally and Amber based on the time and Steven's advanced warning to expect them. He had relocated to the bed where he was propped up in a sitting position with the help of some pillows he had stacked against the headboard as the cyclone of thoughts continued to swirl around his head.

"Come in," he called out in response to the knock at the door.

The girls stepped inside and immediately headed over to the bed and climbed onto the mattress where they each took up positions on either side of Kyle before wrapping their arms around him and giving him consoling kisses on his cheeks.

"How are you doing," they both asked in overly sympathetic voices that made Kyle feel somewhat pathetic.

For Kyle, the whole mood was feeling like there had been a death in the family with people stopping by to offer their condolences. He still wasn't really in the mood for company but the girls were another one of those exceptions who brought a dose of strength and positivity along with them. "I'm doing about as miserably as can be expected," Kyle answered before turning to Amber and adding, "It looks like

Patrick took you're suggestion that we both become porn stars to a whole new level."

"What are you gonna do," Ally asked while unable to think of a better question?

"There isn't much I can do." Kyle looked at the ceiling and shook his head in exasperation. "I started thinking that I could just hide out here for the next few weeks and put this all behind me when I head off to college but then I realized that there is no getting away from this and it's gonna follow me wherever I go. The only way I could escape it would be to fake my own death and go off the grid for a few years. Maybe live in the woods for awhile before eventually returning to society somewhere out on the west coast where I could live under an assumed name," Kyle hypothesized jokingly before returning to his aggravated growl. "Fuck! Patrick really fucked me over on this one! If it was just a simple case of being outed, I could lean into it but how do I lean into something like this? What, am I supposed to walk around in a leather thong with a spiked collar around my neck and an orange ball gag in my mouth? That's not who I am. This whole thing was just a sex game. It was harmless experimentation." Kyle was venting all of his frustration, which had been building throughout the day and the girls were doing all they could by serving as good listeners.

"Maybe you should lean into it," Ally finally suggested after a sustained silence. "I don't mean dressing like you're headed to the S&M club but you could post something on social media as a little damage control."

"I'm all ears," Kyle said. "What did you have in mind?"

"Pretty much what you just said," Ally shrugged. "Own the fact that you're bisexual and put the focus on that while downplaying the whole sex tape as harmless experimentation."

"Yeah," Kyle said approvingly. "And then I could throw in how Patrick likes to wear diapers and dress up in drag."

"Is that true," Ally asked as her and Amber each stifled a laugh?

"Not really," Kyle admitted. "But it sounds good and it would serve him right to put something out there that would embarrass the shit out of him. I know that sounds messed up but what's even more messed up is that I still have no idea why he would do any of this."

"So, you haven't talked to him?" Ally sounded slightly surprised.

"No. And I'm really not sure I want to."

"I have," Amber spoke up. "I talked to him on the phone earlier. Do you want to know what he said?"

"Yes! Please enlighten me," Kyle said as he suddenly saw an opportunity for some answers.

"Well, he never meant for anyone to see the video," she explained. "He said that he released it by accident when he was moving files around and inadvertently placed it in the wrong folder. Unfortunately, that folder contained a bunch of 'epic fail' videos that he shared with some other people online. By the time he realized what happened, it was too late and the damage was already done. Now he's afraid to face you because he feels terrible about what he did and he can't face the thought of you hating him for it."

"Okay," Kyle said, "but that doesn't explain why he even made the video in the first place. Why the hell would he do something like that?"

"He said he wanted to capture the two of you on video so he could immortalize the moment and keep it forever. He also said that he did it without you knowing because the opportunity was there so he took it. The reason he didn't ask you first is because he was afraid you'd turn him down. I know what he did was off the charts inexcusable but if it's any consolation, he's completely devastated over it and extremely remorseful. I've never heard him sound like that. He was choking back tears the whole time we were talking."

Kyle remained silent as he processed the information. He was relieved to know for certain that Patrick hadn't released the video intentionally, which was the worst case scenario that he had imagined. He was also quietly enjoying the thought of Patrick suffering for what he had done to him.

"Then, on top of everything," Amber continued, "Patrick's parents found out and are threatening to cut him off and disown him unless he attends one of those twisted sexual orientation conversion camps."

Kyle was no longer relishing the thought of Patrick's anguish when he heard this distressing news and suddenly he became concerned for Patrick who was suffering some unimaginable consequences of his own.

"Well," Ally said to Kyle, "I can't even think of talking to Patrick right now because I'm so pissed off at him for what he did to you and he's gonna have to earn your forgiveness before I'll ever consider talking to him again."

"I appreciate the solidarity," Kyle said, "but I don't want any other relationships to suffer because of what went down with me and him."

"Okay then," Ally said, "how about this for solidarity? When I go home tonight, I'm gonna come out as bisexual on social media right along with you."

"Me too," Amber seconded as she reached across Kyle to give Ally an opposite hand high five.

"That's sweet of you," Kyle said, "but I definitely don't need anyone coming out on my behalf."

"Well, we're doing it anyway," Ally, said defiantly.

"Besides," Amber added, "it's largely symbolic since we've kinda been out there with the PDA lately so it probably won't come as a big surprise to a lot of people."

"Alright, fuck it," Kyle said. "Let's do it together then. We'll be like the Three Musketeers."

"More like the three muster queers," Ally said and they all laughed.

"I like it," Kyle nodded approvingly as he reached for his phone on the nightstand, "and as a matter of fact, I'm gonna get started right now."

Kyle began typing up his 'coming out' message while Ally and Amber pulled out their phones and went to work on writing similar announcements of their own. Despite the gestures being largely symbolic at this juncture, with the information already out there, Kyle still felt some apprehension over taking such a long awaited step and was comforted by the thought of having a couple of good friends along with him for the ride. He also felt a sense of satisfaction from taking back a moment, which was stolen from him by a reckless thief. When the three companions completed the drafts of their public proclamations, they each took turns reading them aloud to one another for a final critique while simultaneously video taping their testimonials before the ultimate reveal online. Kyle, who had the most to say and perhaps the biggest stake in the game, set the tone by being the first to recite his declaratory address.

"Today I watched in horror as a leaked sex tape, which I didn't even know existed, showed the world a side of myself that I had previously kept private. Not only did this blindsiding bombshell reveal the fact that I am bisexual, it did it in the worst way imaginable. What started out as some harmless fun and experimentation ended up as a nightmare scenario. In an effort to please the needs of a partner, I put myself in a precarious position for, which I am now paying a painful price. So, let this be a lesson to anyone who is participating in this type of sex play. Sadomasochistic activity such as bondage is risky behavior, which can lead to costlier results than having your private moments plastered across people's computer and phone screens. Being bound and blindfolded leaves you vulnerable to potential acts of violence and it's probably never prudent to put your trust in the hands of a sadist. I would like to thank all of the well-wishers who reached out to me in the wake of this ordeal. Your support and concern are greatly appreciated. I would also like to tell all of the homophobic trolls who took the time from their busy bile spreading schedules to turn their hateful rhetoric toward me, that your envy is showing and everyone can see right through you as the louder you protest against homosexuality, the more clearly your true feelings on the subject become. You need to stop projecting your self loathing onto others for having something, which you obviously want for yourselves." Kyle shrugged his shoulders and looked at the girls for their reactions. "So, that's it," he concluded. "Signed, Kyle Jacobs. What do you think?"

"I think it's awesome," Ally praised.

"I think so too," Amber agreed. "Shoot it."

"Thanks," Kyle said as he put his arms around each of them and pulled them close. "And, thanks for doing this with me. So, who's next?"

"I'll go," Ally said as she held her phone up and read her message aloud for the others to hear. "To anyone who is interested: I am writing this message to publicly declare the fact that I am bisexual. Earlier today, I saw a good friend of mine, who is also bisexual, being unceremoniously outed on the internet and I just wanted him to know that he's not alone. Bisexuality is actually more common than most people are willing to admit as the vast majority of us are capable of being attracted to both sexes. Until we're ready to stand up together and say that the emperor has no clothes, people will continue to feed the negative emotions of guilt, shame and envy, which fuel the self loathing condition of homophobia that effects our society as a whole. Peace, Allyson Lynch. And, then I put a little hash tag at the end," she explained as she held the phone out to show them the '#X2' symbol she had placed at the end of her message.

"Hash tag, ex, two," Kyle read aloud. "What does that mean?"

"Actually," Ally clarified, "it's hash tag, by, two, but like b-i-t-o-o, as in, also bisexual."

"Oh, hash tag, bi, too," Kyle said, suddenly understanding. "That's pretty good. Do you mind if I use it?"

"Go right ahead," she said. "It's meant to be shared."

"Okay, it's my turn," Amber said as she took the floor. "Hello friends and whoever else happens to read this. I'm going to make this short and sweet. In case you weren't already aware, I am bisexual and I'm saying this publicly to stand in solidarity with my friends who are also bisexual and making public declarations of their own. Despite the fact that I've always dreaded the idea of people knowing about my sexuality, I'm actually finding the act of revealing the truth to be exhilarating and liberating. Feel the rush! Amber Pierce. And now," she said, taking to her keypad, "for the final touch." Amber typed in the '#X2' symbol with an added '(bi too)' in parentheses for extra clarification. She showed the finished product to Kyle and Ally who applauded her message and both agreed that the '(bi too)' was a nice addition so they tacked it onto their declarations as well.

After posting their 'coming out' messages on social media together, the three of them shared a group hug before Ally and Amber departed for the evening and Kyle climbed back into his bed where he held a pillow over his face for a moment and relished the thought of smothering himself. He wasn't seriously considering ending his life but he did find himself wishing that he could fall into a deep sleep and magically awaken to discover it was all just a bad dream. Kyle knew that he would eventually have to leave the refuge of his basement to face the whispers and snickers of the outside world but for now, he only wanted to curl up in a ball and pretend that the whole thing never happened.

Unfortunately, sleep was elusive with both his thoughts and his body being twisted into knots but Kyle did manage to nod off for a brief period, before he was awakened shortly after nine o'clock by the sound of knocking. He was still groggy and it took him a moment to realize he wasn't dreaming but once his head cleared, he immediately recognized the rapid succession of knocks and knew that it was Patrick who was pounding on his door. He felt a sense of panic grip his body and violently shake him as he heard the sound of Patrick's voice calling to him from the other side of the barricade.

"Kyle, are you there? Please talk to me," Patrick pleaded. "I can't take having you not talk to me."

Kyle could hear the anguish in the muffled sound of Patrick's voice and he was torn between wanting to go to him and needing to turn away. Part of him was aching to feel Patrick's arms around him while another part of him was glad to hear Patrick suffering and wanted to prolong his pain. Regardless of any inner conflict however, Kyle wasn't ready to face him and had no intention of opening that door tonight. He was glad that he locked the door when the girls left although, it didn't matter because Patrick had no plans to enter without an invitation. After an extended period of silence, Kyle heard Patrick's cracking voice say, 'I'm sorry', a moment before the sound of a car door closing followed by an engine turning over and, as Patrick's car was rolling away down the driveway, the tears were rolling down both of their faces.

Finding Our Way Through the Fog
Jonathan B. Taylor

CHAPTER 18, 'AFTERSHOCK'

Kyle awoke the next morning from a restless night's sleep, hoping to feel better about his situation but instead he felt even worse. It was as if all of the previous day's thoughts and musings had come rushing over him like a tidal wave, the moment he opened his eyes and reality punched him in the face. He attempted to focus his attention on the positive aspects from that dark day, such as those uplifting visits from Steven and the girls but the images of the leaked video compounded with his degrading participation in Patrick's follow-up three-way extravaganza continued to haunt him. Suddenly, a chilling thought occurred to him as paranoia played tricks with his mind. What if Patrick had made other videos of their sexual exploits and the next one to drop featured him getting hit from both ends by Patrick and Sebastian on the coffee table? He remembered how Patrick had disappeared for a few minutes right when they were kicking things off that night, which would have provided the perfect opportunity for him to plant some of his hidden cameras around the room while Kyle was busy with Sebastian's dick in his mouth.

Ultimately, Kyle decided that he had enough to worry about without creating additional scenarios in his imagination so, he turned his energy to something more productive like checking his phone to see what kind of response he had gotten from last night's 'out' post. Kyle was shocked by the sheer volume of messages he had received and was pleased to see that virtually all of them appeared to be positive in nature with subject headings like, 'Bye Bi Closet' or 'Ride the Bi Way' although the vast majority were simply using Ally's '#X2' call sign, which was definitely catching on. Kyle noticed that the homophobic trolls who were firing shots at him with both barrels in yesterday's batch of comments and texts were suddenly silent and he wondered if his calling them out on their hypocrisy in his post had turned out to be an effective deterrent. As Kyle combed through the messages and found his spirits buoyed by the uplifting support of the community, he noticed that there were several texts from Patrick scattered among the others. As he read those captions, Kyle saw how Patrick had cleverly found a way to get his message across by posting it in pieces throughout the subject headings. 'You probably won't read this' was the title of the first message, which was followed by, 'but I want you to know' and then, 'that I'm sorry and' as Kyle scrolled down further he found the next message. 'I love you and' Kyle kept scrolling, 'I can't live' finally, Kyle reached the last message but he already knew what it was going to say; 'without you'. Kyle went back and started opening the texts to find that they each contained the same message in it's entirety as the one, which had been meted out through the patchwork of captions. The extra effort was endearing and Kyle felt himself beginning to soften as he was missing Patrick terribly with a twinge of forgiveness slowly creeping throughout his heart. He was about to send Patrick a message to let him know he was ready to talk when he saw that he had an incoming call from Amber, which he assumed was her wanting to discuss the reactions to their 'coming out' trifecta.

Finding Our Way Through the Fog
Jonathan B. Taylor

"Kyle, it's Amber," she said in an urgent tone, which drew immediate concern. "Have you heard from Patrick?"

"No," Kyle answered as dread filled his head and the knots returned to his stomach. "I mean, I got some messages from him but, why? What's wrong?"

"I'm worried," she said gravely. "He called me this morning and I could tell right away that there was something off about him. It sounded like he was wasted and he kept saying how he had hurt the only person he ever loved and there was no coming back from that. Then he told me that they took his aunt off life support and she was probably the only person besides me that he had left and he thanked me for not giving up on him. After that, the line went dead and now, I keep getting voicemail when I try to call. I'm worried about him because Patrick's lived this charmed life and I'm afraid that he lacks the coping skills to handle all of this turmoil. Will you please try calling him? I just need to know that he's okay. I know that he'll pick up if he sees that it's you calling and if he still doesn't answer then something is definitely wrong. So, will you do it?"

"Yes, of course," Kyle said as he processed everything that Amber had told him. "I was actually about to text him right before you called. I'll try him right now and if you don't hear right back from me, it means that I got through and we're in the middle of something."

"Understood," Amber, said. "But please don't keep me waiting for too long. I've got a really bad feeling that it was like," Amber hesitated as though she couldn't say the words.

"Like what," Kyle, asked?

"It was like he was saying 'goodbye'," she finally blurted.

That was all Kyle needed to hear. "I've gotta go," he said, ending the call abruptly and immediately speed dialing Patrick, which led him straight to voicemail. Kyle got an uneasy feeling as he remembered Amber saying that voicemail was an indicator that something was wrong but he tried not to panic and figured there could be a number of reasons why Patrick hadn't picked up. He could be in the shower or maybe he had shut off his phone. Kyle typed out a quick message to Patrick, letting him know that he was ready to talk and requesting that Patrick give him a call. Then he called Amber to let her know what happened.

"No luck," Kyle said with a combination of disappointment and concern. "It went straight to voicemail."

"Shit," she responded with deepening dread. "That's not good!"

"So, let's think this through," Kyle, said. "Where was he when he called you?"

"I'm not sure. I thought he was at home but there was no answer there. I even tried the landline."

"Well, it sounds like a good place to start," Kyle figured. "I'm gonna head over there. I'll call you if I hear anything."

"Okay, same here," Amber said and they both hung up their phones hoping that the next call they received would be from Patrick.

Kyle threw on a pair of shorts and a t-shirt and laced up his running shoes with double knots. He knew that the shortest distance between two points was a straight line and the fastest way to Patrick's was on foot through the woods so he made his way out the door and hit the path at a full sprint. This was the fastest he had ever run as he dodged low branches and hurdled over rocks and stumps like a whitetail deer with a pack of hungry wolves on its heels. For Kyle, it felt like a trip down memory lane as the many times that he and Patrick had spent on these same trails were flashing in his head while he jumped and ducked his way through the forest. It took him just under eight minutes to arrive at Patrick's house where he stood for a moment, slightly bent over with his hands braced on his knees, while he attempted to catch his breath. Once he was finished hyperventilating, Kyle made his way across the vast, meticulously groomed grounds of the palatial Connor family estate toward the front of the house where he observed Patrick's Challenger parked in the spacious circular driveway, which was a good sign that he was home. Unfortunately, he noticed that Patrick's father's green Jaguar and his mother's white Mercedes were also there, which meant that the whole operation could possibly go sideways with a potentially uncomfortable confrontation cued up as the next annoying subplot. Kyle was dreading that scenario and starting to wish that Amber had made the trip over to Patrick's instead of him.

He wanted to avoid ringing the front doorbell so Kyle tried throwing a few small pebbles at Patrick's window in an attempt to get his attention but unfortunately, there was no response. When that didn't work, he tried yelling Patrick's name up toward the window but there was still no sign of him although his efforts didn't go completely unnoticed and he ended up getting the attention of the two people he was hoping desperately to avoid. Suddenly, the front door swung open and Kyle saw Patrick's parents standing on the landing of the intricate stone and mortar staircase that graced the front of their home. They both had a look of disgust on their faces and hatred in their eyes as Kyle felt like a fly, which had ventured too close to the hatch of a trapdoor spider.

Finding Our Way Through the Fog
Jonathan B. Taylor

Thomas and Jennifer Connor were only in their late forties but they looked much older in the harsh light of the mid morning sun. The gray hair, which was normally hidden by their natural blond color, was suddenly more visible as was the toll that their lifestyles, involving her drug use and his stressful world of high finance, had taken on their general appearance. Jennifer's skin, which appeared like parchment from too many cosmetic procedures, was pulled into pleats around the edges of her face while her swollen lips looked as if a swarm of bees had stung them. Thomas's face on the other hand, just looked tired and craggy. They assumed an attack formation with Jennifer taking the lead and Thomas providing backup by standing slightly behind her right shoulder with his arms folded and an angry scowl on his face.

"Look, I don't want any trouble," Kyle said, sensing their hostility and holding his hands up as if surrendering to their madness. "I'm worried about Patrick. Amber got a call from him that was a little concerning and we just want to make sure he's alright."

"How dare you show your face around here after what you've done," Jennifer hissed?

"Excuse me," Kyle said with both shock and confusion. "And, what exactly is it that I'm supposed to have done?"

"You know what you did," she screamed in a shrill tone. "You lured our son into a perverse homosexual encounter and ruined his reputation!"

"Lady, what planet are you on," Kyle asked as he contemplated the alternate universe in, which these people existed where they created their own narratives to suit their surroundings. "I didn't lure anyone into anything."

"Our son was a normal, healthy boy before you got your hooks into him and twisted his mind with your perversion," Jennifer growled.

"What are you talking about," Kyle said in disbelief. "Do you even hear yourself? Nobody's responsible for Patrick being bisexual and it's not an affliction. And for the record, he was already into dudes long before he met me." Kyle instantly regretted saying that last part but Patrick's mother had gotten him so irritated that he couldn't help getting a little defensive.

"I think it's time for you to leave," Thomas spoke up.

"Not a problem," Kyle agreed, as he was more than ready to get the hell out of there. "But I just need to know that he's okay. Will you please check on him?"

"He's not here," Thomas finally revealed. "We don't know where he is. He left earlier and as I said, it's time for you to leave."

"Look, I'm telling you, something is wrong," Kyle persisted. "Don't you even care that your son could be in trouble? We need to find him, now! You've got connections. Have them ping his phone or something!"

"No, you need to get the hell out of here or else I will call the police! On you," Jennifer shouted as they both stepped back in the house and slammed the heavy, wooden door behind them.

"Well, that went well," Kyle, said ironically, as he answered the incoming call on his buzzing phone. It was Amber looking for an update.

"Where are you," she asked.

"I'm at Patrick's," Kyle replied. "He's not here. His parents said that he left earlier but his car's still in the driveway. I'm not sure what to do next but I need to get out of here before I get swatted."

Finding Our Way Through the Fog
Jonathan B. Taylor

"You mean like a bug," Amber asked, slightly confused.

"No, I mean like they're about to call a S.W.A.T team on me," Kyle said as he combed through Patrick's earlier messages looking for clues to his whereabouts. All of the texts contained the same short message until he finally opened the last one, which contained the caption, 'without you'. There he discovered an additional passage, which said, 'If you're ever looking, you will always find me in our place where I'll be forever waiting'. "I think I know where he is," Kyle said, as he hung up the phone and headed for the woods.

Kyle bolted across the lawn and disappeared into the tree line where he raced down the paths with a newfound sense of urgency after reading Patrick's ominous, cryptic text. When he reached the clearing with the plastic lawn furniture, Kyle practically dove headfirst into the crawlspace beneath the wall of thorn bushes as he made his way toward the tip of South Point where he was growing increasingly frightened of what he may find. He could tell that someone had recently crawled through here by the fresh tracks from their dragging feet, which had disturbed the leaves and exposed the dark, moist soil below. The thorn bushes were clawing at his back and tearing holes in his shirt and skin as a result of his haste but he was oblivious to that pain, which was dulled by his adrenaline as he flew through the obstacle course toward the finish line.

When he reached the small patch of sandy beach, which was the site if their first sexual encounter, Kyle's worst fears were suddenly playing out before him. He saw Patrick's lifeless body lying on the same green army blanket they had shared that night with two empty pill bottles beside him and some empty strawberry wine coolers scattered around the scene. Kyle felt his legs give out as he fell to his knees and watched his vision become blurry as his eyes filled with tears at the overwhelming loss he was feeling.

Suddenly, Kyle's lifeguard training kicked in and he scrambled over to Patrick to check for a pulse. He held Patrick's wrist in his fingers and was filled with relief when he felt the twitching of Patrick's heart beating in his veins. Despite his excitement, Kyle knew that the situation was dire. Patrick was barely breathing and his Pulse was nearly undetectable. First, he rolled Patrick onto his stomach and held his forehead up while sticking his middle and index fingers of his right hand down Patrick's throat to trigger the gag reflex and induce vomiting. Kyle was relieved to see the cloudy, pink liquid come out of Patrick's mouth and leave it's chalky film behind where it drained through the blanket. He did this repeatedly until nothing more was coming out and Patrick was merely dry heaving. Kyle then placed Patrick on his side while he called 9-1-1. As he waited for someone to pick up, he examined the labels on the empty bottles and saw that they were prescriptions for Oxycodone, which told him that Patrick must have gotten into his mother's stash. Finally, after what seemed like an eternity, Kyle heard the sound of a woman's voice come on the line.

"Nine, one, one, what is your emergency?"

"I've got an eighteen year old male suffering from an apparent drug overdose. Opiates involved," Kyle spoke in a clear, calm voice despite the fact that his hands were shaking. "I've induced vomiting but he has a weak pulse with shallow breathing and a loss of consciousness. We're located at the southern most tip of Sunset Cove. It's only accessible from the water so you'll need to alert the Harbor Master and make sure that rescue services is ready with the Narcan."

"Roger that caller. Dispatching Harbor Master to your location and notifying rescue services to be ready to administer Narcan. Do you have medical training sir?"

"I'm a certified lifeguard," Kyle replied.

"And what is your name sir?"

"Look, I don't have time for this. Will you please just tell them to hurry." He dropped the phone on the blanket and went back to checking Patrick's vitals. Within minutes, Kyle heard the familiar sound of the Harbor Master's twin engines approaching from the west at full throttle. Nick came racing around the point at about sixty knots before slowing and coming to a stop just beyond the rocks. Kyle stood up and waved his arms as he watched Nick throw out the mushroom shaped anchor and toss the aluminum framed floating stretcher into the water before jumping in himself and navigating his way toward Kyle through the jagged, slippery rocks.

"It's Patrick," Kyle yelled as he watched Nick's expression change from intense concentration to one of deep concern.

He frantically fought against the resistance of the water as he forced his way along and when he got close enough to where it was only knee deep, Nick picked up the lightweight stretcher by its side frame and carried it like a suitcase as he sprinted toward the shore. Nick shouted expletives as he stumbled several times and nearly fell while tripping over the treacherous landscape that lay beneath the surface.

"How long has he been using," Nick asked, as he finally made it to the beach.

"He hasn't," Kyle, answered while they went to work loading Patrick onto the stretcher and securing him with the seatbelt style nylon straps. "This wasn't an accidental overdose. It was intentional."

"What the fuck," Nick said in disbelief.

"I don't suppose you've got any Narcan on that raft of yours, Huckleberry," Kyle asked, as he put his phone into his T-shirt pocket and stuffed the two empty pill bottles into the pockets of his shorts.

"Negative," Nick said, "but emergency services will have it on site at the rendezvous. We just gotta get him to the East Side Marina."

"Well, we better move," Kyle said, as they each picked up an end of the stretcher and carried Patrick toward the boat. "His condition's deteriorating rapidly."

As they struggled to make their way through the perilous obstacles with their awkward load, Kyle was grateful to be wearing his sneakers this time as he tripped and stumbled over the barnacle encrusted rocks, which threatened to sink their teeth into his tender feet when he walked this same path with Patrick all those nights ago.

"My god," Nick said, as his ankles and shins took a beating, "could he have picked a worse place for this? I get the feeling that he really didn't want to be found."

"Yeah, I'd say that was the idea," Kyle agreed.

"Come to think of it," Nick said, as it suddenly occurred to him, "how in the fuck did you find him out here?"

"I don't know," Kyle, answered, as his mind drifted off to the night that he and Patrick had spent here for their first time. "This place was kind of special for us and I guess that I'm the only one who could have found him here."

"Well, he's lucky you did," Nick said as they finally reached the boat.

Finding Our Way Through the Fog
Jonathan B. Taylor

"Let's hope so," Kyle replied with the gravity of the situation continuing to weigh on his thoughts.

Together, they hoisted the stretcher over the side of the boat and attempted to place it gently inside but their awkward positioning caused them to drop Patrick on the deck, slightly rougher than they intended, which led them to both wince at the sound of the thud. Kyle jumped into the boat and tended to Patrick while Nick pulled up the anchor and gave the boat a good shove toward open water before climbing in and getting behind the wheel. He fired up the engines and began to open them up rapidly to full power as he slid the throttle forward and headed for the East Side Marina. It was an unusually calm day and the boat glided effortlessly over the glasslike surface as Kyle kneeled over the stretcher and held Patrick's wrist to feel his faint pulse while images of them in happier times appeared throughout his mind. He saw memories of them kissing and cuddling on the couch or smiling and laughing at the beach, which made Kyle feel like he was watching their life together flash before his eyes as if Patrick was slipping away from him and this was somehow his way of saying 'goodbye'. Kyle had heard of people seeing their whole life pass before them when they die and he wondered if Patrick was sharing these images with him through some kind of telekinetic connection on his way to the other side.

Suddenly, Kyle saw Patrick begin to stir in his aluminum cradle and show the first signs of life since finding him on the beach a short time ago. Patrick was still suffering from the effects of the opiates and in his dreamlike state, he was having trouble connecting with reality. Patrick looked up and saw a shadowy, blurry figure shrouded by a bright light and assumed that he had entered the afterlife. As his eyes adjusted to the glare, he saw Kyle's face looking down on him with the late morning sun appearing like a halo around his angelic face.

"I must be in heaven," Patrick muttered feebly with a strained smile, "because all the angels look like you!" He was referring to his double vision. "Is this really happening," he asked weakly. "Are you really here?"

"I'm here," Kyle said, squeezing Patrick's hand tightly with his own.

"Please don't leave," Patrick, pleaded as his eyes welled with tears.

"I'm not going anywhere," Kyle assured him with his own eyes becoming watery as well.

"I'm sorry! I'm sorry for what I did to you," Patrick barely managed to whisper. "I never meant to hurt you."

"I know," Kyle said forgivingly. "None of that matters now. All that matters is that you're okay."

"Kyle," Patrick said in a final gasp, "I love you." After that, his words stopped but his mouth continued to move like a fish out of water that was gulping at the air before finally becoming still. Kyle watched the life wash out of Patrick's eyes, leaving a dead stare in its wake. He then began to frantically search for a pulse but there was none. Patrick was gone. However, Kyle wasn't ready to let him go and he shouted an agonizing 'Nooo!' as the tears ran down his face. This got Nick's attention as he turned around to see Kyle straddling Patrick's lifeless body and beginning to perform chest compressions while screaming Patrick's name in an attempt to call him back to the land of the living from wherever he had gone.

"Stay with him kid," Nick urged as he wiped a tear from his own eye. "We're almost there!"

Nick turned on the flashing blue lights that were perched on masts above the steering console and activated the high-pitched, urgent, emergency siren to alert any boaters around the marina that they were coming in hot so everyone needed to get the fuck out of the way. All of the background noises seemed to fade into the distance for Kyle as if he were suddenly wearing noise canceling earplugs and the only sound he heard was his own heartbeat pounding out a drum line in his head as he thrust the base of his palms into Patrick's motionless chest.

When Nick pulled up to the dock, he witnessed a sea of red and blue flashing lights from the parade of emergency vehicles that were lined up at the scene, making it look more like a response to a natural disaster than a drug overdose. This was typical in a small town where very little ever happened so that when a call came in, everyone wanted to get in on the action. Nick appreciated their dedication but he felt that the ladder truck was probably overkill.

"He's in cardiac arrest," Nick yelled to the awaiting responders as the boat slid up against the dock. He killed the motor while a couple of officers secured the bow and stern lines and a team of paramedics leapt onto the boat like a band of marauding pirates that were coming aboard to plunder the rescue efforts. Kyle got out of their way and moved to the back corner of the boat while the professionals took over. He was visibly distraught but he managed to compose himself enough to provide the necessary information regarding Patrick's condition. He told them that Patrick had taken a mixture of Oxycodone with alcohol but he was unsure of the amounts although he had seen some chalky residue after he induced vomiting. He also explained how Patrick's heart had only stopped beating in the last few minutes and that he had immediately begun chest compressions.

Finding Our Way Through the Fog
Jonathan B. Taylor

Kyle watched helplessly from the sidelines as the medical technicians went to work. The crew, which consisted of three men and a woman, all had military style haircuts, including the burly female who wore a flat top style buzz cut. Two of the men were tall and wiry with a similar appearance, who Kyle suspected were likely siblings, while the third was average height and looked far too young to be a part of the team. One of the tall, lanky paramedics continued with the chest compressions while the other administered a dose of Narcan into Patrick's nasal passage. The woman, then inserted a manual breathing pump into his airway and began squeezing the bag to flood Patrick's lungs with needed oxygen while the younger member, readied an adrenaline shot, which he injected directly into Patrick's chest. When none of these things were successful, the second of the two taller EMT's stepped in with the defibrillator pads and attempted to shock Patrick's heart back to life. Just when their efforts were looking hopeless, the youngest member announced, "I've got a pulse," and the entire pier of onlookers, which had been holding its breath, erupted in a cheer. There was a chorus of applause and whistles when the team carried Patrick past the crowd and loaded him onto the ambulance. Nick and Kyle hugged each other in a celebratory embrace while tears of relief and joy streaked down their faces.

"You did it," Nick said, squeezing Kyle's shoulders and shaking him like an etch a sketch.

"We did it," Kyle corrected him.

"No, that was all you," Nick said humbly. "You did good today." Nick slapped him on the back. "I'm proud of you kid and I'm gonna recommend they give you a medal for this."

Once things settled down, Kyle called Amber to bring her up to speed on everything that had transpired and she told him that she would be right over to pick him up so that they could get to the hospital and hold a vigil for Patrick in the waiting room. Meanwhile, an overweight police officer named Stanley Simmons who looked like he spent too much time in the doughnut shop, was still on the scene and approached Kyle as he stood with Nick on the deck of the Boston Whaler. Officer Simmons started asking Kyle a bunch of questions that he didn't want to answer so he gave him a lame excuse about being too distraught to talk and saying that all he could think about was Patrick's wellbeing, which was true although his concern wasn't as debilitating as he was making it out to be. For a moment, it looked like the cop wasn't going for it but Kyle got an assist from Nick who intervened and convinced his colleague to postpone his impromptu interrogation for the time being.

"Look, Stan, this kid's been through a lot. Can't this wait," Nick said as he stepped in front of Kyle and shielded him from the wannabe detective's view. "Right now his friend's on her way over to pick him up and take him to the hospital. You know where he lives so there will be plenty of time for grilling him later."

Reluctantly, Officer Simmons agreed to hold off and Kyle was relieved to see Amber's silver Toyota Tacoma arrive at the end of the pier just in time to get him out of there.

"There she is now," Kyle, said as he gave Nick a handshake and a half hug.

"I'll stop by the hospital after my shift," Nick promised as Kyle climbed out of the boat onto the dock and gave Officer Simmons a nod while he made his way down the pier toward Amber's waiting vehicle. As he was walking away, Kyle looked down to see the bulge of the empty prescription bottles in his shorts pockets and he began to worry that the overly inquisitive cop may have spotted them as well. Kyle was expecting him to come running from behind at any moment to inquire about the noticeable objects and he quickened his pace accordingly. When he made it to the end of the pier, Kyle breathed a sigh of relief as he clambered into Amber's truck, which sat comfortably on oversized balloon tires. As he pulled the door closed behind him, Kyle wondered to himself why all of his friends drove such environmentally irresponsible vehicles. Once behind the safety of her tinted windows, Kyle took the pill bottles out of his pockets and stashed them in Amber's glove compartment as he contemplated his next move. He was facing a bit of a dilemma. Kyle didn't want to betray Patrick by revealing what he knew about his suicide attempt or provide any information, which could be used to bring charges against him for drug possession but he had already revealed some damaging facts during the rescue effort that could undoubtedly come back to haunt him. He also knew that Patrick needed help and this probably wasn't the best time to be enabling him.

"What is it," Amber asked, observing the frustrated scowl on Kyle's face.

"It's nothing," Kyle answered. "There's just this nosy cop who's asking a lot of questions that I really don't want to answer. I managed to wiggle my way out of it for now with some help from Nick but let's just get out of here before Captain Curious has a change of heart."

Amber nodded in agreement as they pulled out of the parking lot and headed for the hospital.

Finding Our Way Through the Fog
Jonathan B. Taylor

CHAPTER 19, 'THE AFTERMATH'

When they arrived at the hospital, Kyle and Amber found that Ally was already there in the waiting area, sitting on a mustard colored sofa while thumbing through an outdated architectural magazine, which she had taken from a stack on one of the two Formica covered end tables. Ally had driven straight over to the hospital after being apprised of the situation in a phone call from Amber. Upon seeing each other, they all came together for one of their group hugs before Ally brought them up to speed on Patrick's status. According to his parents, Patrick was in stable condition although he hadn't yet regained consciousness but his prognosis was good because the speed and efficiency in, which he had received CPR made it less likely that he would have sustained any permanent brain damage due to oxygen deprivation.

Kyle cringed at the mention of Patrick's parents as he was suddenly reminded of the fact that they would be floating around the hospital, which hadn't occurred to him before that moment. Now he had to worry about a possible continuation of the morning's earlier confrontation being played out in a public setting for added awkwardness. Kyle told Ally and Amber about his concerns as he recounted the tale of his run in with the hateful homophobes a few hours earlier and they both assured him that they would have his back in the event of a similar scene. This provided Kyle with some degree of comfort, knowing that the girls would be ready to pounce if the Connors attempted to reengage.

The three of them sat huddled together on the stiff, vinyl cushions of the waiting room couch with Kyle in the middle and the girls flanking him on either side just as they had done the previous night in Kyle's bed. The air had an antiseptic smell of medicine and disinfectant, which conjured up images of previous visits during past ordeals.

"I feel so terrible," Ally said, shaking her head in disappointment at herself. "I wasn't taking his calls or answering his texts but I never expected something like this."

"None of us did," Kyle said. "And I know exactly what you're feeling. I've been beating myself up too but you can't blame yourself. Being mad at someone doesn't make you responsible for the choices they make."

"I guess the only one who doesn't have to feel guilty is Amber," Ally said.

While Kyle and the girls leaned on each other and waited for news, he noticed a couple of fairly young, female staff workers dressed in light green hospital scrubs, who were staring in his direction and whispering to one another. "Could they be anymore obvious," Kyle said, as he was suddenly reminded of his newfound local celebrity status as an unintended porn star. This was exactly the type of reaction he had been dreading throughout the previous day when he was hiding out in his basement bunker and now that the moment arrived, he found it to be trivial and meaningless in light of everything else, which had transpired. Kyle wasn't even angry with the two strangers as he found them to be completely insignificant and felt only indifference toward them although he was a little annoyed when it appeared that they were walking by him to get a closer look. As they passed, they both smiled and waved while calling out, "Hash Tag, Bi Too!"

"Well, I guess I totally misread that one," Kyle admitted while Ally and Amber nodded in agreement after being caught off guard by the girls as well.

Suddenly, the lighthearted moment turned tense when Kyle saw Thomas and Jennifer Connor coming down the hallway and appearing to be headed right for him. Kyle stood up and was about to beat a hasty retreat in order to avoid another altercation but something in their expressions disarmed him and instead of walking away, he decided to wait and see what they had to say. Unlike earlier, when he had observed a look of hatred on their faces, Kyle now saw what appeared to be a look of adoration in their eyes.

Unfortunately, Kyle's misreading of the circumstances involving the two female hospital workers moments ago, made him question his ability to make an accurate assessment of the currently unfolding situation. As the Connors drew closer, Kyle could see that Jennifer's eyes were filling with tears and he got a sick feeling in his stomach that Patrick may have somehow taken a turn for the worse. When she was within striking distance, Kyle saw Jennifer's outstretched hands coming at him as if she were going for his throat. He was just about to throw an instinctive block when he heard the words, 'Thank you' pour out of her mouth. She then placed her hands on the sides of Kyle's face and held his head in a tender embrace.

"You saved my baby, you sweet angel," she said, as she threw her arms around Kyle and held him tightly. Kyle was momentarily frozen in a state of shock over this latest twist before eventually, putting his arm around her thin frame and returning the gesture. It was incredibly uncomfortable to be hugging someone who had unleashed a toxic homophobic tirade on him a few hours earlier but this clearly wasn't the same person he had faced off against that morning and he was perfectly willing to accept this kinder, gentler version of that wicked witch of the East Side.

"We should have listened to you," Jennifer cried on his shoulder. "Here we were making arrangements for my sister's funeral and if you hadn't found Patrick and done what you did, we would be having," Jennifer paused, unable to finish the sentence as if afraid to speak the words aloud. She released Kyle from the uneasy embrace but continued to hold onto his shoulders while apologizing for her inexcusable behavior. "I'm so sorry for the way I treated you. I hope you can forgive me."

She then turned to walk away and Thomas looked at Kyle and mouthed the words, 'Thank you' before placing an arm around his wife and escorting her back to Patrick's bedside.

"What just happened," Kyle said to Ally and Amber in a state of disbelief. It was as if the world had been turned upside down in order to right itself. "Could this day get any stranger?"

~

It was sometime after four o'clock when Nick stopped by to check on Patrick and see how the rest of the crew were doing. He found Kyle sitting by himself on the hard, unforgiving cushions of the tacky waiting area furniture. The girls had gone to the cafeteria to get something to eat but Kyle wasn't hungry so he stayed back to wait for some news. He gave Nick the latest update on Patrick's condition and they both stared at the shape of their reflections in the high gloss finish of the hospital's white tiled floors. Kyle wondered how they were able to keep the floors so polished and shiny with all the foot traffic as he wished they had channeled some of those resources into acquiring some decent furniture for their waiting areas. After observing their brief moment of reflection, Nick broke the silence.

"You know, I heard about what happened with you and Patrick," he said, finally addressing the elephant in the room. "I thought it was pretty messed up and I'm sorry you had to go through that. I also have to admit that I was a little surprised to find out you two were a couple," he added, holding his hands up slightly with wide eyes and raised eyebrows as if reliving the exact moment when he first found out. "Definitely did not see that one coming. But I want you to know that I'm cool with it and I hope you guys can work it out."

"Thanks," Kyle said with a smile. "But, what's this; no jokes or wisecracks? I must really be pathetic."

"Would it make you feel any better if I took a couple of cheap shots," Nick asked with some of his digs at the ready.

"Probably not," Kyle shrugged. "Stand down!"

Just then, Thomas Connor came walking down the hall at an urgent pace, which got Kyle's attention and immediately brought him to his feet.

"Come on," Thomas said to Kyle with a beckoning wave of his arm. "He's awake and he's asking for you."

Kyle felt an overwhelming sense of relief followed by a rush of excitement over the prospect of finally seeing Patrick after hours of anticipation. He asked Nick to go find Ally and Amber in the cafeteria and let them know what happened while he headed off to Patrick's room with Thomas at his side. As they walked, Thomas put his arm around Kyle and gave him a reassuring pat on the shoulder that felt like the gesture of a man who was welcoming his future son-in-law to the family. For Kyle, this was just another surreal moment in a growing list of bizarre events that left him questioning his own reality.

Finding Our Way Through the Fog
Jonathan B. Taylor

He felt like he was walking through an endless, vivid dream from, which he expected to awaken at any moment and be lying in bed back in the basement with the sun shining through the windows and the birds chirping outside while Patrick made his way over for their morning workout. Kyle longed for those simpler, carefree days as he tried to decide whether it was more uncomfortable to have the Connors shouting at him with their homophobic bile or to endure their friendly petting.

When they reached the doorway to Patrick's private room, Kyle entered alone while Thomas waited outside in the hall. Once inside the dimly lit room, Kyle saw Jennifer standing over Patrick's bed in the simple black dress and string of white pearls, which she had been wearing that morning while making funeral arrangements for Karen. She could just as easily have been standing over a coffin, Kyle thought as he took in the scene. Jennifer watched as Kyle and Patrick's eyes met, triggering the uncontrollable smiles that were always a dead giveaway of their incredible attraction to one another.

"Well, let me get out of here so you two can have some privacy," she said, taking her cue to leave. As she walked past Kyle, she rested a hand on his shoulder and smiled before going out to the hallway to wait with her husband. Kyle appreciated the one eighty on the homophobia but he was having a hard time adjusting to all of the gentle touching. He wondered if her leaving the room was truly about giving them space or if it had more to do with her inability to see them interacting as a couple.

Kyle approached cautiously as Patrick appeared so fragile that he was afraid of breaking him. Patrick had the adjustable bed raised so that he was nearly sitting up and Kyle leaned in for a slow, sensual kiss on the lips like the first one they had shared on West Beach so many nights ago. The railings prevented Kyle from sitting on the edge of the bed so he took the wooden armchair, which was upholstered in the same tacky, mustard colored fabric as the waiting area furniture, and slid it up to the bed. After he sat down, Kyle looked at the machine, which was monitoring Patrick's vitals and he shuddered as he thought of the horrifying moment when his heart had stopped beating on the boat.

"I was worried they wouldn't let me see you because I didn't know the rules on visitors in these situations," Kyle said.

"I'm not sure what the rules are either," Patrick replied, "but my parents are major benefactors of this place so I doubt the rules would even apply."

To someone else, this may have sounded like bragging but to Kyle, this was just Patrick speaking as a matter of fact. Patrick held up his hands to show Kyle his leather wrist restraints, which limited his movement as he tested their integrity by tugging on them.

"I guess I messed up pretty bad," Patrick said with a curled lip and squinting eye.

Kyle thought about making a bondage joke but figured it was probably 'too soon'.

"I'm sorry for what I did to you," Patrick said with his voice cracking. "Do you think you can ever forgive me?"

"Forget about all that," Kyle said, taking Patrick's hand in a firm, interlocking thumb grip with his own. "I already forgave you so let's just put it behind us and never mention it again."

"Well, I like the sound of that. Forgetting that I ever fucked up this bad would be nice but I'm afraid that we'll be feeling the repercussions from this one for a long time to come," Patrick admitted reluctantly. "By the way, thanks for saving me. I guess I owe you my life now," he smiled. "How am I ever gonna pay you back?"

"Don't worry about it," Kyle waived his hand. "We can work out an installment plan."

Patrick let out a slight laugh but his mood was serious. "I can't believe I did something so stupid!"

Kyle thought he was referring to the sex tape but quickly realized he was talking about the suicide attempt.

"What the hell is wrong with me," Patrick asked the ceiling. "How am I supposed to make it in life if I'm ready to cash in my chips at the first sign of trouble?" Patrick turned to Kyle. "You know, this probably won't last forever," he said, holding up their clenched hands as a visual aid, "and one day I'll have to deal with the pain of losing you. Do you think I'll ever be able to handle that?"

"First of all, you don't know what's gonna happen with us. If we can survive all of this then who knows, maybe we can last forever. Besides, even if our relationship eventually evolves into something completely different from what it is today, I know that we will always have a connection and continue to be there for each other no matter what happens along the way. Secondly," Kyle continued, "this was about so much more than you thinking you had lost me. Your whole world was crashing around you. You lost your Aunt Karen and you thought you were losing your family and friends along with your whole identity. That was a lot to take for someone who's never even had a bad day before. But, things are looking up. We're together and your parents seem willing to accept you for who you are."

"That's right," Patrick smiled. "You seem to have won them over. So," Patrick shook his head, "all of this good comes out of me almost killing myself," he surmised ironically. "How messed up is that? What's the moral of the story? If things go bad, kill yourself but don't worry because your superhero boyfriend will swoop in to save the day and once you're brought back to life, everything will turn around in your favor."

"No," Kyle said, disapproving of Patrick's spin. "All of this good didn't come from you nearly killing yourself. All of this good happened in spite of it. This is the future we almost didn't see and you almost became just another statistic. You may think that the reason I forgave you is because I almost lost you but the truth is, I had already forgiven you long before I found you on the beach at South Point and I almost never got the chance to tell you. So, the moral of the story is; things usually have a way of working out if you just give them a chance and even when they don't, the pain or sorrow you feel today isn't going to last forever because time has a way of healing all wounds. But, enough about that. There's another matter we need to discuss," Kyle said in a serious tone, which gave Patrick pause.

"What," he asked gravely, as if expecting the worst.

"There was this cop back at the marina who was asking a bunch of questions about your overdose. I managed to get out of there without telling him anything but I only bought myself a little time because he will most assuredly be back so I think we need to get our story straight."

"Get our story straight," Patrick laughed out loud. "What are you gonna do? Try to lie to the police," Patrick said as if the idea were absurd.

"Well, I don't want to say anything that could hurt you. It's bad enough that I already told them you took Oxycodone but without those pill bottles there's no proof."

"Oh, fuck! I forgot about the pill bottles," Patrick said in a slight panic. "I wasn't even thinking of that. Those things could get my mother jammed up. Where are they now?"

"They're in Amber's glove compartment," Kyle answered.

"That's good. You have to get rid of them," Patrick instructed. "Or, better yet, tell Amber to get rid of them. That way you can say you don't know what happened to them if you're asked. We can't have you lying to the police because without a poker face, they would see right through you and you could end up facing an obstruction charge or something. Don't worry about incriminating me because I'm going to tell them everything except for the part about stealing the pills from my mother's stash. I'll leave her out of it and say that I bought the pills from some guy in a parking lot outside of a bar or at a concert or something."

"But, if you admit to taking a bunch of pills, couldn't you wind up facing some kind of drug charges," Kyle pointed out.

"No, there won't be any charges. My parents already took care of it. I'm gonna have to go to an upscale psyche ward for 'observation'," Patrick made air quotes with his fingers, "and hopefully, get green lighted out of there in thirty days. It's not as bad as it sounds. Supposedly, the place is like a high end spa with bars on the windows."

"A whole month," Kyle said, disappointedly. The thought of going an entire month without seeing Patrick was extremely frustrating but Kyle pushed those selfish feelings aside and took comfort in the fact that Patrick would be getting the help, which he obviously needed. "Well, it sucks that I won't be seeing you for a month but you need to focus on getting your head right and just think how different things will be when you get back. No more worrying about hiding who we are. Now, we're free to be ourselves."

"I can tell you one thing that will be different," Patrick said. "No more of that one sided domination shit. I swore that if you ever gave me another chance, things would be different."

"Yeah, but I kinda like the domination stuff," Kyle pointed out.

"I'm not saying we should stop it all together," Patrick explained. "But, from now on, we take turns. Just like we do with the blow jobs only now, you get to bend me over and show me whose boss."

"Are you sure," Kyle asked skeptically. "I don't want you to let me fuck you out of some sense of obligation. You have to really want it."

"No, I definitely want it. Make no mistake," Patrick insisted. "I've actually wanted it for awhile but I was letting my ego get in the way. But, I'm over that now. You can even film it if you want and then we can post it online for everyone to see."

"Well, I don't know about posting anything online but I could definitely get into fucking you in the ass," Kyle said as he watched Patrick's massive erection quickly pitch a tent beneath the sheet. "I guess you are ready," Kyle smiled approvingly. "See, our relationship is evolving already. Now I'll have to teach you my pre date douching technique."

"Thanks, but I think I can figure out how to give myself an enema." Patrick gave a sly smirk.

Eventually, the visit came to an end but not before Ally, Amber and Nick all had a chance to stop in and see Patrick to wish him well and show their support. After their brief words of encouragement, the three of them stepped back out into the hallway to give Kyle and Patrick one last moment alone. The boys enjoyed a long 'goodbye' kiss, which neither wanted to end. They would have liked to do a lot more but with everyone standing right outside the door and a security camera on the ceiling watching their every move, the timing wasn't right for makeup sex and they decided it would have to wait for the reunion.

"So, I guess I'll see you in a month," Kyle said as he slowly peeled himself away from Patrick.

"Oh, man, a whole month without seeing you. That's gonna suck," Patrick said with frustration.

"Yeah, but it'll be a hell of a reunion," Kyle said with an optimistic smile.

~

After leaving the hospital, Amber dropped Kyle off at his house on her way to Ally's where she was planning to spend the night. On the drive, Kyle passed along Patrick's request that she dispose of the pill bottles and when she began to tell him how she planned to crush them and drop them in a dumpster, Kyle stopped her abruptly and told her that it was best he didn't know.

Once he was home, Kyle took an overdue shower and climbed into bed. It was only seven o'clock but he was completely exhausted and craving sleep after it eluded him so effectively over the past twenty four hours. "What a difference a day makes," Kyle thought to himself as he lay in bed thinking of how he was so consumed with the gut wrenching scandal of the sex tape the day before, that he couldn't even dream of a day when he would put that whole nightmare behind him. Fast forward to the present and the trauma of yesterday had all but faded into the backdrop, foreshadowed by the much bigger events of today.

Kyle was close to sleep when his phone began buzzing so he picked it up off the nightstand and saw that it was a text message from Claire, informing him that they would be back soon and saying how she had 'so much to tell him'. Kyle laughed at the irony and thought that whatever exciting tales she had in store from her intriguing art world, he was pretty sure he could top them although dancing around the subject of the sex tape could prove dicey. As he finally drifted off to sleep, his mind was awash with thoughts of Patrick, which he hoped to carry with him into his dreams. After witnessing a world without his soul mate, there was a newfound sense of urgency to hold onto Patrick tightly and never let him go again. He didn't know where they were headed or what the future held in store but as long as they had each other, they could handle every curve ball and overcome any obstacle that life was sure to throw their way.

Finding Our Way Through the Fog
Jonathan B. Taylor

CHAPTER 20, 'THE REUNION'

Kyle sat on the edge of the outdated double bed with its burnished brass headboard and tested the squeaky springs by bouncing slightly just as he had done several weeks ago when he visited the apartment with Patrick for the first time back in July. This was Kyle's second week in the new place and he was still adjusting to the never-ending cacophony of the city, which was in stark contrast to the quiet neck of the woods from where he came. Although, he couldn't do much about the constant shouting and horn honking outside on the street, Kyle could at least control the unwanted sounds within the residence like the irritating shrillness produced by the springs.

Kyle made his final decision to remove the obnoxious piece of furniture from the premises, following a visit from Steven and Billy in, which his two guests ended up spending the night on the article in question. After listening to the incessant bedsprings squeaking for nearly three hours in the next room, Kyle was determined to find a solution to his problem by ridding himself of the noisy nuisance once and for all. Unfortunately, this was a furnished apartment with the bed belonging to the landlord so Kyle couldn't just drop it in the nearest dumpster as he would have liked. Upon further inspection, he determined that it was actually the box spring, which was creating the racket and the mattress itself was not an issue. Therefore, the best course of action would be to place the mattress directly on the floor in typical college student fashion and put the antique frame and box spring in their storage space, which was located down in the basement.

It was a good plan but Kyle still wanted to run it by Patrick before making any drastic changes to the décor although he didn't foresee a problem considering Patrick's strong aversion to annoying noises. One example of, which could be seen in his deep dislike for people whistling. That was one of his biggest pet peeves and whenever Patrick heard someone performing this irritating act, he would pull out his imaginary shotgun and chamber a round with the pump action before placing them in his sights and pulling the trigger. The whole thing was carried out with accompanying sound effects.

Kyle looked around the room and thought of how the twelve foot ceilings would appear even taller with the bed reduced to just a mattress on the floor. This was the smaller of the two bedrooms in the apartment and was originally meant to serve as a decoy by being passed off as Kyle's bedroom while he and Patrick would actually be living together in the larger bedroom across the hall. That was the plan when they were both in the closet but now that they were out, there was no need for diversions and Kyle's faux bedroom could simply be known as the 'guest room' just as it was when Steven and Billy stayed over the other night.

Despite the traumatic way in, which his 'coming out' process had unfolded, Kyle was embracing his new life as an openly bisexual college student and finding that all of the dread he felt for so many years over the prospect of people knowing, had been building up in his head for nothing. Just as Amber had said in her 'coming out' message, Kyle found that living in the open was actually a liberating experience instead of the overwhelming one he imagined and all of his anxiety, which he expected to worsen in the aftermath of 'coming out', had in reality been lifted. With the threat of exposure no longer looming and the freedom to be himself finally before him, Kyle was able to feel more comfortable in his own skin than he ever had before. He even found that his own homophobia toward certain members of the community was no longer an issue as he now saw everyone as an ally regardless of their flamboyance or femininity and figured there was plenty of room on the platform for all.

However, any hopes that Kyle had of living in obscurity once he got to college, were quickly dashed by the realization that the infamous sex tape along with his subsequent 'coming out' story had followed him all the way to Boston from the backwoods of Sunset Cove. His renowned story had earned him a level of notoriety, particularly around the LGBT community on campus. 'Hash tag, bi, too' was trending as a growing number of individuals were acknowledging their attraction to both sexes and finally admitting that the emperor had no clothes. Kyle had already met scores of individuals who were using the catch phrase, which Ally came up with and Kyle had popularized.

Although Kyle had always expected the story to follow him on some level, the number of people who approached him to offer their praise and support in the short time since he had arrived at school surprised him. And, while his overall experience was mostly positive, he still had to deal with the occasional issue, which could be considered uncomfortable. Kyle would cringe at the thought of anyone watching the sex tape and everyone who acknowledged a familiarity with his story was essentially admitting to having seen it, which always led to the inevitably awkward moment at the time of revelation. He also had to deal with the random homophobic remarks, which were sometimes made within earshot. In the past, he would have dismissed those types of remarks and never taken them personally but now that he was 'out', he couldn't help wondering if they were being directed at him intentionally.

In another twist, Kyle found himself walking back his previous comments about being unaware of the sex tape's existence in an effort to protect Patrick from being portrayed as a villain. Kyle made a new claim on social media that he actually knew the video was being made at the time but only denied any knowledge of it in an attempt to save face. In making the amended, false statement, Kyle absolved Patrick of any wrongdoing and chalked the whole thing up to a regrettable mishap. This allowed him to clean up Patrick's image while unfortunately, tainting his own in the process.

Kyle stepped out of the spare room and walked down the hall past the bathroom, which accounted for the lesser square footage of the smaller bedroom in comparison to the larger one. He entered the open living area, which contained a couch, two chairs and a coffee table. There were also a couple of small end tables on either side of the sofa. It was a standard layout with a small kitchenette, which had a circular dining table surrounded by four matching hardwood chairs with thinly padded vinyl seat cushions. The place still smelled of musty air and old wood varnish, which Kyle was attempting to air out by opening the windows and pegging the door with a small wooden wedge, which provided a nice cross breeze on this warm, sunny day in late August.

He wondered how Ally and Amber were doing at their new schools. Ally was attending the University of Massachusetts at Dartmouth while Amber was attending at Amherst. Both were living in the dorms, which they had each described as 'prison like'. This made Kyle appreciate the fact that he was living in an apartment off campus. He was excited to begin this new chapter but there was a part of him that missed his old friends and the carefree days of youth that they represented.

Kyle looked at his watch and saw that it was almost noon, which meant that Patrick would be arriving at any moment. This would be the first time they had seen each other since saying 'goodbye' in the hospital over a month ago and Kyle was both nervous and excited over their highly anticipated reunion. Patrick had finally been released from the place, which his parents had referred to as the 'wellness center', on the condition that he continue making regular visits to a therapist. Kyle couldn't help wondering what effect thirty days of intensive therapy may have had on Patrick and whether he would see a noticeable change in him. At one point, he was even worried that a therapist may have seen their relationship as toxic or unhealthy, leading to recommendations that could threaten their future together. However, those fears were put to rest when he spoke to Patrick on the phone that morning and heard the old familiar sound of longing in his voice.

He thought of how fortunate he was to be standing in that moment, waiting for Patrick's return. Although their story had a happy ending, Kyle knew that too many other's didn't. Unfortunately, the suicide rate among LGBT youth far exceeded any other group and Kyle knew that homophobia was the driving force behind those grim statistics. He wondered how many of the lost souls who didn't make it, had grown up in the same type of toxic environment in, which Patrick had barely survived. Kyle was able to take some comfort in the knowledge that Patrick wouldn't be returning to that same household of hate and bigotry, which had nearly been the death of him. For, not only had Patrick's parents done a complete one eighty on their views toward Kyle, their entire outlook on homosexuality had changed for the better. Jennifer Connor had turned her life around by overcoming her addiction to prescription painkillers while becoming an outspoken advocate of acceptance and equality for the LGBT community. While Jennifer's turnaround had restored some of Kyle's faith in mankind, it was his own generation who provided him with the most hope for the future. With twenty percent of Gen Z identifying as LGBT+, they were coming out in droves to lift the veil on sexuality and celebrate the many colors of the spectrum. They were also coming of age and turning out in droves to vote, which was good to see. However, not everyone was pleased with that development. Due to their predominantly liberal views on social, economic and environmental issues, many of these new constituents were seen as a threat to right wing, conservative lawmakers who sought to silence their voices with backward suggestions like raising the voting age or enacting draconian laws, which targeted the LGBT community in vain attempts to drive the perceived sympathizers from their districts and minimize their influence on future elections.

As for his own parents, Claire and Phil were mortified to learn what had happened to Kyle but they took it all in stride as they did with every other upheaval that ever occurred in their lives. They still trusted Kyle to make his own choices and live life on his own terms so they supported his decision to stay with Patrick and continued to view him as one of the family. This was an easy call for them considering how much they adored Patrick and the fact that they were forgiving by nature and never ones to hold a grudge.

Finding Our Way Through the Fog
Jonathan B. Taylor

Suddenly, Kyle heard the sound of the gate opening and then closing on the cage style elevator from down on the first floor. The elevator, which had been out of service when they first visited the place over the summer, was working now and carried passengers to the upper floors through a large atrium that was situated in the center of the building. There was a horseshoe shaped balcony, which ran around the tier and allowed you to see all the way down to the lobby if you were to peer over the railing from Kyle's vantage point on the fourth floor. He considered stepping out onto the tier to have a look but decided to wait and let himself be surprised. He saw that the woman who lived in the unit directly across from him had opened her door and appeared to be waiting for someone as well. She was an attractive woman who looked to be in her early thirties with frizzy red hair that was pulled into a ponytail high on the back of her head. She reminded Kyle a little of Amber and he wondered if the two may have shared some ancestral DNA. They each stood in their apartments and craned their necks as they listened for the elevator to reach its final stop. Although the woman was focused on finding out if her guest had arrived, she was also completely captivated by Kyle's beauty. She tried not to make it overly obvious that she couldn't take her eyes off him as he stood beyond the threshold, wearing only his navy blue, cotton gym shorts with the backlighting from the sun shining through the windows to accentuate his sinewy musculature. On his shorts, he had created a pinkish and a purplish stripe around the top with the help of some bleach, to honor the colors of the bisexual flag.

After a moment of avoiding eye contact, they eventually heard the elevator come to a stop and could tell by the sound that it had arrived on the fourth floor. They both perked their ears up and listened as the mystery passenger exited the elevator and Kyle knew that it was Patrick when he heard those familiar footsteps coming around to his side of the tier. Kyle watched the woman's expression change from disappointment to intrigue when she saw Patrick come into view on the opposite side of the balcony. She began to undress him with her eyes as Kyle watched her and thought to himself, "Wow, this chick is horny!"

Patrick reached the apartment and saw Kyle standing just inside the doorway. When their eyes met, the smiles erupted on their faces just like always, only this time there was no blushing or looking away. Instead, Patrick stepped over the threshold and stood before Kyle as they slowly slid their arms around each other and held on tightly with their heads interlocked at the neck in a reenactment of their embrace on the beach that night in July when they had shared their first kiss. As they relived that moment, Kyle and Patrick were transported back in time for an instant, before a whirlwind of memories from all of their subsequent encounters flashed through their minds and carried them back to the present where they capped off the experience with a slow, sensual kiss in homage to the one, which had kicked it off all of those nights ago.

"You're home," Kyle said as their lips slowly parted.

"I'm home," Patrick replied with a smile. He then looked into Kyle's eyes and said, "Now it's your turn," before turning his back to him and pressing his ass into Kyle's stiffening erection.

Kyle wrapped his arms around Patrick and pulled him close. "I just have one question," he whispered into Patrick's ear through clenched teeth. "Are you clean?"

With that, Kyle kicked the wooden wedge free from the door and let the wind do the rest. Across the hall, the woman with the red hair watched the boys and smiled as the door slowly closed on the scene.

The End

Finding Our Way Through the Fog
Jonathan B. Taylor

Finding Our Way Through the Fog
Jonathan B. Taylor

Author's Note:

I wrote this book in response to what I felt was lacking in other stories of this type that either focused too much on the graphic sexual descriptions while falling short on the storyline or went the other way by telling a compelling story while glossing over the good parts as if people could only be interested in one or the other. In 'Finding Our Way through the Fog', I sought to challenge that theory by striking a balance between intellectual stimulation and the art of erotica in hopes of offering readers the best of both worlds. For all of those who have ever felt like Kyle or loved someone like him, this book has something for everyone with the exception of the uptight or prudish who may want to stick with their sensory deprivation and Bible passages.

With so much material out there these days, creating something that is considered completely original can be a challenge as it becomes increasingly difficult to introduce a concept that no one has ever seen or done before. In the alternative, we strive to be authentic and unique while avoiding the pitfalls of producing played out knockoffs or tired, old clichés.

In creating this story, I've tried to follow two basic principles, which have been passed down by other writers over the years. First, you must throw ego and self-consciousness out the window. Keep it raw and don't be afraid to talk about things that are embarrassing or uncomfortable. You're allowing people to be that fly on the wall so give them the most revealing and intimate details you can imagine. Always make them cringe and get them squirming in their seats whenever possible. Also, try not to get carried away with intricate descriptions. Give them just enough information to set the scene and let their imaginations do the rest. You don't need to describe the color and texture of each individual carpet fiber. Remember that you're telling a story, not painting a picture.

At this time, I would like to thank my friends Scott and Mike whose insight was crucial in the creation of Kyle and Patrick. I also want to thank my other friend Scott for helping me discover and develop a hidden talent from what started out as a social experiment and writing exercise.

WARNING: The use of enemas can strip the colon of its protective mucus lining and therefore, are not recommended for recreational use.

Finding Our Way Through the Fog
Jonathan B. Taylor

ABOUT THE AUTHOR

Jonathan B. Taylor was born October 30, 1969 in New Bedford, M.A. He grew up in the small seaside town of Mattapoiset, MA where he developed a love for writing and the art of putting words together in order to find the perfect formula for what he had to say. In November 1995, he was convicted of Arson and murder and sentenced to life without the possibility of parole. He has always maintained his innocence and continues to fight for his freedom to this day.

Finding Our Way Through the Fog
Jonathan B. Taylor

Finding Our Way Through the Fog
Jonathan B. Taylor

Finding Our Way Through the Fog
Jonathan B. Taylor